THE LEADING EDGE

THE LEADING EDGE

An Anthology of Lesbian Sexual Fiction

Edited by
Lady Winston

Introduction by
Pat Califia

Lace Publications

Lady Winston Series

Library of Congress Cataloging-in-Publication Data

The Leading Edge.

(Lady Winston series)
1. Lesbianism—Fiction. 2. Erotic stories,
American—Women authors. 3. Lesbians' writings,
American. I. Winston, Lady, Date . II. Series.
PS648.L47L38 1987 813'.01'083538 87-4074
ISBN 0-917597-09-5

First Edition. First printing. Cover design by Lace Publications. Cover illustration by Artemis OakGrove.
Lace Publications/POB 10037/Denver CO 80210-0037

ISBN 0-917597-09-5

This book is dedicated to Karen Hays for working so damn hard to keep Lady Winston in typewriter ribbon and to pay her outrageous phone bills. It is also dedicated to Pat Califia for being brave enough to keep on writing to keep us informed and entertained against the odds and some of the most vicious attacks against her from the very press she works to preserve.

Lady Winston wishes to acknowledge the following people for helping to make this anthology happen: Pat Califia, Merril Mushroom, Jewelle Gomez, Dennise Brown and Nancy K. Bereano.

TABLE OF CONTENTS

Lamar
Van Dyke 1987

THE EDGE OF CUNT

PAT CALIFIA

Did your mother ever tell you, "Don't put that in your mouth! You don't know where it's been!"? Don't worry. You can nibble on this introduction. I'm always willing to tell you where *I've* been. The authors in this anthology are, too. But let's sit down and chat a bit before you feast your eyes and imagination on the whole book.

In a letter to me, Editor Lady Winston explained that she had selected **The Leading Edge** as the title for this anthology because:

> I believe that Lesbians tend to be the pioneers in most fields and sexual fiction writing is no exception. The authors who have contributed are in the forefront of what I hope will be a steady flow of Lesbian sexual fiction in the years to come.

In the last five years, an erotic literature written by lesbians for a lesbian audience has emerged. This is very exciting. But I don't think that we have been pioneers in the field of sexual fiction writing. Heterosexuals and gay men have been able to take their own porn for granted for a long time now. Tons of books, videos, movies, and photo-magazines cater to nearly every shade of male sexual preferences. In contrast, much of lesbian literature is polemical, and gives the impression that we are more to be pitied as a bunch of argumentative workaholics than feared as sexual deviants who will steal susceptible women-folk away from male domination. Why have we had to wait so long to celebrate the joy we take in our lesbian bodies?

The sad fact is that in 1987, it still takes a brave woman to write honestly and explicitly about her fantasy objects and the route she takes to satisfy her sexual needs, if her cunt tugs her relentlessly toward other women. Not only is she subject to the same right-wing forces that are trying to eliminate any trace of sexual choice or sexy images from our society, you can guarantee that she will be attacked viciously and personally by some of the very women who ought to be tickled pink to read her steamiest words.

In some quarters of the feminist press, our nascent indigenous porn—**On Our Backs**, **Bad Attitude**, **Outrageous Women**, a few hot-talk tapes and videos, sex parties, women-only strip shows, and the intrepid but outnumbered female entrepreneurs who market lubricants, vibrators, dildo harnesses, and more esoteric delights—is condemned so strongly that you would think they were critiquing the **Malleus Maleficarum**, a manual for Inquisitors, instead of sex manuals for Amazons. And you can guarantee that when these products, ads, books and tapes are banned by women's bookstores or magazines, they are evicted with even more nastiness than a heterosexual male clerk at 7-Eleven would display, if he refused to exhibit such wares to his customers.

This anthology will no doubt provoke a similar reaction. I can just see the headlines on the book reviews. PIMPING FOR THE PATRIARCHY and THIS IS NOT WIMMOAN LOVE and YOU SHOULD ALL BE SPANKED AND SENT TO BED WITHOUT ANY SUPPER are a few that I can easily envision appearing in those humorless oob-stetrical rags. (Well, maybe not the last one, although the tone is certainly appropriate.)

Nevertheless, the main effect of these ringing denunciations will be to alert lesbians who are hungry for clit-to-clit talk to get their mitts on a copy ASAP. The popularity of earthy dyke material demonstrates that there is a great need for it. Once again, the "intelligentsia" seems to be alienated from the "proletariat." Your average lesbian, being smarter than her self-appointed leaders, knows sex is good for her and she wants to hear more about it. Like black lesbian poet Cheryl Clarke in "palm leaf of Mary Magdelene" ("Obsessed by betrayal/compelled by passion"), she would do just about anything to savor and satiate her woman, and knows that vital drive is the thing that redeems and transforms her life.

In this sense, this anthology and the authors it shelters *do* represent a Leading Edge. what a shame it is if a girl who wants to tickle another girl's fancy can't curl up with a bad book if that other girl is out of town. What a shame it is that we can't trot down to the corner store with our Significant Other and Joint Tenant for a pint of designer ice cream and an x-rated videotape—a harmless but invigorating weekend pleasure that most heterosexual couples can take for granted.

The number of mom-and-pop stores that make adult videos available seems to demonstrate that many, if not most, people are fairly liberal about porn. The problem is that liberals, gay and straight, treat sex and pornography and something trivial—entertaining, but trivial. And they defend it on that level. They don't want to be denied access to titillating activities which they enjoy, but they refuse to take censorship as seriously as they do the death penalty or aid for the contras. And they tend to view other people's porn as being extreme, decadent, harmful, or at least dispensable.

On one level, that is exactly what lesbian sex-writers are trying to do—provide their sisters with high-quality, salacious entertainment. But we should not underestimate the value such of recreation in a world where most of us work too hard for way too little money, and wind up too tired at the end of the day to think about much else beyond dinner and David Letterman. Life should be more than a serious of long waits for the weekend.

Arousing lesbian literature has survival value. Its stimulation can give us hope that our true love is out there somewhere, and the strength to keep paying the bills and looking out for her. By giving us a bit of escape from tedious heterosexual reality, it makes our lives easier. Is there a bar-butch alive who has to report to a desk or a cash register nine to five, five days a week, who wouldn't like to burn her business drag and climb into a van with a stud-buddy and go cruising down the highways of Amerika "looking for women to fuck," like Carol and Liz in C. Bailey's "Ride My Bitch II"?

But the fuss that gets made by lesbians who think lesbian porn should not exist makes it clear that there is more at stake here than the question of whether we should spend our spare time reading dirty books or marching to Take Back The Night. (After all, most of us who do the former would still like to be able to do the latter.)

Industrialized, western societies have often been accused of repressing their citizens' sexual energy and sublimating it in compulsive consumer binges funded by wage slavery. It is easy to forget that movements for social change also usually make a bid to control the private lives of their members. A movement that can exercise enough social control has a huge pool of energy which can be used to get petitions signed, pack meetings, demonstrate, write angry letters, raise money and lobby for legislation.

The feminist anti-porn movement is the most germane example of this. These groups preach despair and encourage vigilante action by promulgating an emergency mentality. They do this by identifying the existence of mainstream, commercial pornography with rape and genocide. They promise women that all they need to do to get out from under the heal of the patriarchy is wipe out smut. This is an excellent strategy for guilt-tripping women into committing themselves full-time. A movement that attacks targets which are vulnerable anyway because right-wingers and the minions of the state don't like adult bookstores and prostitutes any more than they like homosexuals or working women or reproductive rights can score enough victories to make women feel that their sacrifices on its behalf are meaningful.

Anti-sex ideology is so widespread that even activist women who have nothing to do with fighting pornography can still feel guilty if they take an evening off to read something that makes them horny. If there were no more pre-orgasmic lesbian activists or lesbians waiting until the revolution to start hopping on each other like bunnies in springtime, this reasoning goes, we would all stay home burning out our Panabrators. We would become shameless electricity junkies. We wouldn't even care if the juice came from a nuclear power plant!

That's just so many red-hot road apples. We are not going to make lesbian lives better by substituting a grim Big Sister for Ronald Raygun's vague and evil smile. When women have enough sex and the right kind of sex, or at least feel that this might be possible to achieve, I suspect that we will feel better about ourselves, have more energy, and be less inclined to take shit or be talked down to. The sexually satisfied woman is not a vegetable, she is a Valkyrie. However, because you have to be "selfish" (this is what our culture calls women who pay any attention to their own needs) and somewhat aggressive to get yourself off on a regular basis, the sexually autonomous woman is probably not going to be a docile follower. She will probably have something better to do than go to five meetings a week to argue about the language of a resolution. She will want to get the damn thing on the ballot already.

And (oh my Goddess) could it be that the real fear of those who want to use sexual repression to fuel the women's movement is that we might actually make so much progress that (gasp!) we would not need to go to meetings at all? I guess some people would just be happier in a world where there's never any time for romantic picnics or week-long orgies. They'd rather caucus than copulate or cunnilingicise. *Un*-fuck them, I say. They've already wished that on themselves anyway.

Now, women really are second-class citizens, and lesbians stand even further down the line. We do not get a fair deal. We are belittled, under-educated, kept back, exploited, abused, and ridiculed. That has to change. But in the process of describing how we are oppressed, trying to persuade other women to see the damage done to them, and pushing for a reallocation of gender-based resources, we run the risk of becoming professional victims.

We must celebrate our strength as well as our frustration the beauty as well as the misery in being a woman, a not-woman, a lesbian. Jewelle Gomez's tender story, "Come When You Need Me," poignantly evokes the hard times of a young, black lesbian newly migrated to Manhattan precisely because it lacks any self-pity. When Gomez's heroine, Roslyn, meets Lee, the descriptions of their lovemaking are deeply touching because the author has told you, simply, without lecturing, just how hard they have to work for the precious time and space to be together.

Just about the only power women have been given is the control over morality in the private sphere, the home—the behavior of other women and children. One of the unspoken, unexamined conflicts in feminism is our fear of giving this domestic power up if we seek more power in the rest of the world. What if we fail? Then we will have no power at all. It is tempting to turn feminism into a quest to extend private feminine power into a public institution, and make the world run according to the proscriptive precepts of Cary Nation and Betty Crocker. Regine Sands' amoral and promiscuous heroine Diana Hunter (who appears here in an excerpt from a recently published Lace novel), is the exact opposite of this sort of moral guardian. Instead, Miss Hunter jetsets about in her high-heeled lizardskin pumps, and hotel maids and stewardesses alike melt in the heat of her complacent, self-confident abandon. Diana Hunter is a self-absorbed, but she is also subversive.

The best lesbian erotic fiction empowers women because it creates new icons, a new feminine system of erotic symbols that has the potential to transform the way all people, not just lesbians, view women and desire. Chocolate Waters' poem "Feminine" points out with devastating irony the need to reclaim this word and soup it up.

Alluring new concepts, previously thought to be mutually exclusive, are being paired. Women who are fuckers, women who are receptive and responsive without being devalued, are just two of these new possibilities. Cass, the highway patrolwoman with notches on her nightstick, and the bitchy blonde speed-demon ("all she has on under that little sundress is her perfume") she pulls over are Anahn Nemuth's contribution to dyke iconography in the story "Fantasy #418."

The new semiotics of lesbian sex imply deep changes in our definitions of what women will become. Lesbian readers want stories about women who are wise, magical, deadly, cunning, and strong—as well as irresistibly come-hither-ish—because we want desperately to be heroes. We want our lives to be adventures, and the patriarchy relentlessly "protects" women from experiencing those kinds of risks and thrills. Women this powerful, whose lives have a truly human scope, seem so unlikely, so far away, that it is not surprising that some of the stories in this book are about women in the future or on another planet. Dorothy Allison's "Predators," Meh and Tesla, are two impressively realistic aliens. But this scary pair are still recognizable as girlfriends as they stalk the dock-strip and leather bars of New York City, bickering and flirting and looking for a bit of human dessert.

Creating a sense of history for lesbian lust, confirming our intuition that some women have always managed to find a way to escape male control and touch, excite, gratify other women, is another function that some of these stories perform. Ann Allen Shockley's "The Mistress and the Slave Girl" is about an interracial lesbian couple in the antebellum South—a time even more hostile to lesbian passion than our own. The common theme of an all-woman society that might have existed in the past is given a rather chilling twist in Linda Parks' "La Femme Chênière," the tale of a band of bloody, bawdy female buccaneers.

Now, I am no separatist. I am a polymorphous perverse lesbian who feels that girls will be boys will be queer will be kinky, and if somebody is wearing a leather jacket with nothing underneath it I don't always check their chromosomes before I start pinching their tits. However, it strikes me as being a bit ironic—a bit strange—a bit inconsistent—that it is ostensibly other dykes who keep telling lesbian sex-writers—lesbian pornographers—that we are ruining their lives and future and movement by writing about what cunt tastes like and chases after and what makes us cum on or in somebody else's cunt. Some of the fiercest homophobes wear lavender t-shirts and labrys necklaces.

I wonder if the porn debates are not a new twist on those old conflicts about how lesbians and straight women were going to work together in the feminist movement (if at all), and the conflict about who exactly is a lesbian. There are an awful lot of straight women out there who can't stomach men. Some of those women have taken sanctuary behind the "political" label of lesbian, but in fact other women have almost no erotic charge for them. I feel sorry for them, and I think feminism ought to be working for a world where women who want to fuck men can do that in peace and satisfaction. I'm grateful to straight feminists who are willing to be dyke-baited without breaking solidarity with us. But lesbianism ought to be more than a haven for the frustrations of heterosexual women who can't abide the way most men behave. It will not solve their problems to gag those of us who want to sing detailed praises of women's bodies, nude, corseted, in uniform, athletic, plump, restrained, free, sweaty, predatory, insatiable, itching, glowing, struggling, cruising, harnessed, working, speeding, teasing, achieving, thighs imploding. To be blunt and probably vulgar, if you don't like to read about pussy maybe you don't like pussy and you should be lickin' something else.

Feminists and gay liberationists who want to normalize homosexuality (i.e., pass) don't like lusty literature because it might make them all hot and bothered when they need to respectfully beg our elected representatives, whose salaries are paid by our taxes, to stop making things so tough for us. Well, we aren't going to achieve any of our goals by being respectable. Even if we don't want to talk explicitly about queer sex, our enemies do. They tell the most outrageous lies about us because they know that we are inimical to their system. They say the sex two women can have is impossible, unfulfilling, disgusting, unnatural, never happens, is too much, is perverse, happens only if men are there, quits happenings if men are there, isn't genital, is too genital for normal woman to enjoy, is really male, isn't real at all. I am sick of having other people tell lies about us. I want us to tell the whole truth about our flamboyant, generous, persecuted, amazing sex-lives. If we have the courage to describe ourselves without shame, whatever our enemies have to say about us will subside to the status of a footnote.

The new lesbian porn is more than entertainment, it is propaganda, outright queer, lezzie, bulldagger, femme-swagger proselytizing, It would be presumptuous of me to speak for all lesbians who write sexually explicit fiction and poetry. I'm sure our sexual politics differ on many points. But I have a vision of what this writing has the potential to achieve.

Lesbian pornographers are working toward a day when no woman in the world will be ignorant of the fact that another woman can make you slither in your panties. We are working toward a day when no little baby dyke of thirteen will think she is the only one in the whole world until she grows up to be a librarian and discovers **The Well of Loneliness** locked up in the Hell Collection. We are working toward a day when no woman will stay with a lover for 15 years without having sex because she believes that sex should not be that important to a lesbian. We are working for a day when no woman will put her own hand over her mouth and masturbate in the dark trying not to wake up her lover because she cannot tell her lover what thoughts and pictures and imaginary dialogue passes through her mind and makes her come. We are working for a day when none of us will be pushed out of the lesbian community or punished in any way because her desire is uncommon or unique.

In short, lesbian pornographers are working for sexual honesty and human happiness. Nobody believes that writing sexy stories is enough to make that happen, but writing which arouses you, dear reader, and sends you prowling through your own libido is dammit-all more radicalizing and liberating than the ACLU or NOW or the FBI or WAP will admit. Besides, honey, we can write such shameless stuff that you can't wait to get home alone and get your fingers sticky. But we can't redistribute all the wealth. I do believe that day will come, but in the meantime, we have to make it through the night.

I don't necessarily like all the material in this book. You probably won't either. Some of the work seems too sentimental to me, or in need of more editing and polishing. But I'm glad there is such a variety of themes and treatments, from romantic to rough. You can't get much more gentle and languid than the bath and banquet scenes excerpted from Merril Mushroom's *Dirty Alice*, in which a mysterious, green-tinted Lady uses her knowledgeable webbed fingers to wring all manner of delicious sensations from Alice's by-no-means unwilling body. And at the other end of the spectrum are tales like Dennise Brown's "Sweet Cecily." Cecily is every bit as curious as Alice, but her mentor, Miss Todd, is somewhat more severe. Cecily only grows sweeter under her controlling care, and when she passes from her hands, it's at the behest of Mistress Amelia, who is a tiny notch more severe.

If you really hate a selection, skip over it and start the next one with an open mind. If you finish the entire book and you are still dissatisfied, maybe you ought to write a story for the next anthology. There are many faces to lesbian desire, and it is not easy to tell secrets like these at all, let alone in a writerly, skillful way. In time, if we are left to develop this new genre of lesbian literature in peace, we will have even better writing, and there will be enough of us publishing it that we can specialize, so that those of us who don't like S/M or vanilla or anal sex or group sex or oral sex or casual sex or butch-femme won't have to tolerate its distracting presence alongside works that speak to our most intimate needs. For now, Lady Winston and Lace Publications have to bundle everything together between one set of covers, and if these stories can bear to be next to one another without hissing, perhaps we can be equally kind to them.

I can't imagine anything that would make our enemies angrier than the spectacle of all of us getting along, despite our sexual differences. It's probably too much to hope for from a book that only intends to seduce and entertain you, but if **The Leading Edge** fosters a little more tolerance and mutual understanding in the lesbian community, it is a pioneering work indeed.

TRAVELS WITH DIANA HUNTER

REGINE SANDS

[Ed. note: The following is an excerpt from the novel *Travels With Diana Hunter*, Regine Sands, Lace Publications]

In the Grab Bag of Life,
She always,
Always,
Reaches for the Bigger
Packages

Cigarette spent. Diana Hunter, thirty years old and stunning, showered. Packed. The scent in the motel room would take the maid a full eight hours to extinguish.

Diana left the key on the bureau. Grateful for the convenience of the airport motel. Grateful that she had sufficient time to make the next airplane, having missed the prior one. Grateful for the silent exit: the woman had left when Diana was in the shower. Diana lifted her suitcase and attaché in one hand, and stood there. Still.

Something, she thought, there was something left to do. She surveyed the room and nothing left behind. She remained. One thing, something left to do.

She placed her bags on the militarily still-made bed, and went into the pink and black tiled bathroom, caught her reflection in the mirror, leaned back against the wall-to-ceiling sliding glass shower doors, closed her eyes, lifted up her cotton skirt, slid her hand into her white panties and slowly stroked the length of her cunt with her fingers.

She didn't even consider the inconvenience of having to sit on the plane with wet panties for the length of the flight if she masturbated now, she preferred it; what if the person in the next seat on board noted the scent of her pre-takeoff activity, all the better; supposing the stewardess confronted her with the fact that she "knew" what heinous act against God Diana had been up to . . . . Yes. Diana could only hope!

Diana felt her already swollen clitoris. Yes, eyes closed, she began to fantasize about her possible encounters on the airplane. Her cunt pulsed, her imagination beckoned, the invitation to fantasize extended itself. She began:

> The flight held promise for Diana. She saw the woman in the seat next to hers. The woman in her late thirties: thin, tight, angular, wearing a grey linen suit and a severely tailored silk-soft black blouse. A jet-black leather attaché, the color of her pumps and purse, rested on her lap, open.
>
> A "Hello, My Name Is" badge lay inside the attaché. The "Hello, My Name Is" part was blackened out with one thick black marker stroke and on the card was written only the name, "Miss Tropic." Miss Tropic. That was all. To the point. Bold. Now came the decisions, Diana calculated. Does she or doesn't she look like a Miss Tropic woman? And what are the implications of the heat of that name? And so the silent interchange between them had already taken flight.
>
> Diana noted that this woman was writing on a notepad. What she wrote, Diana couldn't see. She would soon enough, because the woman finished writing, put the pen in the inside pocket of her blazer, folded the note in half and half again, and turning to Diana in one move, handed it to her. The cabin lights turned off, the plane taxied and took off into the black night.
>
> Diana had only to say "Yes." The woman did the rest.
>
> The woman closed her attaché and placed it under her seat and turned again to Diana. Without so much as a self-conscious hesitation, not one doubtful pause, Miss Tropic took Diana's face in her hands and kissed her lightly on the

lips with her tongue. Before Diana could bring her tongue out to meet the bold, firm tongue of this woman, Miss Tropic had unbuttoned the top two buttons of Diana's blouse, slipped one hand inside her shirt, and most gently cupped Diana's breast through her camisole. Miss Tropic had a most massaging hand. Caressingly it slid along the outline of Diana's breasts, these long and perfectly manicured hands. A fleeting thought flashed through her mind when Diana saw Miss Tropic's long ruby nails—but it made no difference if the woman was straight or not.

Catching Diana most unaware, Miss Tropic whispered that she wanted to lay her lips on Diana's breasts. Her "beautiful" breasts, is what the woman said. Not surprising. Most women had the same thought when they met Diana. Her breasts were full, large, round and much too much for one set of hands to explore. A mouth always fared better.

Miss Tropic's directness was arousing Diana, and she responded to the woman's request (which warranted no response but Diana couldn't remain totally passive) nonverbally: her legs spread apart a slight inch or two. Still ladylike. Still composed. That would soon change.

Diana's breathing though was beginning to give her away. Irregular, heavier, sweet-smelling. She was getting hot. Her legs spread only enough for Miss Tropic's long-nailed, slender fingers to slide up her thigh to her already damp cotton panties. Miss Tropic was pleased at Diana's eager compliance. So was Diana.

Miss Tropic, Diana was certain, would have done what she wanted to do with Diana anyway, with or without her permission. With a woman like Miss Tropic, it was smarter just to do what she was told to do. Like a good girl. And Diana was all for being and seducing good girls. Miss Tropic could expect continued compliance from Diana Hunter.

Miss Tropic returned to stroking Diana's breasts, looking down at her hands on them, desiring them and then looking up to stare into Diana's eyes: a straight, hungry, telling stare. Not asking. With an "enough-time-has-been-spent" look, Miss Tropic lowered her head and lay her ruby lips on the dark hard nipple of Diana's right breast wetting her camisole. . . . The Rush–

The Rush elicited a low moan in Diana that surprised her but not Miss Tropic. Gently kneading Diana's breasts, kissing her nipples now, first one then the other, kissing, slowly sucking in the silk. Then lifting it to kiss the flesh, slowly, slowly with her parted lips, her smooth tongue.

And yes, there were other people on the airplane. Thankfully, it was a night flight. And no, Miss Tropic was not the type to do 'it' under an airplane blanket. And yes, they were watched. Some were too asleep to watch. Some too horrified. Some just too turned on. The sole person watching with focused concentration was the slender, leggy stewardess.

She must have been a California girl. Perfectly Protestant. No more than eighteen. No more than five-foot nine. No more than one hundred and ten pounds. Lean, and physically gifted. She stood by Miss Tropic's aisle seat and leaning in against it, she watched and imperceptibly rubbed her thighs back and forth alongside the seat. From time to time she leaned closer over Miss Tropic's seat to watch, to grow more aroused, and she would whisper, or it might even have sounded like a murmur, "oh yes". And as she grew more excited, "yes, do that . . . I like that".

To Diana, a thrill, the fleeting hope for a ménage à trois. The stewardess would stand straight up again after speaking, to watch. Diana was jaded already at the ripe age of thirty, but jaded or not, a *ménage à trois* was one of her most delicious choices when the choice was offered. Which it was not in this instance.

Miss Tropic placed her hand on Diana's knee and painfully slowly, or so it seemed, moved it up and up the length of Diana's thigh, under her skirt. Diana's skirt barely moved, that is how stealthily this expert hand slid. She could only feel Miss Tropic's soft palm sliding up her thigh to where they both wanted it to rest, tired from its long journey, and at peace.

"No," the stewardess whispered to Miss Tropic, Diana now wondering if they were in this together. "I want to see." Miss Tropic didn't have to turn around to see who was making the request. She knew. Miss Tropic had chosen not to invite the stewardess to join them. Now Diana saw the name tag on the woman's ample uniformed-covered chest, "Veronica". Miss Tropic was to have Diana to herself, for now at least. Veronica was waiting impatiently for an invitation. Too polite, and not assertive enough (anyone paled in comparison to Miss Tropic), she remained a not-too-silent partner.

But Miss Tropic did turn to her. She said calmly and coolly, with almost a deliberate ease, "What is it that you want to see, Veronica?" This question seemed natural enough to those who didn't question Miss Tropic like I did, knowing full well Miss T. knew the answer to it before asking.

Veronica replied, trying very hard to maintain some semblance of control, as she was *only* eighteen, "I want to see you put your hand in her panties." Speaking slowly, her trembling voice continued on admirably with its request, "I want to watch your fingers rub her pussy, and I want to watch her come."

Always one who tried to accommodate every woman's wishes (especially when they coincided with her own), Diana joined in the conversation with, "Let her, Miss Tropic." After, all permission had to be granted from a woman like Miss T.. "I want Veronica to watch," she said, turning to Veronica. When no response came, she continued, "It's okay, doll, you can watch me. I want you to. I'll spread my legs wider for you so you can watch me come."

Miss Tropic turned to Diana with a "you-did-very-well" look on her face and smiled an experienced smile. Superior. Diana had done well, and she was pleased.

"Lift up, I want to slip your skirt up to your waist," Miss Tropic said, and true to her word Diana complied for Veronica's benefit, spreading her legs apart. Her clitoris was pulsing noticeably, her panties were damp through and through and Miss Tropic could sense Diana's wet. Miss Tropic was pleased.

Skirt lifted, in full view were Diana's panties hugging her round, soft hips. A flattering sight. Miss Tropic noted that Diana looked just like she hoped she would. Veronica, too, was grateful. And Diana could have come right then and there, but she knew better than to hurry a woman like Miss Tropic.

"Pull your panties down so Veronica can see. She wants to watch and I want you to show her everything." What a deep mellifluous voice Miss T. had—her words measured, weighed, exact.

Diana did as she was told. She slipped her panties down her hips, down her thighs, calves, ankles and off. Not knowing what else to do with them, she handed them to Miss Tropic.

"You are so good," Miss Tropic whispered to Diana with a seductive hint of a smile. It was intensifying this heat of hers, as it seemed that Miss Tropic knew exactly what turned Diana on.

Legs spread for Veronica, Diana awaited further instructions from the woman in charge. Miss Tropic pushed the button on the armrest of Diana's seat and it reclined back. Diana was almost laying flat, nude from the waist down except for her high-heeled, open-toed pumps. Red alligator pumps. Miss Tropic lifted the armrest between her seat and Diana's and pushed it back flush, out of the way. No obstacles, no distractions now, as Miss Tropic had work to do.

"Now spread your legs wider for me, honey, like I know you can. Like you want to. Spread them very wide, darling, so Veronica can watch." Miss Tropic's hands on thighs, parting them, helping Diana to obey. Miss Tropic placed her hand right on top of Diana's grateful cunt. Massaging. The young married couple two rows back heard Diana's moan. Diana, to say the least, was intoxicated. The closer Miss Tropic's fingers came to the threshold of her wet recesses, the harder she throbbed there. Veronica was motionless. Miss Tropic made longer and longer strokes up the length of Diana's cunt. Miss T. had no intention of penetrating Diana; Diana had every expectation that she would. Diana grew hotter with anticipation, with the touch, with the strokes, with the look of the ruby nails on her this way.

Veronica was not hiding the fact that she was going to come herself at any moment. She had lifted her dress up discreetly, as befits a woman in the proud position of stewardess, and was gently masturbating herself in the dark aisle, facing the two women. Diana was certain to come shortly herself with this vision in front of her. Veronica's eyes were closed, her teeth barely biting her thick lower lip, her breasts slightly moving, and her hands rubbing her own wet pussy. Miss Tropic, once again, was pleased.

Still stroking, gently at first, but now more firmly. Regularly, rhythmically, steadily and more firmly, purposefully and more firmly, watching Diana's every move.

Watching Miss Tropic watching her watch her, Diana was aroused in triplicate. Yes . . . .

Miss Tropic instructed Diana, "Come now. It is time for you to come. Let go now, little darling." With this, Miss Tropic lowered her head to Diana's cunt, kissing her there, and whispering to her in between the gentle wet kisses, "Come . . . You want to . . . I know you want to . . . And you have to now for me . . . ." Miss Tropic's beautiful hands on each of Diana's thighs holding them apart, with Veronica watching, and Miss Tropic's wet lips, throaty voice, full tongue upon her now . . . on her lap . . . between her thighs . . .

Diana came.

Her orgasm must have lasted a bit of time, for in that time Veronica had knelt down, lifted Miss Tropic's skirt up from the rear, and no panties to contend with, slid her more than wet fingers inside of Miss Tropic. Oh God, Yes! This was the scene Diana opened her eyes to, not knowing even that she had closed her eyes when the orgasm overcame her. The look of this sent bliss-filled tremors up her spine, as she watched Veronica tongue Miss Tropic, lick her, taste her from behind. The sight was unmatched: Miss Tropic in her crisp linen suit being taken from behind by Veronica, kneeling in the aisle with her face gently pressed against Miss Tropic's bottom. Miss Tropic was groaning, and not in her usual measured and controlled way.

"Please me, Veronica. I know that you've wanted to . . . Come, sweet thing, do it to me." Miss Tropic began breathing harder and continued with her instructions. "Yes, Veronica, that's right, yes, please me . . . ." And Miss Tropic cooed other things that neither Veronica or Diana could hear. She was seducing herself with her own words, her own voice.

Diana, still laying still, turned on her side and let Miss Tropic's head rest in her lap, with, "Lay your head in my lap, Miss Tropic, and let me hold you." And Miss Tropic obeyed—both giving and receiving wet fingers kissed and tongued Miss Tropic, Diana caressed and stroked and Miss Tropic's hair, her face, her breasts. Her hands were everywhere arousing, arousing.

Miss Tropic came violently and Veronica did not so much as ease up or slow down, as one might expect, but continued to do it to her more firmly, knowing Miss Tropic would not ask her to stop even though she might have wanted to. Miss Tropic reveled in the smoothness, the grace of Diana's hands, and told her so. And before long, Miss Tropic shuddered with the second coming.

"Good," she said, the sound resonating from her most wet and swollen lips that were buried in Diana's wet and fragrant lap. And all were pleased . . . .

Coming as no surprise to me, Diana came at the exact moment she fantasized Miss Tropic's final parting word "Good". Without the passion of the orgasm with her tropical woman friend in her imagination, but with enough knee-weakening force to sate her temporarily.

Diana opened her eyes and found the hotel housekeeper, a blond girl of no more than twenty, leaning against the closed bathroom door, watching her. The girl had been watching Diana masturbate. This was a delightful surprise. Sometime during her semi-conscious state of fantasizing, the girl apparently entered the bathroom, shut and locked the door behind her, leaned back against it, and not more than seven feet away from Diana masturbating, watched. Oh, most definitely, yes!

"What is your name, little one?" Diana asked.

"Whatever you'd like to call me" from the girl, told Diana everything she needed to know for now.

"PREDATORS"

DOROTHY ALLISON

"I hate this place," Tesla growled. The heavy mist had collected on her piled braids and was trailing down her forehead. She had to keep shaking drops out of her eyes, cursing every time. "I fucking *hate* this place."

Meh shrugged. "You hate cities, all cities." Her voice was so soft Tesla had long ago developed the habit of tilting her head perpetually in Meh's direction, straining not to miss the faint whispery voice. "It's all these overhanging walls." She shrugged again. "Why don't you try thinking of them as cavelike?"

"Too bright." Tesla gave up and used the back of one heavily-ringed hand to wipe the accumulated water from her face. "I like my caves nice and close and dark," she paused to watch a pair of hunch-shouldered men stumble past their doorway, ". . . and unpopulated. *Sweet Suffering Mother*, they're certainly an ugly bunch, aren't they?"

Meh gave the two men a slow look, shrugged, and used her right thumb to skim a line of moisture off her eyebrows. Tesla had been talking about how ugly the people here were since they had arrived. It wasn't a conversation she wanted to reopen. Maybe it was time they gave up waiting and tried the bar again.

Of course, that had its own complications. No one paid them much attention hurrying past in the rain, but in the more comfortable atmosphere of the bar, Tesla drew every eye. These people weren't used to extraordinarily tall coffee-colored women who wore their hair tied up in tightly coiled braids and razor-edged rings on every finger. Worse, Tesla had already acquired a taste for whiskey and on two glasses would start to croon through her teeth and get amorous. A little whiskey and Meh would have to decide whether or not to try sobering Tesla up with strong coffee. But coffee seemed to turn her melancholy and mean, and there was nothing like a half-drunk, sad-eyed, horny and irritable Tesla to complicate a task.

Meh sighed and gave Tesla's belt an affectionate tug. "When we finish this up, you and I will take some time off together, spend some cash on ourselves for a change. Maybe take another desert trip? Or do a few weeks in that port city you liked so much?"

Tesla's back stiffened, adding two inches to her height. "There," she hissed, "that look like the one you wanted?"

Two figures were coming up the uneven brick walkway, one of them kicking at occasional scraps of trash with booted feet. The other was gesturing and apparently arguing in a low intense mutter, too absorbed to really watch where it was walking. The booted figure kept putting out one hand to steer the other around pieces of lumber and patches of broken glass. The angry one never noticed and never stopped talking. Meh gave a soft grunt of interest.

Both were dressed casually in the typical jeans and jean jackets of this neighborhood, but atypically both of them smelled female and yes, the booted one did look something like the one Meh had come here to find. The one in the soft-soled running shoes certainly wasn't.

"YOU DON'T GIVE A FUCK ABOUT ME!" The angry one had stopped suddenly and was screaming at the other. "YOU DON'T GIVE A FUCK ABOUT ANYBODY. YOU AND YOUR GOD-DAMNED PRIDE . . . ." She was trembling all over, waving her hands in the air, rising slightly up on her toes. The booted one stood perfectly still.

"YOU THINK YOU'RE SO . . . ."

The hand snapped up and out beautifully. Both Tesla and Meh heard the crisp sound of the slap from thirty feet away. Both smiled and gave each other a pleased glance. Yes that *might* be the one. Running Shoes stumbled, staggered and fell back against a rusted garbage can. Boots said something that neither of them could hear.

"Goddamn you," the other one moaned.

"Stay away from me." Both of them heard Boots this time. "You come near me again, and I'll kick your ass into the East River."

Meh and Tesla eased slightly out of their doorway, watching. Meh drew both of her hands up so that her palms rested lightly on her collarbones. Tesla laced her fingers together so that the filed and pointed nails rested lightly on the rings that marked her knuckle joints. For a moment they resembled nothing so much as two tigers who had scented blood; then without exchanging a word or glance both of them drew back and became almost invisible in the doorway. Only a faint gleam from the street lamp showed on Tesla's rings before she tucked them into the shelter of her armpits.

"Ahhhh," Tesla breathed, a low rumbling pleased sound.

"YOU . . . ." Running Shoes tried again, shoving the garbage can around and toward Boots, a foolish move since the other was much more agile. A kind of turn and jump and Boots was over the can and had taken Running Shoes by the collar and slammed her up against the filthy loading dock on their left. Both Tesla and Meh caught the gesture that brought one hand down to a boot and then seemingly reconsidered, closed and became a fist that slammed the other one face down into a scummy puddle at the edge of the dock. They couldn't make out the words this time either but the threatening hiss was clear.

"Maybe," Meh said softly, "maybe so."

Sputtering and struggling, Running Shoes was wholly unable to either wiggle free of her captor or get her face more than partially out of the dirty water. "ALL RIGHT," she suddenly yelled hoarsely, going limp and allowing herself to be shaken loosely, "I'm sorry." Her voice sounded like she was about to cry. The booted woman let go of her and walked away without a backward look. Tesla and Meh exchanged a wordless glance and separated immediately; Tesla striding off after the sodden victim and Meh carefully following the stiff booted figure toward the dim glow of the bar's doorway.

"Goddamned Bitch." Annie blew her nose roughly into one hand and wiped it on her jeans, then looked back to see if she could see Jay, but the woman had already disappeared into the bar at the end of the street. "BITCH!" Annie yelled, and heard her own voice crack. The urge to cry made her throat hurt. There wasn't a damn thing she could do to Jay, not a damn thing.

There was a man coming up the street now, carefully not even glancing in her direction. Another goddamned leatherman, cap and all, with that same stiff booted stride Jay was so proud of. "Nothing but a man in a pussy body," Annie heard herself mutter, and the thought made her feel better. That's all Jay was, a caricature, a clown. Madeline had called it, Madeline had warned her. What had she said?

"No normal woman, no self-respecting lesbian would spend all her time in those dark smelly faggot bars, acting like a faggot, sucking up to faggots."

She would give Madeline a call, go see Madeline. Annie wiped her nose again and hurried up the street, carefully not looking over at the dark-visaged leatherman passing her. She hated them, hated most of all that nothing she could do would affect them, just like Jay, like some of the teachers she had had in school, some of the women with whom she had tried to be friends. The hardest thing about it was that she kept on wanting to be near them, to get them to like her, to talk to her—to respect her, and take her seriously.

It wasn't sex, not really. Sex was something different; sex was fucking. Hell! She and Jay never even talked about fucking, though sometimes Jay did talk about the women she *fucked* in a tone of voice that sent chills right through Annie's belly. But even then, Annie didn't want to be one of them, one of those "bitches". A bitch who would beg for it, a woman who would literally get down on her knees and stare up like a hungry puppy dog—the image horrified Annie. She couldn't stand the idea, the thought of herself on her knees crying for those gloved hands on her body, her mouth open, her thighs wet, her howls loud in her own ears.

Annie shuddered. She wasn't like that. For her it was something different . . . it was all that unspoken stuff, a kind of tingle all over her, a feeling in her throat not her cunt. *Not sex, it wasn't sex*, she told herself again. But when Jay acted so tough it *did things* to her, made her feel special and privileged just to be allowed to watch. Sometimes afterward, when she was actually rocking on Madeline's soft breasts, she would remember it, something Jay had said or done, the shine on her boots or the way her belt slid through the loops with a sigh when she pulled it out. Annie would remember it and a flush would ripple all over her body. She would feel suddenly sexy and powerful, feel like somehow she had become Jay or even one of those men in one of those bars. It was horrible and wonderful, and because of it she had hung around and let Jay treat her like shit, laugh at her and watch her with those cold expectant eyes. Annie knew Jay was waiting for her to get down on her belly and beg for it, but she wasn't like that. She really wasn't like that.

"I'm not like that," Annie told herself once more, for the thousandth time. "I'm not."

"You're not?" The tone was ironic, the words sibilant and threatening. It sounded as if someone had stepped up and hissed them right into the hollow of her left ear.

Startled, Annie swung around peering into the gloomy mist that was quickly turning to rain. There were four big identical white trucks lined up along the platform to her left, and a row of empty battered garbage cans scattered along the sidewalk on the right. The arc lamps at each corner threw great circles of light that almost met in the center of each block. Annie knew that if she kept going a few more blocks, the ramps would disappear and traffic would pick up. This place was only busy in the early morning when the trucks loaded up and pulled out, and the early afternoon when shipments were restocked. Evenings and nighttimes, it was deserted except for people walking west to the leather bars and the diners that hugged each entrance to the highway, not very many people actually, and not the kind that worried much about being harrassed on the street.

Annie crossed her arms across her chest and hugged herself. Somehow she had never paid much attention to this walk with Jay, but now she realized that this really was a pretty deserted desolate area, the perfect place for a mugging, especially this late and in this weather. She made herself take a deep breath and start walking again. She must have imagined that she heart the voice. All she had to do was keep walking quickly and calmly a few more blocks.

Down between two of the white trucks something moved. A shadow flickered and Annie felt the hair on the back of her neck rise. Determinedly she kept moving but edged closer to the other side of the street, nearer the garbage cans. Whoever it was wasn't going to take her by surprise. They'd find out. She wasn't entirely a fool. Her teeth started to chatter and she clamped them together painfully.

"I am not afraid," she told herself, and then realized that she was starting to shake all over. "It's the rain, the cold," she whispered, and then saw one of the garbage cans suddenly unfold and stand up, becoming an impossibly tall dark figure.

"Oh, mama," Annie moaned.

"Nooooo." The figure had a strange throaty hiss to her voice. It was a woman but not like any woman Annie had ever seen. This one had to be six and a half feet tall, at least a foot taller than Annie, and she had something funny-looking coiled all over her head, something ropelike and sparkling. Her clothes were kind of shiny too, a glossy wet leather that wrapped her body in strange contours. The shirt-jacket didn't have a zipper or buttons but crossed in front over the belly and wrapped around the back to come back to a tight knot in front.

"I can not even imagine," the woman whisper-hissed, "what might have mothered you." She took one step forward and Annie felt herself automatically backing up. There was something *wrong* with the way this woman moved, the way her big hands with those impossibly long fingers came up, flexed and linked themselves almost in front of her throat. Bright silver rings on every finger and thumb caught the glow of the street lamp and flickered. Annie found herself thinking nauseously of a coil of baby snakes, wet and hungry, their slender bodies linking and unlinking. The woman chuckled and Annie looked up for the first time into that brown smiling face, the teeth white and sharp, the eyes a strange hazel, almost yellow in the dim light, exactly like a cat's.

Exactly like a cat's eyes, a snake's eyes, pupils slitting open side to side, not widening as an iris.

"Oh, my god."

"You don't like what you see, motherless thing?"

Annie couldn't move. Those hands, those great long arms came out and caught her, her shoulders were gripped and lifted. Shuddering, Annie felt her whole body recoil, and those little snake images blossomed again before her eyes. Involuntarily she pitched forward, her stomach cramping in nausea, a terrible feeling of violation and . . . wrongness going all through her.

"No, no, no, no," her own voice was mewling like a kitten far off and helpless. This enormous thing was hefting her into the rain, laughing delightedly in her terror. The little snakes flickered again and Annie suddenly knew that this creature was inside her head. Knowing what it was made the feel of those mental tentacles too horrible. Her arms flopped and Annie felt her bladder give way, then her sphincter. She opened her mouth and felt as if a wave were coming up to spew out there too, but closed it again suddenly when she was dropped painfully to the bricks. Desperately, she rolled over onto her belly and tried to crawl away.

"Such a small small world in your mind," that hissing voice whispered. "So tight and predictable and sad. Can't you ever open your mind's eyes, little thing? There are worlds and worlds and all of them wide, and waiting for you, little thing. All of us . . . waiting for you."

The monster woman laughed again and half danced, half jumped right over her. Annie turned her head up, saw the figure in the air, those great hands and silver rings flashing over her, down toward her, the silver edges catching the light, catching her cheek, ripping skin and flesh, opening up little rivers of blood. Annie screamed then, no words, nothing intelligent, nothing human.

"Nothing human," the monster whispered with enormous pleasure right into the deepest part of her brain, and the little knife rings cuts her again.

* * *

Meh waited a long couple of minutes before following the booted woman into the bar. When she and Tesla had come here before, they had had a moment's trouble at the door. The people here had some odd notions about who exactly they allowed to engage in some of their social pleasures. Women, for example, were not automatically welcome in these bars. But then Tesla and Meh, while *women*, were not exactly what the doorman thought of when he started to tell them "women aren't welcome here." On good nights, he didn't put it that way. He took a moment and said something like "you wouldn't be comfortable here". But then the tall one had given him this strange amused glance and a little chill had shot right up from his ankles to his balls. He had paused a moment and taken in the fact that both of them were dressed in leather, and the little one had a particularly long and fascinating blade strapped half way up her right thigh. He had stared for a moment at that and then into her preternaturally bright black eyes, and backed off without a word. It was similar to the way he greeted the woman in the boots, except to her he gave a nod of familiarity.

"Strange people," Meh told herself again. The man at the door hesitated again when she approached and she felt clearly his desire to make her go away, but again he stepped aside. She was wet all over from the mist that had turned to rain but she resisted the urge to shake herself. Instead she drew the braid of her hair up out of her shirt and dropped it down her back, willing herself to relax. She would dry soon enough, and hopefully Tesla wouldn't take too long with the other one.

* * *

Waiting for her beer, Jay took a moment to carefully inspect her nails in the light from the back of the bar. The nails were flat, even and steady. It was the steadiness that pleased her. She had not, after all, lost her temper. When she looked up at her own face in the mirror, it was as impassive and calm as that of the man two stools down on her left. Good. She tucked her left thumb into her belt and reached for her beer with her right hand, giving the bartender an appreciative nod and an almost smile. He returned the nod before stepping away. It had taken her a long time to earn that even unexceptional glance of approval that most of the men in here never even noticed. Scenes like the one with Annie always made her feel unsettled, as if some of the hysteria and weakness could attach itself to her. The bartender's cool but impassive familiarity reassured her, reminded her who and what she was.

Not Annie.

A woman of pride and strength and discipline, that was who Jay knew herself to be. Years of keeping her mouth shut, her tongue pressed against her teeth; her muscles worked and ready; her mental stance both engaged and detached—Jay knew she had made herself who she was. Twice she had apprenticed herself; once as uki to the top ranked Judo competitor in Massachusetts and once as a virtual slave to the meanest woman she had ever known. In both cases her apprenticeship had lasted only until she had known that she could overcome and defeat her erstwhile superiors. She had achieved the first in open competition in Boston, the second in a street outside a bar in New Orleans, and if the story could be told, it would be the second that she would speak of with the most pride.

Most of her best stories could not be told.

Jay sipped her beer and used the battered mirror over the bar to look over the room. She knew perhaps seven of the dozens of men there but most of the men knew about her. For those who didn't, the bartender would offer a few quiet comments. If it came down to it and there was a scene with some drunk who would challenge her right to be here, she had long ago developed the habit of waiting it out without saying a word. The odds were then that one of those seven would intercede, and if they didn't she had no doubt about her own ability to handle any confrontation that reached the physical. With neither height nor visible muscle mass, she was still harder and faster than most of the men in the room could imagine—except for the ones who had seen her in action.

That speed and skill was important. No matter what Annie thought, it wasn't a matter of pride. It was more essential than pride; it was self respect. She hadn't started out with it, she had earned it, manufactured it out of nothing but her determination and force of will. Sometimes, looking into other women's faces she would see their lust and recognize an old edge of her own. Not that they wanted *her* so much as what she had made of herself. They took her as a measure of what they could be, while she took their glances, their hunger, and used it to make herself even stronger, harder, more their obvious superiors.

The worse thing that anyone could say about her was that she took her lovers by that measure, choosing always women who had some one thing—either strength or skill or experience—that she did not have. By the time the relationship had run its course, she would have it. She would better it, and them, and prove it to them. Afterwards they would not be lovers, and only occasionally could they go on, as her apprentices, slaves or followers. She could not change that about herself, no matter how lonely it made her life.

Jay had gotten so used to the loneliness, she never even thought about it any more. She only knew that it was harder and harder to find women who truly drew her, women to whom she could breathe the precious word "lover". It was not that she did not value the women who followed her, the women who worshiped her, who begged for her hard hands or her whip. She wanted them, of course, and respected them, particularly those few who could challenge her and acknowledge their own desire but the ones like Annie were a kind of challenge too.

She always managed eventually to force them to ask for it, to admit exactly what it was that they wanted, sometimes to their own shock and horror. Each of them came to her pretending to themselves that they were not what she knew them to be, clinging to the pretense that they did not have those contemptible desires for her impassive cruelty. It was wonderful when they finally gave in, when they finally opened themselves up and begged without shame or denial. It was delicious to watch their mouths fall open and the hunger show naked in their faces.

Jay loved that, loved everything they suddenly became willing to do, loved, too, gradually upping the ante—that form of submission they would have to offer her to earn her attention then. She even loved the moment when they broke and ran from her, when she found the one thing they could not force themselves to endure. That was the loneliest moment of all, bittersweet and terrible and past the understanding of the men here who seemed to understand all the rest of it. It was the flaw in her, and she knew it even if no one else understood exactly how it functioned—how much she wanted the lover who would go all the way with her, who would love the life as much as she did and who would, out of that love for the life and her, become hers in a way she had always dimly sensed was possible. The lover she dreamed of would be the woman who could truly match her, the one who would come to her wanting everything she had and willing, wholly willing, to do all that was required to achieve it. But where in all the world was the woman who could match her, match will and nerve with lust and fire?

The topmen here who truly respected her and whose respect she returned watched her dramas indulgently and chided what they called her perfectionism while honoring it. "If there were no code who would we be?" Malcolm had told her. "Just posturing images acting out self-indulgent rituals. No, the soul of leather is the pursuit of the ideal, that ruthless standard we measure ourselves against."

She had nodded, agreeing, but swallowing the words she really wanted to say to him. There was no man in the world capable of hearing what she knew to be the truth—that her search, her pursuit was the hardest and the most impossible. The men around her—that blond for example, in the vest watching Malcolm so intently—never understood what her life was like. Malcolm himself, who had once forced a young man who was rude to her to kiss her boots, didn't really appreciate what it was like for her.

When she was younger and she had walked down here, with her stomach in a knot and every piece of leather she owned drawing stares and challenges from every corner, it was the loneliness that had done her the most damage. If she could have had back then the friendship she had now with Malcolm it might have helped, at least to keep her hope alive. But it had taken her years to prove herself to the few friends she had and all of them were men—distant, alien, impossible. There had never been a woman for her the way there were men by the score for each of them.

Jay had always been the only one, the only queer of her kind. No matter how hard she had searched, she couldn't find another. All the ones who came after had her as a stalking horse. She had nothing but the men and no matter what they shared, they might as well have been another species.

Jay turned the bottle up and took a long drink. There was really nothing going on here tonight. Maybe the blond would get it up enough to approach Malcolm, but like her, Malcolm had an innate reserve that made it unlikely he would do anything with the blond out here. She'd had her own blond here a few weeks ago, another arrogant young boy who'd half drunkenly challenged her right to the corded whip she wore coiled on her left front belt loop. He's pretended to a great amusement, but it had taken her not very long to ascertain that he wasn't even tipsy, but knew of no other way to approach her. She had had a moment of lust for him as a woman, a momentary fantasy of stripping away his denims to find a woman's breast and cunt. But for that small cowardice of pretending to be tipsy, he had been superb—defiant, beautiful and the kind of challenge she dreamed of a woman offering her.

She still wasn't sure if he had known what he was getting into with her, but he had played it out anyway with a mock show of respect that never quite crossed the line into insult, but tried to cover his own embarrassment at even approaching a woman. He had wanted her as a man, she knew. The irony of it was vicious as well as delicious and she had been all the more cruel for it. Someone had told him about her of course. Malcolm, perhaps? Someone had even explained that she almost never wore her leathers anymore. Though no one could have told him why. No one knew why.

No one knew the rage and grief with which Jay had locked her leathers away into her cabinet, the frustration and grief that she had stubbornly swallowed and hidden, the grief with which she had finally decided that none of the women she had driven away from her were going to come back as she would have if she had been them. No one could have guessed that half the skill she had used on that boy's back and ass had fed right from the well of her knotted loneliness. They couldn't know. They were surrounded by their kind, reflections of themselves or the selves they aspired to be. Even the ugly and the weak had a place here, had a right to the place itself. All she had were her will and her eyes and her hands, the proof of her own body and endurance.

The greater endurance was never of the body. It lay in her unrelenting pursuit of what appeared not to exist at all—the woman who could match her, the woman who could walk down here the way she had walked down here.

Jay had a sudden urge to order another drink, to go on drinking and do what she had never done, get drunk on her ass, dangerously roaring drunk. She grinned at the idea of walking out of here drunk, staggering up those dark wet streets like a fool looking for her own destruction, but then she frowned, disturbed. Someone was staring at her—a shadowy figure at the far end of the room leaning against one of the rough wooden beams that braced the entry to the back rooms. Black eyes reflected back the light like mirrors, a sharp boy's face too young to have even a shadow marring the cheek, thick dark eyebrows, hair pushed straight back from the face—either oiled or wet. It was a hungry face that watched her, an intent unwavering gaze that made Jay steadily more uncomfortable. She had never grown used to being stared at however much she tried.

Jay looked down at her hands again, taking even more care that her face remain impassive. That face reminded her of a woman she had been watching lately—a very young woman up at the 78th Street Dojo, a precise and altogether pleasing warrior who had a particular talent with those long and difficult bamboo poles. Someone said she had been a ballet student who had grown too tall too fast and been weeded out for awkwardness. It was the rage that had first caught Jay's eyes—the outrage that had burned in those dark self-possessed glances. The boy leaning against the beam had the same look about him, a condensed and self-involved distance that tempted every instinct Jay had ever allowed herself to admit.

As Jay watched, the boy moved, pulling away from the wall and straightening slowly before stepping forward with a loose smooth stride. Short, no more than 5′4″ with very small features and hands. Jay was unaware that she had pursed her lips and narrowed her eyes, that her concentration had sharpened so that the moving figure was all she saw. She was unaware, too, of the shock that suddenly widened her eyes and drew an almost imperceptible flush to her cheek. She saw the glint of light at the leg, the knife riding the long ridge of muscle up the thigh, the long blade and silver pommel against the smoky black of the leather pants. Her eyes followed the line of the blade up the thigh to the hip, the curve of the waist drawn in tightly, the curve and slope that screamed female against the flat-edged proportions of every other hip in the room.

It was a girl!

No. Jay pulled her eyes away, looked up again at her own features in the mirror. Not a girl, it was a woman. The youth was an illusion of those unmarked cheeks. The eyes in that face were not young. The confidence in motion that marked every pivot of that hip, the way the hands drew unerringly across the thighs and lower belly, the aura of silence and darkness that rode the shoulders and sharp clearly defined cheekbones were not to be found on the young and untried. Jay took another pull at her beer and knew without looking that the woman would approach her, knew, too, that if she did not, Jay would have to go to her

The woman was her mirror, in spirit if not in flesh, and the hunger that swelled in her throat at the thought was almost unendurable. The loneliness that she had endured for so long, that had been so much a part of her armour, had become with one glance a weakness, a flaw she could not bear and did not even know how to face.

"We have not met," the voice spoke softly at her left.

Jay set her teeth and turned, keeping her right hand loose on the beer bottle. Show nothing, her instincts screamed. She showed nothing.

"No." Careful, careful. Who is she? What is she? Why have I never seen her, heard of her before?

The pupils of those black eyes were enormous; they reflected the light so intensely. For the first time, Jay regretted how dim the lighting in the bar was. She wanted to see this woman clearly. She wanted her naked and exposed, every muscle turned up to the light, everything showing from the edges of her teeth to the curve of her pubic mound. How strong was she? How fast? Where did she come from and what did she want?

"You are drinking?"

"Becks."

A nod, almost a smile.

"Can I buy you another?"

Jay did not want or need another now, but this was a ritual move she knew well, and momentarily it relaxed and reassured her. She nodded, not wanting to speak more than she absolutely had to.

"Excellent."

Was the accent German? Clipped anyway, and unfamiliar. Jay resisted asking the woman her name, where she was from.

"My name is Meh."

May? A Chinese name, the hair was black enough and worn tied back in a single long braid, but the eyes had only the smallest slant. Probably right out of Newark, Jay told herself with a slight inner smile, no sense in guessing. She turned her hip so that she slightly faced the woman and carefully let herself look her up and down.

The boots were odd, without heels, like slippers but sturdy and supple at the same time. The pants were leather, nothing exceptional, mostly dull and grey-black though glossy where they still showed the rain. The belt was wide and she noticed there was a narrow cord that ran down from it to the inside thigh and the fine harness that held the knife. The blouse was a heavy silky fabric as dark as the pants, tucked in tightly with a knot showing at the left hip and another at the left shoulder. It did not seem to have buttons but fastened with those knots. No rings, and the bracelet on the left wrist looked more like an iron cuff than jewelry. No earrings, but the lobes themselves appeared to have been slit in several places. It must have been done long ago for the lobes were perfectly and cleanly healed with the left one divided in two and the right by three. After a moment Jay realized that there was a small indentation at about the point on the left ear that corresponded to the slit on the right.

"They didn't get that one." With a nod, Jay indicated the left ear.

Meh gave a slow wide smile, drawing the bartender over with a slight extension of her left hand. "Becks for both of us," she told him and turned back to Jay.

"No, but I had to sell it later. I was young then and I liked the feel of the biggest rings I could find. I didn't think how easy they would be to tear off."

The bartender set the bottles down with a soft clink and looked expectantly at Meh. Instead of reaching for money, she just gave him a long glance in return. In turn he looked suddenly confused and turned immediately for the far end of the bar.

"You appear to have been wiser." Her eyes wandered to Jay's ears and then down to her throat, down further. Jay felt a heat rise slowly up through her body, her throat go dry. She drank again. She had never worn earrings, never.

Meh watched Jay's eyes, the little lines that came and went as she turned her face and narrowed her eyes, the confusion that was written there as clearly as the desire. Involuntarily, her own hands clenched on the beer bottle and the cuff on her left wrist made a small sound on the wooden bar. They both looked at it, the heavy scarred metal bluish grey in the bar's light. It had slipped down on her wrist. From under one edge of it fine white scars showed clearly against the brown of her wrist. It was just tight enough so that it could never be slipped off without breaking the bones of her hand, just loose enough that a thong could be slipped between it and the skin.

A speculative look came into Jay's eyes and she looked down

again to the knife on Meh's thigh. The silver was highly polished, a small ball of reflection on the leather.

"Were you wearing that knife then?" Her voice was very soft.

Meh still wore the smile but her eyes seemed to grow even brighter. "No." She reached across with her left hand and laid it across the pommel. "I didn't get this knife until I'd had this"—her right forefinger tapped the cuff—"for a while." The forefinger slid across the bluish metal until the hand cupped the cuff almost tenderly and began to rotate it around the wrist. In the dim light Jay could not have been sure, but she could see no hint of a seam, no ridge to show how the cuff had been closed.

Meh kept turning the cuff idly and watching Jay's face. "I've taken my time to get what I need," she whispered.

Jay felt a slight shiver in her belly, a deep uncertainty slowly sinking under her own curiosity and desire. She felt as if the two of them were moving in a slow motion, as if every sentence traveled light years to reach the ears. She lifted her left hand and it was as if she were pushing the weight of the ocean in front of her. Her left forefinger touched the cuff between Meh's spread fingers. It was surprisingly warm. She closed her hand over Meh's, pressing the metal beneath Meh's hand and then slipped her fingers back slightly to form a kind of flesh cuff beside the metal, close and solid. Meh's eyes were flames in the poor light. Her mouth opened slightly to show the teeth parted and the tongue pressing them.

"And you," Meh spoke softly, "how often is it you get what you need? How often?" She smiled again, "How often have you had anything as good as you can be?"

Her eyes wandered slowly down to Jay's belt. Her right hand just as slowly dropped to the whip that hung there. Carefully, respectfully, she stroked the braids with her knuckles. For a moment Jay felt almost drunk and frankly giddy, as if those fingers were stroking not her whip but her sex itself, the suddenly moist folds of her labia. Meh's face was very close, the breath palatable on Jay's cheeks. Jay closed her eyes and drew a deep breath.

The cuffed hand freed itself and pulled away. Meh stepped back, the beer in her right hand, the smile lazy and inviting. She strolled away toward the darker back of the bar, the dim reaches whose depths were marked by the rough towering beams that framed doorways and support posts. There was a ripple of whispers that spread out from the bar's entrance, a ripple of interest marked by men who turned and looked over their right shoulders.

Jay never looked. She took the nearer of the two bottles in her own right hand and followed Meh through the doorway, into the deeper stillness lit only by occasional absurdly small lights. Meh looked back. Jay followed. Both of them had curious half smiles. Neither paid any attention to the men they passed, the sounds around them, nor did anyone look at them. Each was too intent on his own prey, his own desire.

Jay's left hand curled around the corded whip on her belt and stroked as if remembering the touch of Meh's fingers. Meh kept moving deeper and further away from the men and the lights, but as she moved she kept glancing back, drawing Jay on. Her eyes kept dropping to the hand that stroked the whip and the hunger on her face was so strong it made Jay want to purr with satisfaction.

The corridors gave the illusion of going on forever though they had actually been constructed around a series of twenty or so rooms of varying dimensions. Most were cubicles a few square feet in size with rough unworked pine walls. A few were fairly large and nearly star-shaped. Sound carried from one to the next so that stepping into any of them one was surrounded by a chorus of moans, sighs and groans. Most were entirely dark. A few had those tiny dim lights. Meh chose a small empty one with a bulb glowing in one corner. She took a stance in that corner directly under the light, one foot drawn up so that the sole of her boot was flat against the wall. Turning the bottle up, she drained it and watched Jay step into the room after her.

"Ahhhhhh," she breathed. She rocked the bottle loosely in one hand, her smile wide and welcoming, the other hand posed provocatively on her hip. "Found what you were looking for?" she taunted.

For a moment, watching her Jay imagined Meh was going to break the bottle against the wall and fall into a crouch. She was almost disappointed when, instead, Meh bent and set the bottle on the floor, then drew herself back up and slipped her thumbs into her belt. Her face shone under the light, glowing with lust, and ruefully Jay knew her own features must have shown the same intense desire. How long had she waited for, hungered for, someone like this? She imagined the ridges of muscle and sinew under that blouse, the heat beneath those pants. Jay stopped a foot away from Meh and, sipping her own beer, went on stroking her whip.

"Show me how much you want it," she ordered.

There was a moment of stillness, then the thumbs came out of the belt, rose and began to work at the knot at the left shoulder. When it came loose, the flap of fabric dropped, exposing the small right breast and the hard puckered nipple. Jay began to uncoil her whip from her belt. Meh's expression never changed. She just dropped her hands to the knot at her side and began to work it loose. She had to step away from the wall to free the fabric that was pulled seamlessly across her shoulders and back. Then she dropped the blouse beside the beer bottle and watched Jay pull the whip free and trail it through her fingers.

It was a small whip, supple from use and oily sweat—about two and a half feet long, a good three inches round at the base but narrowing to a wicked cutting point at the tip. Jay held it by the base and the tip with her right hand. The loop it made held that way resembled a noose. She drew the loop up Meh's belly between her breasts to her throat, turning her hand so that the thick base pushed Meh's chin up, the head back.

"Was it me—me you were looking for when you came here?" Jay whispered the words to Meh's glowing eyes. "Was it me you expected? My whip you wanted?"

"You," Meh whispered. Her hands rose and settled on Jay's hips, hot and sweaty against the denim.

A turn, an arc, Jay used her left hand, palm open to backhand the pale glowing face. It was a repeat of the slap she had delivered on the street earlier. Meh's hands dropped flat against the pine wall. Jay slapped her again, watching the head move loosely, the mouth open, the eyes fall half-closed, the lips tremble. Meh's braid fell forward across her breasts. Jay took it in her left hand and wrapped it round and round the knuckles until she had it in a tight grip. Ruthlessly, she bent Meh's head back, pressed forward and gripped her ribs, using her nails to dig into the skin.

"You." She repeated Meh's last word, unable to even voice all she was thinking and feeling. Her pulse was so strong she could feel it against the strands of Meh's hair. Her teeth felt sharp and sensitive, the whip in her right hand as smooth and powerful as part of her body as her hands. She had a flash of what Meh would look like bent over, on her knees, her mouth open refusing to scream. Of course, she would refuse to scream. She would fight and fight not to fight, but still . . . . She would take her home. This one she would keep. This one, this image of herself and all she had ever made of herself. It was as if for a moment a sweet electrical current were flowing all through her, resonating most in her belly and cunt. Everything, everything was finally all right. Everything made sense. Everything she had ever done had been in preparation for this moment and all the moments that would follow.

"You," she whispered again. "You will have to work very hard to show me what you are made of—what I am going to make of you." Was that what she had always wanted to say or what she had always wanted to have said to her? It did not matter. Meh's eyes were great liquid pools as wide and deep as her desire. Meh's body arched to press forward against Jay's body, against the whip at her throat.

"Oh yes, make of me . . . ." Meh pressed and reached, and deep inside Jay something that had always been knotted and tight loosened. A warm melting feeling enveloped her and she felt suddenly how soft and tender her own skin was. It was that feeling that made the great brown hands that came around her more than a shock. The very concrete beneath her boots seemed to give way. She saw the hands flatten against the pine on either side of Meh's face, Meh's face as it twisted in disappointment and impatience, the mouth that opened and gasped.

"No!"

Those hands were too big, massive in the dim light and strange in every sense of the word. The fingers were too long, showing clearly an extra joint on every one, each joint marked by a bright silver ring, each ring marked by a crescent, and the crescents themselves showing razor edges on the points.

Jay tried to turn but her left hand was still caught in Meh's hair, and the body behind her was pressing too close. With a look of exasperated resignation, Meh's hands came away from the wall and up to grab Jays neck just below her ears.

"WHAAAAT . . ." Jay couldn't finish it. Her eyes settled on Tesla's glowing pupils and still-wet flushed cheeks as they bent over her and all the breath drained out of her body.

"AHHHHH," Tesla mocked her and Jay was overcome with a startling vision of snakes reaching up innumerable tiny hungry mouths. A sensation almost electrical crossed her scalp. She staggered and closed her eyes but under her eyelids those other eyes still glowed.

"Oh, yes. You're perfect."

The fingers on Jay's neck pressed and dug in. Desperately she tried to fight them but Tesla merely lifted her clear of the floor while keeping her head close enough for Meh to press her fingers even tighter. There was no way to resist. Jay's eyes rolled back in her head and immediately she seemed to be falling, sliding, roller coaster fast and straight down. Far below her was a great glowing ball, a world in miniature like the globe her seventh grade teacher had kept on her desk. But the one she was falling toward was not green and blue but grey and red, marked not by seas and forests but by deserts and great stone city clusters.

"You'll love it," Tesla promised her. Jay tried once more to scream and had the clear impression that Tesla had swallowed the very impulse like a treasured and tasty delicacy. The little hungry snakes that were Tesla's mental image seemed pleased and gloating as she went down into darkness.

"I didn't know you were here," the man in the doorway paused and turned slightly so that his shoulders, broad and muscled, filled the entry. The leather he wore was so black he almost disappeared and the cover he wore low over his eyes hid any expression.

"Oh, we'll be going now," Tesla told him, lifting Jay lightly with one hand and settling her loose body across one shoulder.

"Yeah," Meh sighed and began to pull on her blouse, "though I wish you could have waited just another little while." She twisted the lower knot tight, leaving the top of the blouse loose, her damp and flushed breast bare to the air. She grinned ruefully, "Maybe even a day or two."

"Now, don't be greedy, small one." Tesla laughed lightly and slipped one hand into Meh's blouse, turning the hand so that the ring's points lay against the flesh. She twisted the hand steadily until Meh gave a low breathless moan.

"We got what we came for, and when we get it home, I'll let you have all you want of it." She drew her hand out and then slapped Meh's rump affectionately, pushing her toward the door. They slipped through and past the man easily, Tesla still holding Jay with one hand and chuckling.

"Good hunting," she called back to him as they walked away.

"Oh, yeah." He tilted his head back and watched them through yellow slitted pupils.

"Yeah."

THE MISTRESS AND THE SLAVE GIRL

ANN ALLEN SHOCKLEY

"My god, it's warm!" Heather breathed miserably in the heat of the moving carriage. It was April and already the heavy southern sun dominated the sky. She could hardly wait to get home and take off all those cumbersome clothes.

"Ah-h-h, different from Boston, eh?" her brother, Ralph, observed caustically, slumped in the corner of the seat opposite her. The odor of whiskey permeated from him, mixing sourly with the humid air.

"Yes, *quite*," she retorted, fanning her ankles with the layers of skirts. Ralph had never gotten over their father sending her away to school in the North, where she had chosen to stay until recently. Looking back, she suspected that he had done it to relieve himself of the task of bringing up a daughter after his wife's death.

"Heather, I am very much aware that you don't relish living here," Ralph said, jaws tightening.

If it weren't for you, I wouldn't have to, she almost blurted out. Their family lawyer had written to her, beseeching her to return to try and save the plantation. Only eight months since their father's death and Ralph's mismanagement had threatened a bank foreclosure. He had no interest in business matters, which was clearly evident at the cotton mill this morning. She had to practically force him to come with her, tearing him away from writing his poetry. Because of his literary bent, he stood out like an abolitionist in the south, a place where slave masters not only outnumbered poets, but had little use for them.

"Ralph, please. Let's not bicker," she pleaded, her anger slowly subsiding as pity took its place.

Saying nothing, he half turned to focus his attention outside the carriage. Watching him, she marvelled at how much they looked alike. They could almost pass for twins, except she was a year older than his twenty-one. Both were slightly built with burnt-auburn hair. His extended into side-burns down a weak, but handsome face. Her skin was fairer than his, and her features more refined. Besides their physical appearance, they were alike, too, in another way that each kept silent about.

When the carriage slowed down, Ralph sighed. "We're nearing the slave market."

How she detested passing the scene, seeing the throngs of bargaining hard-eyed men, but most of all, the pathetic sight of the Negroes. Their driver, George, must hate seeing it too, having been in bondage all of his fifty years. Impatiently, she leaned forward to tell him to push ahead, when the sight of a beautiful young slave girl on the auction block diverted her.

"A likely wench!" She heard the black-suited auctioneer describing loudly. "Seventeen years old. Healthy. Good teeth."

The girl stood like a statue before the men, staring vacantly over their heads. An aura of sadness surrounded her. She was a mulatto with cream-colored skin, and long, black wavy hair falling down her back.

"One thousand!" someone shouted.

Heather found it difficult to take her eyes away from the girl. A pink silk dress hugged the fine curves of her body. She remembered being told that they purposely dressed the good-looking ones that way. Swallowing hard, she experienced an almost forgotten familiar sharp sensation coursing through her like hot lava. The carriage had just about come to a halt because of the milling crowd.

"Come now, surely she is worth two thousand!" the auctioneer challenged. "See!" Abruptly, he bared a breast, exposing a perfectly molded mound with a brown nipple. "A find one for the house!" he smirked, using his whip to lift the girl's dress to shapely legs.

As the men surged forward, fury stormed within Heather. "Ralph, come! I'm going to buy that girl."

Ralph turned to her in astonishment. "But, my dear sister, I thought you weren't going to purchase any slaves. 'Slavery dishonors the human race,' " he quoted her mockingly.

"George, stop the carriage," she ordered. Climbing out, she pushed hurriedly through the huddled spectators. "Two thousand!" she called out.

The men stared at her in amazement. Ladies in these parts weren't in the habit of outwardly bidding for slaves. That was a male perogative.

"Twenty-five hundred!" proferred by an oily looking man smoking a cigar.

Heather recognized him as the town's tavern owner with the brothel above. "Three thousand," she advanced, voice strong and clear.

"So-o-o, you're attracted to her too," Ralph whispered beside her.

"Four? Do I hear four thousand?" the auctioneer bartered greedily. Hearing no takers, he barked, "Sold! To the lady for three thousand dollars!"

"That Heather Blakely's got a mind like a man's for business," she overheard someone remark from the crowd.

"Ralph, go fetch her for me." Triumphantly she returned to the carriage. This was one slave girl who wouldn't be thrown to the wolves for a white master's breeder or concubine, she thought delightedly.

"She's up front with George," Ralph informed her. Climbing back in, he pulled a silver flask from his coat pocket.

"Must you?" she lashed out in exasperation.

"I *must*!" he snapped back, deliberately taking a healthy swig.

"Now, tell me, what do you intend to do with your expensive beauty?"

"She will work in the house," Heather responded crisply. No more was said between them during the remainder of the journey home.

* * *

Washing the road dust from her face, Heather twisted her hair up off her neck and changed into her usual plantation attire of riding breeches. Then she had Carrie, George's wife, longtime surrogate mother and cook, to bring the newly bought slave girl to the library.

The girl stood before her desk, hands clasped loosely in front of her. Once again, Heather's body warmed at the sight of her. To offset the unsettling stirrings, Heather looked out the window. The sun was fading and twilight was approaching. She glimpsed the slaves leaving the fields to go to their cabins. All of them had belonged to her father. Now she had become a slave owner. The idea did not cheer her.

Clearing her throat, she asked gently, "What is your name?"

"Delia . . . ." The answer was barely above a whisper.

"Delia," Heather repeated, frowning, for she had said it without a "ma'am" or "mistress" as slaves ordinarily did. There was certainly nothing servile about her, Heather detected, sensing the quiet air of dignity about her. She was reminded of the Negroes with whom she had attended the private all-girls' school in the north, daughters of free blacks, as well as southern white slave owners whose consciences pricked them to educate their illegitimate daughters.

"What can you do? I mean . . . ."

"I know what you mean," the girl replied evenly. "I can sew." Pride was in the answer, heightened by the flashing of her dark eyes. Her voice was well-modulated with no trace of the slave dialect.

Heather's eyes lingered on the tilt of her head which made her hair curtain one side of her face. "You're very pretty, Delia," she said, the words slipping out on their own.

The girl gave her a quizzical look, brushing her hair back from her face. As she did, Heather saw the dark bruise by her ear. "How did you get that?"

"I was struck by the slave trader."

Heather's lips pressed together. Getting up, she went to her, reaching out a tentative finger to the spot. Immediately she was sorry, for the girl's skin was like velvet, soft, smooth, exciting, triggering want. "I'll never strike you," she promised huskily. "Never."

The girl's eyes softened. "Thank you." A small smile curved her mouth, relaxing the stiffness of her body.

Heather looked quickly out the window again to hide the stark desire in her eyes. This girl, Delia, had brought up emotions that she had tried to keep submerged, only to find them rising once more, stronger than ever. The unhappy school affair years ago had devastated her. After that episode, she had vowed there would be no other.

"You'll be my personal servant, Delia. I know you're tired, so I'll talk more with you in the morning." Only when she heard the girl leave, did she dare to look with longing at the space where she had been.

Ralph, even though intoxicated, had managed to make it downstairs to dinner. Carrie's ample form, clothed in a white apron and headpiece, hovered over him, trying to coax him to eat the ham and rolls she had prepared. Seeing her brother picking at his food, Heather wished that she could persuade him to get away from the South with its engulfing power for weakening men with artistic strength.

"Carrie, are you getting Delia settled?" she questioned, helping herself to the food.

"Yes'sum, Miss Heather. She in the kit'chin eatin'."

"What do you think of her?" Surely the girl would be less reticent among her own.

"Hum-m-m—" Carrie's dark face grew solemn. "She quiet, like she cryin' hard inside 'bout sumpin'." Pausing, she poured hot coffee for Ralph. "She got real soft hands, like she never done no kind of hard work befo'."

"If that's true, I'm certain my sister doesn't intend to break her work record," Ralph interceded, stirring sugar into his cup. "Too bad she doesn't have a brother of comparable beauty. I might be tempted to buy a slave myself," he laughed shortly.

Heather flashed him a warning look, while Carrie's face assumed the mask of the house slave: see nothing, hear nothing, think nothing. Heather ate her meal in silence, mind occupied with the next day when she hoped to find out more about Delia.

* * *

The morning's early heat stalked the bedroom where Heather sat at her dressing table. Turning to Delia, she asked, "Have you cut hair before?" When the girl answered in the negative, Heather handed her a pair of scissors. "Let's give it a try anyway."

Surrounded with cut tresses on the floor, Heather scrutinized herself in the mirror. "It's much cooler this way," she determined in satisfaction, running her fingers through the short strands. "Don't cut yours," she said to Delia, reaching up to finger her hair and graze her hand along the girl's face. Quickly she drew back, for it was like touching a flame. For a long moment, the girl's deep brown eyes grew darker, appearing to drown Heather in their depths. Heather fought not to embrace her, to kiss the sweetness of the face she had felt.

Suddenly the room became unbearably hot to her. "I'm going downstairs to breakfast," she said brusquely.

Ralph was slouched at the table, shirt open at the collar, eyes red-rimmed, drinking his coffee. "So, you've cut your hair!" he noted immediately. "What role are you trying to play, dear sister?"

"I'm *not* playing *any* role," she snapped. "But since you mentioned it, what I would *really* like to be is an abolitionist. Free the slaves, sell this plantation and go back to the North to live!"

Ralph shrugged indifferently. "All right by me. Do what you like."

"Then," she added, voice softening, "you would have enough money to go to Paris and write."

"And not be an oddity among the southern patriarchy," he uttered grimly.

Sympathy welled up in her for him. If only he would let her get closer to him. They were two people in the wrong bodies for this age, oddities among others. Eating her breakfast hurriedly, she summoned Delia to go for a walk with her. The morning was shaded by an overcast sky. Walking with the girl, Heather perceived how small and delicate she was, barely reaching the tip of her shoulder. The girl followed her down a dirt path lined with trees, her breasts rising and falling from the quick breathing caused by trying to keep up with Heather's sure-footed long strides.

"Let's sit here for a while." Heather motioned to a large oak tree where a robin was perched, cocking inquisitive bright eyes at them. "I used to sneak out here as a child to get away from everybody."

When they dropped to the ground, the robin, sensing his intrusion, blessed them with a chirp and flew away. Leaning back against the tree, Heather asked curiously, "Where did you come from, Delia?" Like a strange being dropped from the sky into her life, she wanted to know more about her—this beautiful girl who affected her senses so deeply.

"New Orleans . . . ."

"That's a good distance from here. Virginia."

"You go where they take you," she replied, lips trembling.

Perceiving her painful dilemma, Heather changed to a lighter vein. "Who taught you to sew?"

A shadow crossed the girl's face. With downcast eyes, her slender fingers plucked at the grass. "My mother . . . ." Choking on the words, she seemed on the verge of tears.

Heather automatically took her hand to comfort her. The hand fit like a small bird in the palm of her own. "What's troubling you?" she asked gently. *Besides being a slave*, she thought to herself.

"Nothing . . . ."

"Something *is*," Heather insisted, squeezing Delia's hand. "Someday, I hope you'll trust me enough to tell me." Thunder rumbled a bass warning in the sky. "We'd better go back," she said regretfully, "before it rains."

The rain stayed with them all day, steady, refreshing, cooling the air. To get Delia out of her mind, Heather busied herself with updating the plantation records, filling in expenses, slave births and illnesses. Things were beginning to look much better, and the bank was willing to wait.

Towards evening, she grew tired and went to her room to lie down. What she needed to relax her was a good book. She asked

Delia to go down to the library to get Elizabeth Barrett Browning's poems.

Waiting, the though struck her like an electric shock: Slaves weren't supposed to be literate. But Delia had gone for the book! When she returned, Heather said quietly, "You can read."

Delia stepped back, fright on her face. Then, sensing no hostility from her mistress, she replied hoarsely, "Yes. My mother sent me to a free school."

Heather sat up quickly on the side of the bed. "Was she a slave?" She had to have more answers to piece together this puzzling enigma of a girl with whom she was surely falling in love.

"*My mother was not* a slave," Delia stated firmly, tossing her head back proudly. "She was a free woman!"

"In that case, *you* were free," Heather said slowly, knowledgeable of free issue. If the mother was free, the child was born free.

"I–I was kidnapped by slave traders when my mother died."

"How horrible! What about your father?"

Delia's voice lowered. "He was my mother's master. He set her free before I was born. I don't know anything else about him." She began to cry, letting the pent up ordeal of suffering come out into the tears.

Heather went to hold her closely. "You're going to be all right," she hushed, "here with me. You'll sleep in the alcove off my bedroom. Be here at all times. Close to me."

The girl's sobs subsided in the protective circle of her mistress' arms. "You're so kind–so very kind to me."

That night, Heather could not sleep, blaming it on the rain, but knowing it was because of Delia in the other room. She could hear her tossing restlessly in the bed, muted sobs escaping, provoked by her dreams.

Restraining the urge to go to her, Heather buried her head in the pillow, hugging its softness like a woman's body. Delia's face spun a disturbing vision in her own dreams, the haunted look and midnight eyes that were beginning to glow at the sight of her. Yearning made a warm cradle in her stomach. She did not fall asleep until daybreak.

The accident occurred in the afternoon of the next day. Ralph's horse reared up and plunged wildly across the field, knocking Delia down while she was gathering flowers for Heather. George carried her into the house, followed by a stricken Ralph.

"I'm sorry, Heather," he apologized in the library where Heather had been working. "It was a new horse. Skittish." His eyes begged for forgiveness. "I know how you feel about here. I know—."

From the turmoil of her thoughts, Heather looked up at him in a daze. One thing stood out in her mind: she had to go to Delia. When she got up shakily, Ralph reached out his arms to solace her. Kissing her lightly on the cheek, she rushed upstairs to where Carrie was tending Delia.

Upon seeing her worried face, Carrie smiled reassuringly. "She goin' to be jest fine, Miss Heather. Didn't do much harm. Jest scared her to deaf."

Bending over the bed, Heather asked anxiously, "Are you all right?" *Dare she touch her forehead? Smooth her hair? Lean closer?*

Delia nodded, smiling, seeming pleased that Heather was there.

"I'm glad," Heather's fingers were lighter than a snowflake on Delia's cheek.

When darkness fell, Heather went to her, a shadow seen moving across the room in the lamp's yellow flame. "Would you like to sleep with me?" She caught her breath in fear, holding it until the answer came. She couldn't order, demand, for it wouldn't be the same.

The girl's face expressed surprise, then changed to a rare happiness, blooming in the dimness like a flower opening to the sun. "Yes—." A quiet response that meant so much.

The fantasies in Heather's dreams had come true. Together in the large canopy bed, Heather drew her close, basking in the warm curves of Delia's body pressing into her own. An exploratory fingertip traced a solitary pattern on Delia's face, pausing at the eyes, narrow nose broadening at the nostrils, and the full sensuous lips.

"My Delia," Heather breathed into her ear, "You know, some women can feel about one another the way men and women do."

The girl was still in her arms, head nestled against Heather's breast. Finally she whispered softly, "I know. Now." Tenderly she looked up to cup Heather's face, taking a picture with her eyes as she did. When their lips met, it was a fusion of soft petals wet with dew.

Leaving her lips a baby's breath away, Heather asked, "Do you like my kissing you like that?"

"Yes . . ., yes!"

Heather felt gladness winging in her heart. Gently she kissed her again, opening Delia's lips with her own to slip her tongue into the chamber of Delia's mouth. Breathing hard, Delia's arms wound tightly around Heather's neck, as she shyly returned the kiss.

Slowly Heather began to remove Delia's gown. "My sweat, I want to see your beautiful body." Then, Heather took off her own gown. Naked, they embraced, body to body, warm flesh blending as one.

"Delia, say my name," Heather urged, nibbling on an earlobe.

"Mistress—"

"No! I'm *not* your mistress!" Heather retorted, half angrily. "I am your *lover*!"

"Lo-ver. Heather."

"And, you are my love." Lightly Heather caressed Delia's breasts and round stomach. "Darling, you're so delicate, like a precious jewel." She kissed her forehead, tasting the dampness of her skin with the tip of her tongue. The trembling of the girl's body imparted the message she wanted to know. Fired with passion, Heather kissed the brown nipples of her breast, mouthing each tip with her lips. Next, she stroked the tapering thighs, stopping to fondle between them. The wiry pubic hair tickled her palm as a middle finger eased into the moist entrance to another wet warm mouth. The girl moaned as her legs parted to better receive the instrument pleasuring her.

Withdrawing her hand, Heather bent down below to place a kiss on the small sunken hollow in the middle of Delia's stomach. When Delia's hands tightened in her hair, she moved her lips to where her hand had been. There she blew warmth into the furry patch before sending her tongue on its lascivious journey.

"Oh-h-h," Delia gasped in delight.

Heather rose from the fountainhead of ecstasy to cover Delia's body with her own. Gently she improvised a slow sensuous movement, sealing bottom lips with an excruciatingly sensuous gratification almost akin to pain. Delia's face contorted as the sweetness of loving swept through her. As if she had been born with the knowledge of this kind of love-making, her body moved in perfect harmony with Heather's cadence.

"This is the way I like it," Heather murmured in her ear. "Loving as one—together. You with me, and I with you. My wonderful dark princess, I love you!"

"And I, you!"

The heat of sex ignited a tumultuous fire between them, causing an agonizing paroxysm of joy. Simultaneously they came with stabs of blinding goodness overpowering their bodies on a comet of happiness.

* * *

Months later, Heather freed the slaves and sold the plantation. Ralph went to Paris to live, and write, where there was a heritage of those like himself. Heather moved to Boston, taking Delia with her. There they shared a house sheltered by love. No one knew they were lovers, only that the white and black women, who lived together, were terribly devoted to each other.

NOVICE

NATALIE JEENE

be still now
my darling,
let us love
for all our worth.
come
lay down beside me,
let me be your first.
softly
i will touch you
may i kiss
your lips
with mine?
smooth—
your flesh
upon my flesh,
your breast—
may i touch
with mine?
slowly . . .
let us envelope,
our bodies
and
our minds.

slowly . . .
with intense emotion,
love swelling
endless with time.
presently—
my lips
more gently,
touch
hidden lips
like mine.
movement—
so sweet the motion,
come—
taste of sweetened wine.
still now
we linger,
clinging—
two bodies wet.
will we be
together always . . .
sweet smell,
salty sweat.
tenderly
caressing your hair,
covering your face
with gentle kisses,
you gaze
with questioning eyes
wondering all this time—
knowing now
what you've been missing.

FANTASY #418

ANAHN NEMUTH

Dusk was Cass' favorite time of the day. When the sun was setting the eyes played tricks on drivers as they went speeding down the lonely stretch of road Cass patrolled. Her white patrol car appeared to fade into the barren landscape until it was too late, then its distinctive outline would jump out at them as they raced by. It was an old trick Cass knew, but it worked. In just one night she could surprise enough speeding drivers to write a week's worth of tickets.

Tonight was unusually slow for a Friday. Cass didn't mind. She lighted a cigarette, stretched her legs under the steering column and rested her head lazily against the headrest sighing contentedly. A fraction of her attention lingered casually on the crackling noises and voices coming from her police monitor while another portion of her alert mind was devoted to scanning the road. Her hand idly and lovingly stroked her long night stick. From time to time her fingers explored the notches carved in its grip. Cass was at peace yet as readily poised as a stalking cat.

From the distant horizon a movement caught Cass' eye. She ditched her cigarette and picked up her radar gun to aim it at the oncoming car. Her heart rate elevated with the excitement of the possibility of a chase. As the car came closer she knew this was the beginning of another easy Friday night. This car was hovering around 100 miles per hour. What fun, Cass thought, I hope it's a woman.

She turned over her engine, took one last reading—108 mph—put the speed gun down and hollered like a cowgirl on a bull as she took off after her game: a shiny new Corvette. How she dearly loved ambushing hot rod drivers. Siren blasting and lights flashing, she hunted down her prey with ease.

The low-slung vehicle came to a screeching, fishtailing halt at the side of the road. Cass had to slam on her brakes to avoid overshooting the place in the road just ahead of the offender. "Smart-ass," she swore under her breath while turning off her lights, siren and engine. Then she looked in her rearview mirror and smiled. There was a woman driver in the 'vette, and a damned pretty one at that. And she was alone. Ahh.

Cass straightened her cap and tie, grabbed her ticket book and stepped out of the car. She sauntered (yes, girls, she sauntered) back to the Corvette she'd herded into her trap. The vibrating rumble of the car's engine excited her. She wished she didn't have to ask the driver to turn it off. She knew that somewhere in Detroit a little man had gotten rich by developing the formula for packaging a real live, fire-breathing dragon in every Corvette engine. There was nothing like that very tangible sound that shook the earth beneath her Wellington boots.

She tapped the car window with her pen. After an appropriate pause the window was lowered electronically. Cass bent over and instructed clearly, "You'll have to turn the car off, Miss." A pretty hand reached to the ignition and peevishly snapped the key. The sudden silence was Surrealistic. The driver had yet to look at Cass.

There was still enough light for Cass to peruse her very tanned, very blonde captive. God, I'll bet all she has on under that little sundress is her perfume, Cass ventured. Halston, she noted both with her mind and her groin. That sexiest of fragrances was sure to move her every time.

"May I see your driver's license, registration and proof of insurance, Miss?" Cass kept her question controlled and polite to mask the improper thoughts racing through her mind. Unconsciously she fondled her night stick.

Milissa Calais quietly handed the papers and license to the officer. Her mind was working feverishly to find a way out of this situation. If only the officer had been a man, she thought. Milissa had always been able to charm male officers into overlooking her excessive speeding. It had been the female officers she'd encountered who had written all the tickets appearing on her tarnished record. As she watched Cass return to her patrol car to check on that record, she worried about the outcome. Daddy will throw a *fit* if my license gets taken away again. She knew Daddy would probably take away her car, too. The idea of being twenty and without wheels didn't appeal to Milissa. The idea of getting a *job* to earn the money to buy her own car didn't even occur to Milissa.

What *did* occur to her was how terribly handsome Cass was in her dark blue uniform. Each step Cass took on her way back to the 'vette found Milissa rooted in fascination. Cass' cap rested confidently on her short, light brown hair; her face had strong, I'm-used-to-getting-my-way features; her gun and holster rode threateningly on her hip; her Wellington boots completed the stirring picture, adding just the right measure of stylish authority to Cass' outline. Milissa hadn't expected to respond physically to the situation or Cass. She told herself that her nipples had grown taut because it was fully dark now and a cool breeze had kicked up. She was *not* attracted to this policewoman. So much so that she didn't notice Cass wasn't giving back her license or papers but was smiling arrogantly.

Cass opened the door to the sports car. "You'll need to join me in the patrol car, Miss Calais. It seems there's a problem with your driving record." Where *do* those legs end, Cass wondered as her eyes trailed up to the hem of the pastel yellow dress.

Look afraid, Milissa reminded herself. If you look angry or rebellious you'll lose your license for sure. This cop looks like she *enjoys* taking them away. She took her little clutch bag from the passenger seat and maneuvered her legs out of the car.

Then the wind suddenly shifted . . . in more ways than one. Milissa's skirt billowed revealing more than was ladylike. Cass gasped and nearly lost her reserve right then and there. To cover her display of surprise and need, Cass reached for Milissa's hand to help her out of the car.

Milissa pretended she hadn't noticed Cass' reaction and walked innocently and obediently to the patrol car. *Now* she knew the rules of the game. And few could play this game better than Milissa. She turned to rest her buttocks against the car door, challenging Cass to make her move.

Cass stared at her with narrowed eyes. She hadn't had this much fun in a couple months. Her hand toyed with the notches of her stick, then grabbed the handle firmly. She let the business end of it travel up Milissa's thigh, taking the light skirt with it.

"Get in the car, Miss Calais. You're about to lose your driver's license," Cass warned menacingly.

Eyes widened, confused, Milissa did as she was told. She was certain she had found a way to get out of this mess, now this cop was scaring her. Maybe she really *was* going to take her license away. Damn, she thought. That means I'll have to leave my car to be towed and ride into town with her. Instinctively, Milissa read Cass' badge: #418. The name on her shirt pocket was Conifer. Oh, no. Milissa panicked. Her father is the Chief of Police! She was a goner for sure. The fact that her own father was a prominent banker was not going to help her any here.

But then Cass slid onto the seat next to her and Milissa was really confused. The dome light was on and she could look around Cass' domain. The high-powered rifle drew her attention; it reminded her that Cass had all the power in this situation. Milissa was beginning to feel quite helpless.

Cass' eyes were drawn longingly to the hard brown ends of Miss Calais' breasts. They showed distractingly through the light fabric. Just above them were square white buttons that held the bodice together, a simple affair that posed no obstacles to Cass' eager hand. "You've got quite a driving record, little lady," Cass taunted. "I'll have to take you into town . . . ." She left the threat to dangle in the air between them to see just how badly this woman wanted to find another way.

Milissa searched Cass' eyes, looking for the chink in her armor. Desperately she pleaded, "Must you?"

A slow smile moved in on Cass' face. She took her night stick and passed it over Milissa's pert nipple. "Not necessarily," she replied darkly.

They both watched as Milissa's breathing deepened, pushing her breast into the black pole.

Silently, Cass unbuttoned Milissa's top and let it fall. The sharp outline of her tan made a triangular frame for her dark points. Cass pushed Milissa down on the seat and began to lavish wet, sucking kisses all over the soft pillows. Her moans pulled Milissa's moans to the surface. In no time Cass had the blonde's knees up and legs parted to let her large hand in to roughly roam the planes of thigh and belly. Her finger forged into the light-colored fur.

"You're so wet!" Cass wailed passionately.

"Yesss," came the reply. Milissa was suddenly overcome with desire, born out of the tension and fear she'd been feeling only moments ago. She pulled Cass away from her breasts and onto her mouth. Cass responded with a diving tongue and more moans.

With a furious urgency Cass pulled up, breaking the engulfing kiss. She held herself just above Milissa—her eyes grew hard and unforgiving. "You need to be taught a lesson," she proclaimed. "Little girls like you need to learn that speeding can get you into trouble."

Before Milissa could respond Cass pulled her night stick from her belt and meanly thrust the end into Milissa's wet cunt.

Milissa made a small scream and tried to wrestle away from the surprise attack. But Cass overpowered her using her weight and determination to pin her captive down. Again she went for a breast, sucking it into her mouth and biting the nipple.

Milissa cried out but soon she found herself swept away by Cass' unleashed desire. The night stick filled her completely. In and out it thrust—quickly—sliding more easily now as her arousal mounted and her cunt became even wetter.

"Fuck me!" Milissa demanded. "Harder!"

And Cass fucked her harder and harder. Milissa bucked and squirmed and moaned. "Oh, please. Oh, I'm coming . . ."

"Come, bitch! Come!" Cass growled fiercely.

Milissa tensed; her eyes opened; her breath caught. She grabbed the stick to force it deeper inside, then held it there as her body gripped it with massive contractions that forced screams of release and delight from her throat.

Cass raised up, sweat glistening on her face, eyes glazed, as she proudly watched Milissa convulse orgasmically.

This was a Friday night to remember, and Cass knew exactly how she would remind herself.

Milissa was calm now and looked on curiously as Cass withdrew the night stick from her satisfied cunt, then produced a pocketknife from somewhere

No longer aware of Milissa's presence, Cass lovingly eyed the weathered notches on the handle then used the knife to carve . . . another . . . notch.

THE HUNGER

MADONNA

my mind turns on you:
a revolver
revolving,
playing russian roulette

with my fervor.
so saturated with you
i am   you are
like blood inside my body

let   me grate my heart
over the dish of your dreams,
and would that you
could eat this:

licentious desire
engorged and growing—
take a bite and taste
my lust and let it run

through your veins
like you run through mine,
running raw with bleeding
bleeding persistently with the

wounds of wanting you.

THIS IS THE FAMOUS BATH SCENE FROM DIRTY ALICE—REVISED

MERRIL MUSHROOM

"Wait for just one moment." The child released Alice's hand and disappeared into the undergrowth. Alice looked about. She had no idea where they were, how she had suddenly appeared in this forest, naked, nor where the small child had come from. Before her confusion could take hold, however, the child emerged from the bushes holding two large spheres. "Here." She handed one to Alice and bit into the other.

Alice watched as juice gushed forth, trickling off the child's chin and down the length of her small body. Alice followed her example, taking a small, experimental nibble at first, then biting deep into the fruit, burying her mouth and chin in the succulent, juicy meat. She ate greedily, and the sweet nectar ran in clear streams down her chin and over her breasts and belly. As she finished the last delicious swallow, she blotted her fingers in the sticky trails drying on her body. "I need a bath," she laughed.

"You can bathe when we get to my sister's home," the child said. "She lives on the lake, and sometimes in it or under it as well." She reached out and took Alice by the hand again. Her little fingers were slick with the juice from the fruit. "Come, now."

Alice followed her, spellbound by the beauty of the forest around her. There were trees and shrubs of every description, flowers of every hue, delicate bracken and mosses. Bright-plumaged birds flew about, singing and calling to one another, and now and then Alice would catch a glimpse of soft fur and black eyes as some small animal peered curiously through the brush at them.

At length they arrived at a large lake that was blocked on one side by a huge beaver colony of dams and bridges. The child stopped by a large hollow stump. "This is where my sister lives, and here is the door to her house."

"Where?" Alice looked about, seeing nothing that even vaguely resembled a house. She suddenly felt strange, insecure, and she wondered why she felt such trust in this little girl.

The child swung open a section of the stump to reveal a steep staircase. "Here." She began to descend the stairs, holding her hand out to Alice, and slowly, with much trepidation, Alice followed.

The staircase opened into a large, bright room with floor, walls, and ceiling of hard-packed earth. In the center of the room was a low wooden table. A fire burned in a fireplace which had been cut into one wall, and over the fire hung a pot which gave off delicious-smelling clouds of steam. Across from the fireplace was a doorway hung with strands of bright beads through which, as Alice stared in amazement, a woman entered the room.

"Good day, my dear." The woman's voice was low and sensual. It seemed to flow from her throat with the same fluidity that her body had as she moved across the room. She was tall and strong-looking, with silken hair that hung down her back to her knees, hair that seemed to be all colors at once, changing hue as it rippled with her movements. Her smooth skin had a pale green tone and shone with her energy. The one skimpy garment she wore was bright blue, draped in gauzy folds from shoulder to knee, and did little to conceal the lush body beneath. Her legs were muscular, her feet bare, and Alice realized with a start that the woman's toes were webbed, as were her slender fingers. Her gaze rose to the woman's breasts, full and high, dark, ripe nipples outlined by the flimsy fabric. She flushed and raised her eyes to the woman's face only to find that the woman was watching her intently.

Alice flared scarlet with embarrassment. She was suddenly acutely aware of her own nakedness, and a slow bubble of panic began to swell within her.

The woman laughed at Alice's discomfiture. She crossed over to where Alice stood, took her face in her hands, and kissed her on the lips. "You are indeed a treasure, my dear," she murmured, her lips soft against Alice's mouth. Then she moved away. "Come, my little one," she said, taking Alice by the arm, "and bathe."

In a half-trance, Alice followed the woman. Her head was spinning, and the beating of her heart threatened to throw her off-balance. She could still feel the gentle pressure of the woman's lips against her own, and she was aware of a scent and taste of violets on her mouth. The woman drew her down a long passage and through a low doorway into a smaller room, and Alice was startled to see a number of large rabbits scampering about on their hind legs and carrying various objects in their forepaws. The woman stroked her hair, soothing her, sending tiny currents of energy to prickle their way into her belly where they formed a little nest of excitement.

Don't be afraid, sweet Alice," the woman said. "My little servants have been preparing your bath. Here," she drew aside a curtain to reveal a wooden tub filled with fragrant, steaming water. As Alice watched, spellbound, a rabbit poured scented oil into the tub and stirred it around with one paw. Then it scattered a basketful of flower petals on the water, nodded to Alice, and left the room. "Now, into the tub with you," the woman ordered. "I will help you bathe, and this will clear your head." She lit a censer which stood on the table near the tub, and clouds of heady smoke billowed forth and spread through the room.

Alice climbed into the tub and allowed her body to relax in the hot, soothing water. The heavy scent of the flowers, oils, and incense filled her head, and as she breathed deeply, she felt herself recover from her surprise and shock. She was no longer concerned with where she was or how she had arrived at this place. She felt happy and at peace, ready to accept all and everything that might come her way. Lazily she stretched her limbs through the caressing fluid and sighed with pleasure.

Now the woman bent over the tub holding a large, sudsy sponge. She slipped her hands under Alice's arms and raised the girl to a sitting position. Alice's nostrils quivered delightedly at the heady, violet aroma, as the woman leaned close to her, lathering Alice's back, shoulders, arms, and chest. Suddenly she dropped the sponge in the tub and slid her slippery hands over Alice's breasts. Alice gasped at the sharp jolt of pleasure which coursed through her body at the contact. The woman massaged the lush fullness of Alice's breasts, rubbing the delicate webbing between her fingers over Alice's puckering nipples, then moved her hands down over Alice's belly and through the hairy triangle between her legs. She pressed the throbbing lips apart and probed into Alice's secret place, slipping her fingers deep inside her sex, while she massaged the girl's stiffening clitoris with the heel of her hand.

Alice felt as though she were about to be consumed by the raging heat of her passion. She moaned loudly and thrashed her body about in the water. Suddenly the woman's hand was gone as she retrieved the sponge and began to lather Alice's legs, lifting first one and then the other out of the water. "Oh, no," begged Alice, as waves of heat and cold washed through her, "please don't stop touching me. Please."

The woman smiled. She leaned close to Alice and again kissed the girl on the mouth. Her lips were cool and soft, with a steady pressure which slowly parted Alice's own lips. Alice closed her eyes and opened her mouth to receive the woman's soft tongue. The woman drew away. "Don't close your eyes, Alice," she murmured, her voice heavy with passion. "Look at me." With one swift motion, she stripped her flimsy garment over her head and tossed it away from her.

An overwhelming shyness swelled through Alice, and she lowered her lids so that her lashes masked the vision of the woman's nakedness, but the woman took Alice beneath the chin and pressed the girl's head up and back. "Look at me, Alice," she ordered; and Alice cried aloud with longing as she raised her eyes and viewed the woman, devouring the lush body with her vision.

Now the woman laughed, turning about and posing for Alice, her own breath growing more rapid as her desire mounted. Her skin was indeed green, smooth and firm-fleshed. Her breasts were large with lush, dark-brown nipples. Her waist flared into generously rounded hips and a muscular belly. The hair which covered her private parts was a shiny copper color, and Alice could see a glimmer of pink moistness where the woman was beginning to open in excitement. Alice realized that she was the cause of the woman's mounting passion, and the thought aroused her more than the memory of the woman's touch upon her body. She felt a throbbing in her chest and between her legs, and she reached out a soapy hand and stroked the woman's sleek thigh. The skin felt like hot velvet beneath her fingers.

At Alice's touch, the woman tensed and began to make a low crooning sound deep in her throat. She climbed into the tub with Alice and pressed the girl's knees apart. She sat down between Alice's legs and wrapped her own legs up around Alice's waist. Alice began to tremble as she felt a soft tickle of hair against her inner thigh. She raised her knees high, moving her throbbing vulva forward, and pressed her heels hard against the bottom of the tub. Then, with a violent shock, she felt the woman's intimate flesh pressed hard against her own inner membranes, the woman's belly squeezed close to her own, the woman's arms holding her tightly, the woman's breasts crowding hers, their nipples rubbing over one another, as the two of them ground their bodies together, the oils in the bath easing their movements.

Faster and faster they moved against each other, panting and moaning. The woman massaged herself between Alice's legs and squeezed the girl's body rhythmically with her strong arms. Alice watched the woman's face, seeing her own passion reflected there. The woman's eyes were slitted, her nostrils flared. Her mouth was slightly open, and her tongue moved about between her teeth and over her lips. She sang their rhythm of lust with soft, moaning grunts, while Alice accompanied her with a high, keening wail.

The woman mashed her mouth against Alice's, grinding their lips together, thrusting her tongue deeply into the girl's throat. Alice sucked hard on the woman's tongue and bit her lips, as her passion mounted uncontrollably. Hot flashes streaked through her thighs, and a great weakness descended through her arms and chest. She tightened her grip on the woman's body and dug her fingernails into the flesh of her back. She was dimly aware of the woman trembling violently in her arms. Then her entire body went rigid, and a blinding light exploded in her brain. Through the roaring in her ears, she could hear the woman's loud cries a half-octave deeper than her own screams. She buried her face against the woman's wet, fragrant neck, sobbing, as her tremors slowly subsided.

Water splashed over the side of the tub as the woman disengaged herself and moved away from Alice. "I could remain in this tub with you for the rest of the evening, delighting myself with your enchanting body; but dinner will soon be ready, and the others are waiting for us."

"Lady," spoke Alice, gathering all her courage, "by what name may I call you?"

The woman laughed, kissed Alice lightly on the eyelids. "I have no name, my dear. However, if you must, you may call me by any name that pleases you." She stepped out of the tub, and Alice caught her breath as the sight of the woman's nakedness sent a pang of remembered pleasure shooting through her. She gave a little whimper and pressed her hand against her throbbing cunt. The woman laughed again. "Sweet, little Alice," she said softly, "I promise you more delights later on. Now get out of the tub."

Alice stood up and stepped from the water. "I shall call you 'Lady' then," she said with satisfaction. "Where are the towels?"

"Towels? I have no towels. Never mind, our bodies will dry in the warm air. Come on, now." She took Alice by the hand and led her back into the passageway. "It's time to eat."

The floor climbed gradually beneath their feet and, finally, opened into a huge room with domed roof. "Ah!" Alice hesitated in the doorway, spellbound. Gigantic candles standing on the floor illuminated the interior. The walls and ceiling were hung with magnificent fabrics and tapestries, and the floor was littered with cushions. A large silver burner hung from the high lintel, and from it billowed clouds of the same incense which Alice had smelled in the bath.

Slowly, Alice entered the room and walked over to one of the curving walls. She pulled a curtain aside to better peer out of the curiously-shaped aperture over which it hung and gave a loud squeak of surprise as she discerned in the fading light that they were over the waters of the lake. As she looked further out, she realized that they were inside what she had earlier thought was a beaver dam.

The woman walked up behind Alice and embraced her, and Alice was intensely aware of the woman's breasts boring into her back and of a soft, fuzzy tickle against her buttocks. "Do you like my house, dear Alice?" she asked, her warm breath stirring in Alice's hair and against her ear.

"Oh, Lady, yes," the girl stammered.

"The beavers built it for me when I came to live at the lake. The rabbits, moles, and woodchucks dug my tunnels through the earth, and all the little animals serve me. It is their pleasure; and it will be your pleasure, too, sweet Alice, if you wish." She stroked Alice's belly loins with her fingertips, and Alice wanted nothing more right then except to serve the lady for the rest of her life. She clutched one of the woman's hands and brought it to her lips, feeling the soft, pliable membrane of the webbing between the woman's fingers against her mouth. Her heart pounded in her chest, and her eyes brimmed with tears of joy.

The woman laughed and danced away from Alice, breaking her grasp. "Do you love me, Alice?" she demanded.

"Yes, Lady," Alice's voice was husky with her longing. "I do love you."

"Good!" Lady whirled over to a table of carved wood inlaid with gemstones. Her silken tresses, caught the light from the candles, rippling down her back in a kaleidoscopic stream. She picked up a tiny bell and shook it. Delicate, silver tones rang out, permeating the room with a microcosmic tintinnabulation.

At the sound, the same child who had brought Alice to this place appeared in a doorway hung with a long drapery of sea-blue, billowy, diaphanous fabric woven together with tiny slivers of abalone. She pulled the curtain aside and bore in a tray holding a small bottle and two tiny goblets. She set them on the floor near a pile of cushions and then, without a word, retreated behind the curtain. The woman beckoned to Alice. "Come, my dear, and sit with me." She drew Alice down beside her onto the soft pillows and handed her a goblet filled with sparkling amber liquid. "Refresh yourself. Then I want you to dance for me."

Alice raised the goblet to her lips, sipped, then drained the cup of the cool draught. It was delicious! She was relaxed, content, and she wanted nothing more than to please Lady, to do as Lady wished. Rising to her feet, she swayed sinuously before this most beautiful of creatures. Her thick, black hair crackled about her as she arched her back and drew her fingers sensually up her thighs, her flanks, her belly. She touched her breasts and ran her hands down her sides, feeling desire rise hot inside her. She danced before Lady, watching the woman's face, seeing the flush that rose beneath the emerald complexion. Alice danced, feeling every cell of her body tingle with desire. She knew that she was beautiful, that Lady liked her dancing, and she was happy.

Then Lady reached behind her and pulled a cord which hung from the ceiling, and a heavy drape fell away to reveal a large, curved mirror. Alice stared, spellbound, at her own naked reflection and that of Lady, magnified and illuminated by some magical quality of the glass.

"Enough!" ordered Lady, and Alice stopped dancing, stood quivering with restraint. Her body felt as though it were being consumed by cold flames, and a heavy moisture seeped from between her thighs. Lady took her by the wrist and pulled her down to the cushions, pressed her back so that she must look upon her image in the mirror, and descended upon Alice's cunt with a hot, greedy mouth, taking her suddenly, fast and hard.

"Oh!" screamed Alice. "Oh, Lady!" And then she had no more breath for exclamations, because Lady was doing the most amazing things to her with her mouth and fingers. Suddenly, she stopped, and Alice moaned and sobbed and tried to grind her cunt against Lady's mouth; but Lady was only turning her body, taking a moment to swivel about so that she could present Alice with the magnificence of her sex. Reverently, Alice touched the hot, throbbing flesh with her fingertips. Then, with a loud sigh, she bent forward and buried her mouth in the sodden copper hair, sliding her tongue between the swollen lips to taste the woman's succulent wetness, feeling Lady's thighs trembling against her cheek.

The woman crooned her pleasure, her voice muffled against Alice's own cunt, and the vibrations of the sound palpitated Alice's inner membranes, sending little flashes of delight to shoot up her thighs and into her chest and belly. She felt her own sounds of moaning deep in her throat, and she drew Lady farther into her mouth, seeking to merge their flesh together. Faster and faster they

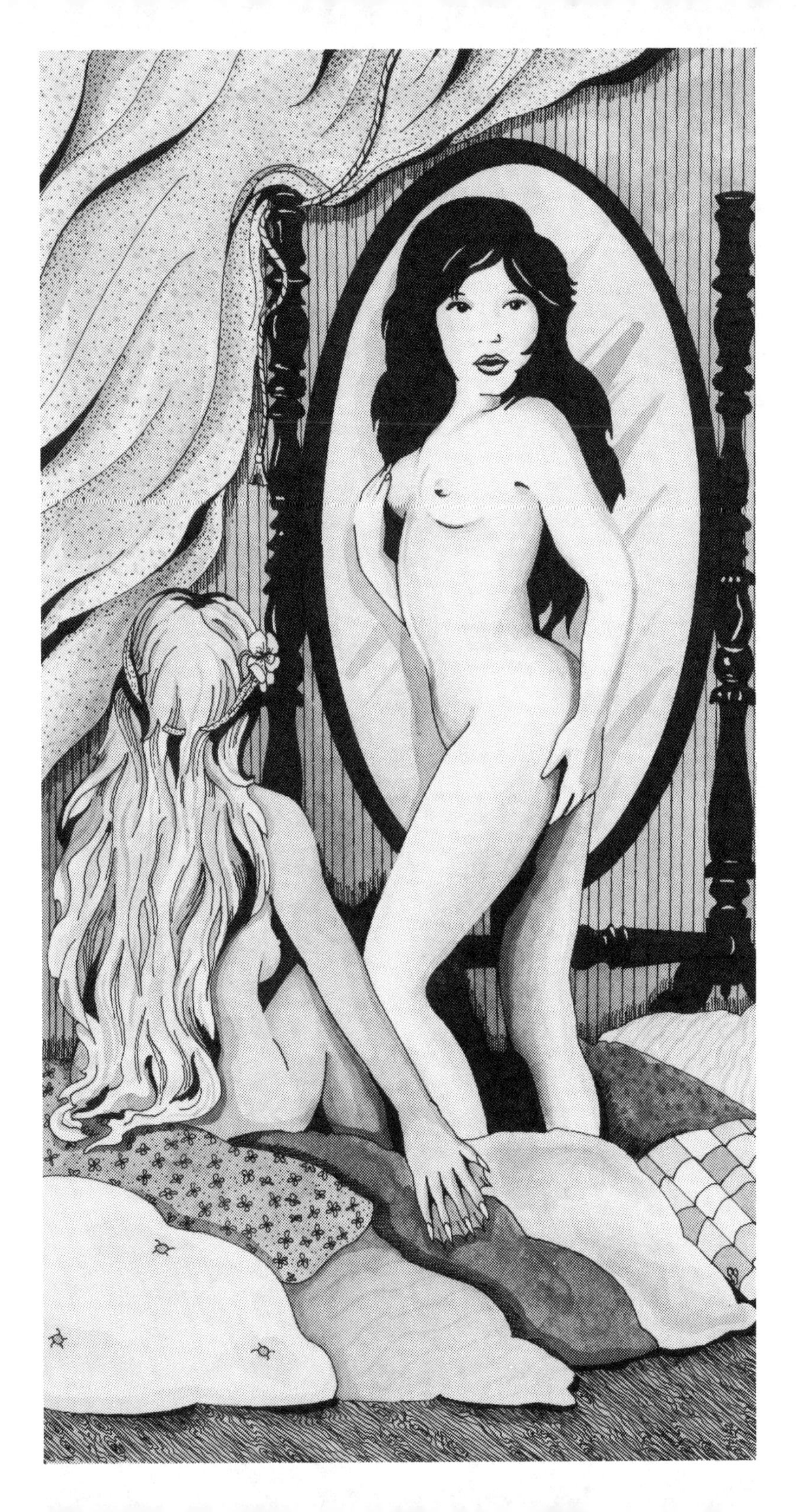

moved against each other. The nectar of their sex ran down their chins, and they smeared their faces and hands in it. They they were coming, coming, riding each other's pleasure in spasm after spasm, filled with the feel, the sounds, the tastes, the scents of themselves and each other, coming harder, harder, and then, after one brief, transcendent lull, coming again.

Lady rolled away, turned around again, and propped herself on an elbow. She looked down at Alice's face. The girl lay still, drained, exhausted. Lady laughed. "Poor Alice. We'll have to work on building up your stamina, won't we?" She bent and kissed the girl on the mouth, and Alice could smell the scent of her own sex on the woman's cheeks and taste her own juice slick upon the woman's lips. She moaned, feeling a fire begin to rekindle in her loins, but Lady pulled away and laughed again. "Later, dear Alice. I, for now, need a *real* dinner. Come with me and eat some of my food." She rose to her feet, reached down, and drew Alice up after her.

RIDE MY BITCH II

C. BAILEY

Iris's blue Toyota wouldn't start. Donna had been promising to look at it, and could probably even fix it. "I guess I'll hitch to Reaton," Iris muttered to herself. "Maybe Donna'll be home. She could bring me home, and we could have supper together, later."

It was Iris' day off from work, and she was restless, as if not quite prepared to fill an empty day. She pushed her brown hair, with its occasional glints of red and blonde, off her face. Iris sighed, shrugged on her pack, and trudged down her long, dirt driveway. Aimlessly she kicked a few rocks.

Coming to the main road revived her spirits. She crossed to the right-hand side and set a brisk pace on the graveled shoulder. A car approached and passed her by. Iris dropped her extended thumb, resumed her brisk pace. Another car, no, a van; the heavy beast swept past, then braked sharply, pulling to the shoulder. Iris ran to the door already yawning open, climbed in, slammed it shut, breathing her thanks and a grin all at once.

The driver was a woman with rolled-up sleeves above muscular forearms. Her short hair was covered by a cowgirl hat shaped with sweat and finger touch. Her eyes were startling: a fine, sharp blue that Iris found to be most unusual.

"Where you going?" Iris asked the driver, whose blue eyes flicked in her direction.

"Just out driving, mostly. We're traveling . . . thought we'd drive some back roads today . . . maybe go up to Portland tonight."

Iris wondered who the "we" was, and glanced around. Another woman slept in the back, curled up, knees tucked to her chest, a slender woman dressed in jeans and a tee shirt, with one hand lying open on the blanket. Her fingers were small, and her wrist, yet obviously strong.

"Where're you from?" Iris asked.

"Out East." A bemused smile rode the driver's lips. Neatly she switched subjects. "You know much about Portland?"

"Sure. I used to live there. Portland's a great place. Of course that depends on what you're looking for."

"Any good bars?"

"Women's bars, right?"

The driver chuckled, lifted her hat, then resettled it low on her forehead. "Yeah, women's bars."

"There's two," Iris replied, glancing sidelong at the driver, admiring her faded jean shirt belted into faded jeans, and the worn boots on her feet. "Portland has a good-sized women's community. There's a bookstore, and a restaurant; pretty much everything you'd want, I guess."

The driver murmured, "I wonder." After a moments silence, she asked Iris where she was going.

"Just into Reaton. I'm hoping my friend Donna'll be home. My car won't start. I'm going to get her to fix it."

The driver watched the road and chewed on a toothpick. "Me and Carol work on cars; maybe we could look at it for you if your friend can't."

"That would be great!" Iris exclaimed enthusiastically.

"Guess I should introduce myself," the driver said, and put out her right hand. "I'm Liz, and that's Carol in the back."

Iris shook hands with Liz, liking how her dry, calloused palm felt against her own. "I'm Iris," she said shyly, and blushed. "If you're willing to work on my car," she ventured, "maybe we shouldn't even bother Donna. She's always so busy. I could cook dinner. We'll have to stop at a grocery store, though."

"Sounds good to me," Liz said agreeable. "Which way to the store?"

Carol slept until they parked in front of Safeway. Awake, she was decidedly not delicate. She reminded Iris of a very old bent nail, stubborn about letting go from the wood. Uneasily Iris shook hands with her, too.

After shopping, the three women drove to Iris's house. It was small and private, a sheltered nook with crumbling shingles and bird sounds resounding from the trees. "We'll take a look at the car, first," Liz said when Iris invited them in. Iris sighed with relief; mechanical disorders just made her tense. "I'll start dinner," she replied happily, and disappeared inside her home.

Later, Liz knocked, then entered before Iris could come to the door. Carol followed Liz into the kitchen. They cleaned their hands while Iris opened beer for them all.

"Got her running," Liz announced through water she rubbed on her face.

"What was wrong with her?" Iris asked, feeling light and bubbly at the news.

"Some wires were loose," Carol said as she dried her hands by running them through her hair. "And the battery needed cleaning up. Nothing special."

"Yep, she's running like a charm," Liz said, settling herself at the table.

"I can't thank you enough," Iris bubbled happily, as she put the food on the table. She had created a delicious Mexican tofu pie, and a garden fresh salad. Carol commented twice on how good everything tasted.

"I don't usually like tofu, but I like this," Liz said when the meal was over and the plates had been pushed to the center of the table. There was something hot in the way she fastened her gaze on Iris. Iris could feel the heat lingering on her throat, descending along her breast lines. Gulping, she met the gaze with her own; aroused desire intermixed with fear caused her breath to stall in her chest. Flustered, with a fluttering heart, she stood to clear the table. Carol gripped one of her wrists loosely to stop her.

"I'll do that," she said rough-kindly. As she piled the dishes and carried them to the sink, Liz demanded Iris's attention with her intent, blue gaze. Iris laughed nervously, yet she was pleased that Liz seemed to want something from her.

"What are your trying to say with those beautiful blue eyes of yours?" Iris asked shyly, playfully. To keep herself breathing right she examined her hands as she waited for an answer.

"Iris." Liz's voice was low and deep.

"Yes?" Iris whispered.

"I want to fuck you."

Unannounced, heat rushed Iris's crotch. It spread deep into her cheeks. Her heart skidded; she experienced the sharp change of the evening as a tight grabbing in her stomach. She didn't know what to do. Just that morning she had fantasized a tall woman taking her in the pasture behind her house. Was Liz somehow related to that fantasy?

Liz shifted her hat onto the back of her head. In much the same grip that Carol had used, but tighter, firmer, she took Iris's wrist. "You want that, Iris?"

"Well . . ." She tried to ease the tension with a joke, but couldn't think of any. Suddenly Carol was standing right behind her. Iris's heart bounded, rebounded. "Is this a joke, or what?" she croaked. Carol leaned against Iris's back. There was something in that pressure that weakened. Iris's knees and heightened the throbbing in her cunt.

"Carol and I drive the country in our van looking for women to fuck."

"You what?" Iris glanced quickly over her shoulder at Carol, back to Liz. "All over the country?"

Liz nodded. Carol slipped one arm around Iris's neck. Iris gasped, thinking that Carol's skin was very warm, and that she should try to get away. But the arm contained such strength, and her cunt was acting wild; her breasts ached to be touched. Instead of pulling away she stayed very still, eyes wide open, waiting.

"You want to be fucked, Iris?" Liz's voice was steelier. "Huh, Iris? I'm not going to give it to you unless you want it. You've got to want us or we'll leave."

“I, yes . . . but this is so strange . . . .”

Liz spoke again, each word deliberate, obviously not to be used again. “Do you want to be fucked, Iris?” Liz leaned across the table, slid one hand through Iris’s clean smelling hair. Her other hand cruised Iris’s breast, catching the nipple with an easy flick of the finger.

Confused by the eager hunger of her body and the sharp contrast of her cautious mind, Iris closed her eyes. If she didn’t look at them maybe she wouldn’t think about it and could be as hungry as she wanted. “Yes,” she whispered.

“What, Iris? I didn’t hear you.”

“Yes.”

“Yes, what?” Liz crooned.

“I want you to . . . to . . . fuck me.” The last two words were almost unintelligible.

Liz’s grip tightened in Iris’s hair as if urging her to open her eyes. “Such a lovely face, Iris,” Liz said, and there was naked sincerity in her voice.

“Take your shirt off,” Carol said in a voice that had turned husky. She stroked Iris’s blouse with her free hand, down across her breasts. “Come on, show us your breasts.”

Clumsily Iris undid the buttons of her blouse, shyly wanting to please Liz and Carol. It seemed that she did. Once her shirt was removed her skin was caressed. Their hands handled her with delight. Carol rested her chin on Iris’s head as she roused each nipple. Iris could feel Carol’s heart against her back.

“Take her pants off,” Carol said, her breath and words thickly mixed.

Here again was that roughness that Iris longed for yet feared. She made as if to protest, but Carol was quick, pinning her face down across the table top. Iris struggled, but Carol twisted her arm behind her back, effectively taking command. Iris could feel Carol enjoying taking command. Iris could feel Carol enjoying the roughness, and whimpered, more grateful than afraid. Liz stripped away her pants, then there was a long pause in which Iris felt not at all degraded as the two women coveted her greedily.

Iris felt almost wantonly exhibitionistic with her round ass stuck up high. For once she did not think of her thighs as heavy, but lush, curves that inspired lust. But her mind wouldn’t leave her alone.

Who were these women, really? Did they actually fuck their way across the States? Carol told her to step out of her pants and she did, not wanting to know what would happen if she didn't. Without warning Carol pulled her up off the table. Liz stood before her with a small braided whip in her hand.

Iris's mind plunged into an agony of thought. She tried to struggle, but Carol simply angled Iris's arm higher up her back, and that was the end of that. Were these women into S & M, Iris wondered, panicked. She had explored some with lovers. Once she had tied up Donna, once Donna had spanked her, but nothing with whips.

Liz unbuttoned her own pants and took them off. Her legs were less masculine than Iris had expected. They were soft at the hips and her inner thighs touched. Liz leaned against the table. "Come here, Iris," she said. "I want you to go down on me. Suck me, baby." It wasn't an invitation, it was an order. Liz's fingers played with her public curls, and her eyes were dark blue, smoky with lust. Iris hesitated only as long as it took Carol to release her arm then sharpen her instincts with quick slap to her cheek. Iris's instincts bade her taste Liz's flesh; her thick calves, sturdy knees, the soft growth of hair leading into Liz's cunt. Iris's fingers trembled as she lifted Liz's shirt tails. This was what she loved, tasting woman flesh, the damp odor on her tongue.

"Iris, you do this so well, don't stop. Fuck me!" Liz said to the rhythm of her heavy breathing, tangling her fingers in Iris's thick hair. She looked at Carol, as much as if to say, "Ok, partner, I'm ready to buck now." Carol grinned. Her eyes were green beneath dark brows. She picked the whip up off the floor, handling it tenderly, crowded Iris's ass with her legs, then laid her leather snake lightly across Iris's skin. The snake bit into the world of lush, wet licking, snapping an element of fury into Iris's tongue. Then Liz's voice snagged her, "Come on, My Bitch, nothing pretty now. Eat me, Baby!" Iris was in a frenzy to please, to devour. Strangely, she craved the lick of the leather, reminding her of heat and flame.

Carol knew Liz's needs and urged Iris to quicken the tempo. Iris responded, gurgling, biting, swirling circles around Liz's clitoris. She felt Carol's hand glide down her back, to her crack, further to her moistness, and hoped terribly, vividly, that it was time for her fucking. She wanted her vagina filled and filled. Faster her tongue flicked, then Liz was groaning, her large body tightened with a dark, red flush, and vaginal gulps became pelvis thrusts as Liz held Iris's face between her large hands.

Iris was sure she was exhausted. She collapsed on the floor, but there was no time for rest. Carol plucked her upright, slipped a leather circlet over each wrist and tightened them. Before Iris could voice her doubts, she was tied to the railing of the stairs, her arms outstretched. Liz, having gotten back into her pants, recocked her hat and licked her lips.

"You ever been fucked in the ass, Iris?" Carol asked. She had stuck the whip in her back pocket; it hung down like a tail.

Iris tested the strength of her bindings. There wasn't even any give. She couldn't decide if she was embarrassed or titillated being strung up, her nipples pushing erect against the wood railing, her backside exposed. Nothing she could do about covering herself, or the wrinkles of her thighs. There was a cool, firm hand on her neck.

"You have a lovely ass, Iris," Carol whispered in Iris's ear. Iris was pleased though she didn't want to be. She wasn't sure she liked Carol. "I want to fuck that lovely ass."

"No, please, I'm too tired." Uneasily she remembered a time with Beverly. One night Beverly had turned her over onto her stomach; hoping to be taken from behind, Iris had humped her ass high into the air, begging to be fucked. Even moaning deliciously. It wasn't her vagina Bev entered, but her ass. She remembered still the pain, her fear and humiliation, especially when she realized she kind of like it.

"I'm not too tired," Carol said. "You too tired to watch, Liz?"

Liz chuckled and touched Iris's clit. "You're going to enjoy this," she told Iris. "Carol's good at this stuff."

"Oh, god," Iris moaned, fearing the structure of her knees were weakening. Liz's finger slid back and forth along the uppermost ridge of her clit. Carol wetted her fingers with her spit and began kneading Iris's asshole, nudging the tight muscles to relax.

I can't go through with this Iris thought with acute panic. "Please, fuck my vagina," she moaned, trying to twist away from Carol. Carol stayed with her like a rider will stick with her horse, and pretty soon Iris was rocking into Liz's hand, then back into Carol's hand. They made her feel like an animal, thoroughly in heat, unmindful of proper posturing. "Oh, god, do with me what you will," she cried fiercely.

That was Carol's cue. Her muscles vibrated like taut wire as she found entrance for her thumb inside Iris. Inside the glove of her ass. Iris's moans were garbled by half screams; she sighed and grunted all at the same time. Sweat beaded on Carol's forehead and stained her teeshirt; she wrapped her left arm around Iris's middle, then used her pelvis to thrust her thumb deep. Slowly she withdrew, thrust in. Liz played with Iris's wet; Iris rubbed her nipples hard against the rails. Her ass ballooned open, welcoming how much of Carol's hand she didn't know; she didn't care. There wasn't anything but riding the fuck waves, spreading out, driving down onto those fingers. Then coming and coming and coming until she sagged.

When they untied her wrists she slid onto the floor, ready for sleep. Drowsily she listened to them moving about, took a mental check of her body. Her ass was one huge pulse, a pleasant throbbing. Her cunt itched, for she had no relief, nothing but tease and more tease. Iris opened her eyes, about to make a protest, when Liz took her arm and raised her to her feet.

Carol was naked and busy spreading the couch blanket on the kitchen table. She was all over lean except for small, full breasts. Iris felt a rush of love for this woman who had shown her such pleasure.

"Hey!" Liz shook her lightly. She had taken off her shirt, her hat sat at the back of her head. "You're not too tired are you, Iris? I'm going to give you what we promised." Her voice was like a direct touch, Iris groaned beneath its sweet drip.

"Oh, Liz, I can't take anymore. You two will do me in!"

"Oh, Baby, we're professionals, didn't you know? If you can't trust us, who can you trust? So get up on that table, Bitch." Liz knew how to knife edge her words when the sweet-talk began dulling Iris's arousal.

"The table? The kitchen table? Why not the bed?"

"Because I want you on the table and Carol wants you on the table. Now," Liz urged roughly, giving Iris a small shove.

Carol had been testing the table's strength and decided it was satisfactory; Iris wasn't so sure, and approached it hesitantly.

"Don't dawdle, now," Liz murmured from her new position, sidling her crotch along the skin of Iris's ass. "Or we'll just tease you the rest of the night until you're begging, but we won't give out."

Iris didn't doubt her, and scrambled up on the table without delay. Surprisingly, she felt much more exposed than any other time that night. They stood looking down on her from either side of the table. She realized she could almost feel them silently communicating, could almost hear a humming as they charged their batteries together. Iris shivered, and not because she was cold.

"I want your mouth," Liz said, and Iris wanted to giggle, but smothered the giggle with her hand. In synchronized motion, her wrists were gripped, then pinned above her head to the table, Carol taking one, Liz the other. Liz licked the corners of her mouth as if clearing away crumbs. There was nowhere to go, she could not flee the nibbles and bites, Liz's tongue calling on her own. The sucking and slurping made her blood roar in her veins and beat against her skin, making her heart work hard to keep up. Liz climbed onto the table, and sat on Iris's pubis.

Please make this table strong, Iris prayed silently, then thought of it no more for Liz began to suckle her breasts. Light as a bird, Carol joined them on the tabletop, planting her knees on Iris's outstretched palms, holding Iris's shoulders down with her hands. Carol's cunt hovered above Iris's face, just out of reach. She cried out, every cell, for ravishment, but could do nothing to bring it to her. Cunts and fingers and nipples and promises hovered, just out of reach. "Fuck me," she sobbed. She tried to thrash free and could not. A new panic entered her; she would explode, she would never get what she wanted.

Before panic could drive Iris from arousal, Carol freed Iris's hands, and knelt down so her wet lips met Iris's eager mouth. Liz crouched between Iris's legs, eased her thighs apart, and entered. Colors exploded in her brain, her muscles stretched long and supple in all directions. She pressed up into cuntal wet licking and sucking and lightly chewing until Carol's wire tension melted to resiliency. She bucked onto Liz's hand, spread her legs wider than wide, played her own nipples until Liz slapped her hand away, and took to sucking them herself. Her cunt accepted the breadth of Liz's first, and the force with which she gave it in, drew it out. In and out. There was some kind of wave action toppling her over into fathomless warmth, and an edge, like the lip of an oncoming tide, that she could hang on to. It pulled her through layers of pleasure, each layer more piercingly pleasurable than the last, until it became a new kind of tension. One she would not resist for anything.

Iris came in gulps and spasms and gutteral screams, clinging and gripping and crying. Then there was a long moment of utter stillness, a sensation of suspension in which she felt complete. She needed nothing else.

Liz and Carol carried Iris to her bed and gently tucked her in. She as too sleepy to know. "Iris, Dear," Liz whispered, "we're on to the next state." Liz grasped her partner's hand and they left.

THREE WOMEN

D. L. HARRIS

We agreed, late one warm summer night
this fantasy we could share,

The room crackled with anticipation
you built two fires, one begins to flicker
promising false starts

The fire within me roars, as you stoke me
with your touch:
I watch thru passion laden eyes as you enter
another
wanting to watch, wanting to be her
wanting to be the sweat that glistens on your back
that glides on the surface of your skin,
I taste it, hoping that it will quench
my thirst for you
until it's my turn . . .

I respond to the pleasure that her mouth is giving me
while your hands reassure me
I moan from the passion, that sears my brain
leaving me marked,

You look so lovely and taste divine
I'm sure that you are ambrosia
then I touch, your secret place, you shudder
shall we share everything?

For a moment, there is a silent awkwardness
reality, is trying to enter
the flames are trying to die out,
then our eyes meet, there are the flames!

We scream and collide in spasmodic rhythm
collapsing in our ashes, energy spent
we three lay like the cooling embers
with our fantasy . . . .

THE ELECTRIC GHOST MACHINE: AN IMPROPER STORY

CHARLOTTE STONE

Patricia glanced at the woman who sat beside her, steering the transit van along the narrow country lanes. She let her mind wander back over the recent past—to try to lay the ghost of her intense feelings. For the last few years she had lived free and easy, screwing around as the guys in the lab called it, enjoying her youth. When she was twenty-five or so she'd settle down; that was the plan. But the coming of Carla had shocked her out of her plan. She never called her Carla—she was Dr. Swallow to her face.

She remembered the first day she had seen her. Carla Swallow had been a new girl—back from the States where she'd done some post-doctoral work. A rumour had gone round that she was a nutter—researching ghosts or some such idiocy. Patricia had expected a weird mad-scientist type—nothing like the woman who walked into the lab that morning. Dr. Swallow was tall, dark-haired and dressed smartly, with a classic style, rather than fashionably or sexily. In her late thirties, thought Patricia, who felt suddenly childish in her tarty red trousers.

"Miss Baptiste, our T. O." the professor had introduced her. A chap behind giggled because Miss Baptiste had tripped on her high heels. The awkwardness vanished however, as soon as Carla Swallow smiled.

She didn't wear much make-up, just a pale lipstick that softened her lips. She seemed as surprised as Patricia—whether because the bright-trousered technician was the only woman or the only black one, Patricia wondered. The smile was far from patronizing. One sensed something stirring through the irony, a vulnerability or perhaps it was just friendliness. Indeed Dr. Swallow needed a friend, and even more an ally.

In the cliquey atmosphere of the information technology department, Carla had difficulty in getting anyone to work on her job, whatever it was. And the lecture she gave was a disaster—people laughed openly. She bore it with dignity, finishing her very last transparency and turning to ask for questions, as if there hadn't been a whisper. A post-grad who saw himself as rather a teacher-basher raised his hand and asked if she was going to hold a seance next.

"No, sorry, but you could probably find one advertised in the local paper, if you're really keen," she answered without a flush. And thus she was, mocked but unbowed—something of a fighter.

For all that, Patricia had been annoyed when the professor had called her to his office.

"I don't think Dr. Swallow is getting full cooperation from the technicians, Miss Baptiste," he'd said, as if she was to blame. He just smiled when she protested and asked her to offer her services to the new staff members.

To think of the ridicule! They called Dr. Swallow "Don Quixote" around the lab. She could well have the sweetest smile in the world, but who wanted to become her fat little Sancho Panza? And sure enough, there were the others' sniggers when they heard: "You going to be her little slave?" . . . "Fancy becoming her witchling!"—She already felt an outcast. But there was nothing to say. Patricia went along to Dr. Swallow's office, cursing the day the woman had set foot in the department. She remembered that with shame. How things had changed!

It had worked instantly between them. She couldn't tell exactly why she found herself two hours later still in Dr. Swallow's office, telling her all about her life, past and present, her job, her friends, her self-doubts. Green eyes kept looking at her—deep sleeping waters—and the words just flowed from her mouth. She had never talked to anyone so freely, and perhaps above all, she thought, so honestly. The woman gave her that special smile at the end—half-mocking, half-loving. It was enough for Patricia to fall under her spell. Only later did she realize that the confidences were all hers, and she didn't know much more about her new boss at the end of the interview.

"Well, no doubt you've heard of me," Dr. Swallow had started in her low poised voice, "the old stick who's trying to raise ghosts or whatever, but I'd better explain what I'm up to." And all she had talked about—maybe all she cared about—was her work.

"You have probably read about N-rays, discovered by Nancy in France, and abandoned later as non-existent. I think people jumped the gun. Just imagine that they did exist, but that their interaction with the human brain makes them impossible to prove. I might see them and you might not, or vice-versa. Although objective proof is out of the question at the moment, I'm sure I can show they are real somehow, and furthermore, use them to do some quite exciting experiments."

That was how their relationship had begun. Patricia was to make the apparatus, a frame which was to capture and read those elusive N-rays, "the electric ghost machine", as Dr. Swallow called it facetiously for the technician's benefit. Funnily enough, from then on Patricia never doubted that theory would succeed where the French had failed, and open the way to those 'exciting experiments' her new boss had alluded to.

Carla Swallow was a hard but fair mistress. She would tick Patricia off it she made silly mistakes, or when she was late—after a lewd night it usually was. But she did it calmly as one who always respected the technician for her work. At first Patricia had been a bit standoffish—perhaps a reaction against her initial abandon. There were moments when warmth returned though, when Dr.

Swallow helped her on very complicated jobs: soldering the mass of tiny connections, for example.

It was amazing how much practical knowledge she would show for a theoretician. Patricia quickly learned that it was no good trying to bluff. She had been attached to Matt Watkins, the brilliant software specialist, and more than once she had tricked the man into betraying his ignorance of hardware. She had enjoyed that, and their daily flirting, though he was no Tarzan. But there was no trick and no flirt with Dr. Swallow. She was there every day like an infallible and beautiful robot, except for some unpredictable smiles with which she thanked her assistant. It should have been very boring. And yet Patricia had found it more and more difficult to tear herself away from the lab at the end of the day.

It had crept upon her; she was not sure when it happened, but she could remember when she realized it. She was expecting Stephen—he came late, usually after the pubs were closed. She felt so randy, she ran to the door naked when the bell rang, liking the feel of her breasts leaping up and down, and the warm draught on her pubic hair. It was meant to excite him as well—anyone could see him greeted by this nude siren, neighbours, passers-by. Of course the chances were against it, but still, it sent a thrill between her thighs.

She froze. Her supervisor stood on the doorstep. They looked each other in the eye. Dr. Swallow might have been in the lab asking Patricia for a measurement for all she betrayed—except one tiny eye movement, brief yet not really furtive, down low enough to take in belly and breasts, then up again.

"Sorry, Patricia. I wanted the key of the terminal room. I've mislaid mine. I need to get in."

Patricia had done something she wouldn't have expected with a woman, covered herself, one arm thrown across her breasts hiding the nipples, swollen as they had been and a hand moving over her hairy triangle although not daring to actually touch it.

"Oh yes . . . I'll get it . . . ." She had blushed, hoping her dark skin and the night kept her secret. Her boss had the leisure then to watch the plump but muscular brown buttocks swinging as Patricia walked away, not unconscious of her rear end. When she returned with the key, she wore a wrap confidently.

"Thanks. I'll give it back tomorrow." Carla Swallow had made to go, then turned back again with the hint of a smile and a shake of her head. Then she was gone into the night.

Although Stephen found Patricia warm, wet and willing, when he arrived, he felt that somehow her mind wasn't on the job. She didn't beg him to stay the night as she had the last time, which made him quite keen to do so. In fact she found him almost pathetic in his attempt to entice her—a sure sign that she was beginning to tire of him. She realized what was wrong after he'd gone. The face of Carla Swallow was on her mind—the beautifully controlled face and how it had flushed just the tiniest bit at the point of the cheekbones. It was an irresistible thought—that cool scientific attitude of hers shattered by Patricia's nudity. And her little glance, as if she couldn't be sure she was even interested. Patricia went to sleep still brooding.

Nothing was ever said at work, but from then on Patricia had felt Dr. Swallow's nearness as a living thing. To be close to her, even if it was just to read the terminal display, that was all she wanted—unlike her other affairs, an ideal sort of love that sex wouldn't spoil. So she thought until that day when Dr. Swallow's body pushed against hers as they squeezed round the back of the rack to find a fault. Patricia felt the sudden wave of heat pass down her belly, the thrilling twitch at the fleshy join of her thighs; suddenly to her complete amazement she was turned on. And as she smelled her companion's fresh-washed aroma, she had been painfully conscious of her own nipples hardening under her tight bra. It was like a light brutally switched on in a dark room. Even now she had not yet recovered from the shock, and it was no fault of trying.

Oh, the subtle torture that it was, like that first time when they had tested the apparatus together. The idea was that past events were stored in the masonry, metal and timber of the building, their vibrations dying away only very slowly. Those vibrations, being N-rays, should be detected by the "ghost machine". With rising hope they had downed the lights of the laboratory, switched on the field-frame—a big cubical frame wherein the N-field was supposed to be generated. The Patricia tapped out the tuning commands that ordered the micro to notionally twiddle a thousand knobs as the present program searched for coherent signals in the void. After ten minutes nothing had been seen at all. Dr. Swallow put on the light.

"Hm, this doesn't look too promising." She had sat and momentarily held her head in her hands. She cut such a forlorn figure that Patricia went to her and put her arms around her without thinking. The scientist looked up with a smile.

"It's alright, Patricia. I know they're there but we haven't got it right yet. I didn't expect it to succeed first shot. Did you think I was about to collapse?" Patricia had laughed to cover her embarrassment.

"Sorry, you must think me stupid."

"I don't. I think you're a very loyal and charming assistant though . . . . Thank you." She had pressed her hand. If only she had known what invisible flesh she had touched all of a sudden, what deep delicate nerves she was moving with hardly a stroke of her hand, and why her "witchling" had tensed up like a bow at her contact – god knows how it would have horrified her, thought Patricia. She had turned cold with fear, standing so close and feeling the pulse of blood in her groin. It was a delicious torture.

They had tried again, a few days later, and that time she sure remembered. According to Dr. Swallow, the brick should be the best medium for N-rays, and they had moved to the dark brick-built store room adjoining the lab. It was there they suddenly saw a mass of shimmering dots in the space inside the frame. Both women had cried out in excitement. Sometimes the dots were just random, like motes of dust in a sunbeam, other times they took form just visible as non-random. And at one incredible moment, for an instant, they saw a faint image of a man walking – only just discernible but undeniable. Dr. Swallow's objectiveness had gone. She was an exultant as Patricia, her green eyes radiant.

The occasion demanded a celebration. They walked through the damp spring sunshine to a large pub where university people went. The Arboretum was crowded at that time, and Patricia nodded to student acquaintances, proud to be seen with her mentor. She had never been anywhere with her before. There was excitement of all kinds in the air, and from her smart navy trouser suit to her bold eyes, Carla Swallow, too, seemed strangely affected by what had happened.

"Let me buy you a drink. You deserve that at least."

Patricia asked for a tropical cocktail she had had the week before. Her companion took white wine. They sat in a cosy alcove, thoughtful until Patricia broke their silence.

"This could make you the most famous scientist since Darwin, you know. It's just incredible—like a dream!"

"That's half the trouble. Though *we* know what we've seen, would anyone be convinced on that evidence? We can't get a record of it. It has to be demonstrated, but much much better . . . ." She sipped from her glass. "And it will. I've got an idea how. I've a very old friend, from fifteen years ago . . . ."

"You can't have, " Patricia blurted out. "You aren't old enough . . . ."

Dr. Swallow laughed at the compliment. "So it is however. When we were girls at school we were very close but we drifted apart when we grew up. I was too much of a grind for her liking. I guess she was a bit of a flirt . . . a sort of butterfly. She got bored of me after a while."

"I can imagine that."

"Thank you!"

"No. Not that way. Because she sounds so stupid." Patricia nearly kicked herself for that ridiculous remark.

"Actually she was very nice. I suppose we just weren't suited. She lived with her father alone in a crumbling old ruin. It must be one of the oldest houses in England. The grounds were a paradise for a couple of thirteen-year olds. There were overgrown lily-ponds that smelled exotic, laden with perfume of nuphar . . . statues covered in ivy . . . mystery paths . . . and best of all the old Roman temple in a cave . . . ."

"Gosh! Really! Roman!" said Patricia who had never suspected how interested in history she could become. The Romans! The word spoke of orgies, conquests and slaves, probably mostly black like her—a whole fascinating world that was glowing in the intimacy of their conversation. And the idea of Dr. Swallow as a child was a strange one. She saw a long awkward creature, staring at plants, rocks and stars whilst her friends when to discos.

"Yes, and we liked that because it was ours alone. Sarah used to do all sorts of outrageous things just because we wouldn't be caught. She stole sweets from the local shops and kept them there. And we had Roman feasts." A smile broke on her face, and she laughed. Such uninhibited laughter she could have away from her ghost machine!

"What is so funny?"

"Oh, the sight of us solemnly eating Turkish delight, and drinking Pepsi which was supposed to be wine. And Sarah would undress, which seemed wickedest of all."

Patricia's eyes opened wider. "Why?"

"Just to be naughty, I think. And, of course, Roman ladies were a bit like that, we thought."

"And did YOU?"

"Well . . . I think I kept my briefs on, I can't really remember, but we were playing."

"Thirteen is quite old for that though, isn't it? I mean, when I was seven we used to run around naked in the garden squirting each other with the hose, but not at thirteen."

"No, I suppose you're right. We would have looked very silly if anyone had caught us. But it was a lovely thing really. She was such an imaginative creature, and I guess because I didn't make friends as easily as she did, I was grateful to her for taking me up. My own school holidays would have been a bit of a disaster if it hadn't been for her."

"Why?"

"Oh, it isn't something to go into now. But Sarah, her father and their house were wonderful." A shadow had passed, the moment of nostalgia and secrets had gone. Carla Swallow had locked herself away again. Patricia was only too aware of it when she heard the calm familiar tone.

"Anyway back to our subject. That temple is just the place for our machine. Light can hardly get in the ruin. It must have lain fallow for hundreds of years. If I could set it up in there, I'd see something indisputable. And I'm sure Sarah would cooperate. I shall contact her next week. If it works, then we'll invite a party of scientific bigwigs to witness it."

Patricia stood uneasily wondering if she'd get invited to this reunion. Dr. Swallow hardly needed her now, she would probably prefer to set the machine up herself in the company of that dreadful Sarah.

"I suppose I won't be needed?" she mumbled. Her companion looked at her, her eyes twinkling.

"Of course you are! You're part of the apparatus now, aren't you?

"I don't know."

"I do. We'll stay overnight, you'll enjoy it, you'll see."

It was that, or the heat, or the rum-laden cocktails, she suddenly felt drunk, enough to lean against Carla Swallow. She would have liked to rest her head on her shoulder. She could have simply kissed her. As it was, just their shoulders touched—the woman seemingly unaware of the contact. Patricia leaned a little more heavily against her.

"Have you often seen her since?"

"Not often. Once a couple of years back."

"And did you still like her? I mean, was she the same?"

Dr. Swallow glanced at her. It wasn't easy to see whether she was mocking or serious.

"Yes, I still liked her."

Patricia looked at that face, again and again wondering what emotions were concealed behind it. The greenish eyes were on her, but for once, just once, she did not retract her gaze immediately. There was a complete silence, and she felt a strange sensation as the cool fearless eyes, so far from betraying any weak reference to the past, just bored into her.

She felt completely exposed, more so than when her body had been nude before Dr. Swallow. She felt her nipples swelling up to sensitive cones of rubbery flesh. She felt weak in her tummy, and her lips seemed ready to tremble. She turned away. No one's gaze had ever devastated her as quickly and completely. She glanced back, defensively, but Dr. Swallow was smiling.

"You seem very interested in my past." Her hand suddenly reached out and very gently, almost casually stroked Patricia's cheek. "Curiosity killed the cat!"

The contact was an electric shock, a thousand volts. There was an unbearable throbbing in her chest. And for the first time in her life she felt a great twitching in her panties without any physical stimulus. If people knew, if SHE knew, that's all she could think in her panic. Thank god it was so difficult to guess a woman. Dr. Swallow had withdrawn the hand as quickly as she had extended it, but before her now sat a quivering jelly.

"Enough of me!" She was laughing now. "Let's drink to you now, my brown beauty! It couldn't have happened without you."

That "brown beauty", it had nearly killed Patricia.

* * *

The van was packed up with the EGM and a portable power supply—all mounted on a trolley. Patricia and Dr. Swallow had set out very early. They stopped for a drink and a sandwich in a pub. They cut off the main road onto the network of country lanes that ran over the ancient downs. The house was difficult to find—the gateway was a ruin, overgrown with brambles and bracken. But there was a new barbed-wire gate in the open position and a track had been flattened along the old drive. Trees hung over the track making it seem a dark tunnel. The drive ended by a semi-ruin of a once great English home. From the door, came a woman of striking beauty, tall and well-dressed with deep red hair blowing around her face. Her eyes were widely set, her lips thin but beautifully shaped. She waved to the van and as Dr. Swallow got out she ran to her.

"Carla! How lovely! You haven't changed at all!"

She held her for a moment and they kissed on the cheek. Patricia was almost shocked to see the warmth of the greeting. Then Lady Sarah looked at the assistant. For a moment her eyes were cool, questioning. Then she smiled and turned to Dr. Swallow.

"Aren't you going to introduce your pretty friend?"

"Yes. She's my technician and assistant, Patricia."

"Oh, I see. Only you didn't mention her on the phone."

"Didn't I? Well, sorry. She can always stay at a local pub if it isn't convenient to put her up here."

"Oh, not at all! She's welcome. Only conditions are a bit primitive here, I'm afraid. The house has been reopened for only a couple of months. Before that it was closed for three years, since my father died. I aim to get it straight though so that we can move back here. Siger fancies himself an English gentleman. Now please come inside . . . I've been looking forward to this. Lunch is served."

On entry they passed through a great marble-columned hall lined with statues, mostly of naked women. Both the columns and statues showed signs of great age with rough porosity disfiguring the surface. Some of the huge beams and cross-members were blackened with scorching.

"I see it still hasn't collapsed." Dr. Swallow was looking about her and up. "It takes me back so far . . . it could be yesterday. The smell of the lilies seems to linger here . . ."

"What could be yesterday?" Lady Sarah had stopped and asked

the question pointedly. Dr. Swallow turned and, smiling agreeably, shrugged.

"Oh, everything . . . ."

They mounted a staircase which had obviously been renovated.

"The old one finally fell down then," remarked Carla Swallow.

"Yes. Luckily no one was here. I had it mended last month."

The dining-room had a huge bay window overlooking a lake on the grounds to the rear of the house. A lunch for two was set out, with wine, caviar and many other delights. Patricia immediately felt unwanted.

"Look, I'll drive down to the village. There was a nice pub there and I can come back with a sandwich and start setting up the machine."

Lady Sarah looked only a little uncertain. "Well, are you sure?"

But Dr. Swallow instantly reacted. "I'll share everything with Patricia. She's had a long journey."

"Oh, nonsense! We'll have another plate, it's not problem." She rang a bell, and footsteps from a passage preceded a side door opening and the appearance of a servant. Shortly afterwards a third plate had appeared on the table. Lady Sarah poured the wine and they began lunch.

"You waste your epicurean tastes on me, Sarah. I daresay this is an excellent vintage, but any wine suits me, provided it isn't the very worst."

"That's where you're wrong, Carla. This one is especially for you; it comes from the vines on the estate. Apparently they are very old and may be related to vines of the Roman period. That's what an expert, friend of mind, told me. He made this out of them . . . look!" She indicated the side of the bottle.

"Castle Aizoia." The label showed a woman standing legs akimbo, bunches of grapes in each hand, unclothed and with devil-like figures behind.

"Let me guess who designed the label," mocked Carla Swallow.

"You're right, but the wine has been a great success, you know. The grapes seem to prosper here, and my friend Vincent knew a lot about making the best of them. This stuff is five-years old—a grand cru!"

"To the ghost-machine!"

They drank and ate, while a mute Patricia picked nervously at her plate. Wasn't it so terribly obvious that she had no experience of such a lunch in such a house? The food was delicious, the wine dark and smooth, yet she had hardly warmed up when Lady Sarah's question stirred her up again.

"Have you told Pat about the Aizoians?"

"No, but she knows a little about the temple, don't you, Patricia?"

"Yes, oh yes . . ." she stammered, and as both women seemed to wait for more, she went on with hot cheeks, "but the Aizoians sound more interesting."

"They were." said Lady Sarah with an ambiguous smile. "This region was the absolute centre of a cult that enveloped both northern Gaul and the whole of Britain as far as the Romans went. Here was the great temple of Aizoia, long destroyed, but where a small chapel was kept going throughout the dark ages in Europe by dedicated acolytes. It was the worship of a goddess, Aizoia, Iza or Aiza, maybe even developed from Osiris who was a god, not a goddess. The worshippers were all women. They had a hierarchy, and the lowest female members were treated as slaves, even though they were in fact in some cases Roman-British ladies of some standing."

"What did they believe?"

"Ah, no one really knows. That the true god was female seems likely. That women could conceive by women. And a lot of seemingly silly goings on with ceremonies."

"Women conceive by women?" Patricia gasped, forgetting her self-consciousness.

"So they thought. But since they no longer exist, what does it matter? A little more wine, Pat?"

That was it. Patricia nodded and held her glass up. She was part of their clan suddenly. She had to show it somehow.

"You both used to play here, didn't you?" she asked knowingly. Lady Sarah looked up sharply and turned to Dr. Swallow.

"Did Carla tell you about that?"

"Only that we used to play in the temple," said Carla, curiously almost apologetic. Lady Sarah stared at her.

"But that was all years ago."

"It was indeed." Dr. Swallow sighed. Patricia felt the past uniting them against her again.

After lunch Dr. Swallow set up her microcomputer and began to do the necessary calculations for the running of the machine. It was agreed that Lady Sarah and Pat would go and check the site. They drove the van down several lanes of the estate and over rough ground to where the famous archeological site was situated. Patricia saw an outcrop of rock, the edge of a large geological feature that ran right through Lady Shadwell's land, with an old rotten wooden door covered with rusting iron reinforcement. It swung open when Lady Sarah pulled it.

With some difficulty they unloaded the frame and down they went propelling the trolley with the strange apparatus along rather a dank corridor cut out of the rock. There were curious doors and forks, but according to Lady Sarah they were dummy ends to fool an intruder. She led Patricia through an arch into a great open space with a stone bench—the altar. They stopped, in awe of some spirit, it seemed. The mosaic floor was damaged, but its original design—two naked women kneeling—was still discernible. The force of the past must have overwhelmed Lady Sarah as she spoke of it again, dreamingly.

"We played some really silly games in here. We used to undress. At least I did. Carla used always to keep her panties on. She was older than me and more inhibited." Her words, the way she looked, were making Patricia uneasy.

"I know," she said quickly. "She told me about that."

"Did she? Indeed! I though she kept those memories to herself. You must be very close to her."

"No. I'm not really. But she only said what you said told me." She, too, felt the need to apologize.

"She didn't tell you about the last time?"

"Last time? No, not at all."

Lady Sarah had a sudden excited grin.

"Do you want to know what happened?" But she didn't wait for an answer. She really seemed possessed by something, thought Patricia—the ghost of her childhood. "We were in here one summer afternoon. Aunt Zenobia was staying. I liked her, she always bought me presents. We played "The Game". I used to be the slave. I'd take everything off. I was twelve at that time. I like to be naked, I guess I was a little exhibitionist. She was fourteen and she stripped to vest and panties. She was the queen and wore a tiara I had found in the house. But this time she wasn't satisfied. I had to kneel before her, feed her grapes and sweets. If I was bad, she'd smack my behind. Very lightly, you see, we were only playing – I used to enjoy it, that's why I was often bad.

That day I was a bit less into it than usual . . . I really wanted to go and see Aunt Zenobia and I told Carla. But she said suddenly, "The queen must be naked, too." I was curious to see her, because she seemed very big compared to me, almost a woman. She took her vest off, and she was still very uniformed, just a slight swelling where her bosoms would come. But when she took her drawers off, I was spellbound. I had no pubic hair and my bottom was still girlish. But she had a big black bush of hair, and her bottom seemed enormous to me.

I knew there was something funny in the air. We both looked down at her hairy triangle. I reached out and touched it, out of curiosity. She laughed. I said I thought she wasn't ticklish. She laughed again. "It is ticklish there," she said. So I began to tickle her. And she lay beside me, so I could carry on. No more mention of queens. I began to rub her because I could see how much she liked it. She closed her eyes and opened her legs. I remember it so well. She was like a great cat purring. I knew it was wrong, or at least felt that if we were caught there'd be trouble. Her sex seemed huge to me, woman-like, though I daresay it wasn't really. But I had an absolute instinct to go on playing her with my hand, watching it open and let out juice. She had an orgasm – probably her first ever. But as she was having it we were caught.

I don't know how my Aunt Zenobia had the idea of looking for us here, but she stormed out of nowhere and pulled us apart. She dragged Carla by her hair. Poor thing, she was trembling with a mixture of fear and ecstasy as she was called a "little pervert." She was sent away. That was the end of her visits. I was very sad, you know, but being young I soon got over it. And it wasn't long before I found out I could do to myself what I had done to her, with similar pleasant results. Poor Carla, I bet that ruined her psychologically for the rest of her life. Does she have boyfriends, do you know?"

Patricia stood petrified before the woman. A deviless, that's what she was, with her red hair, leading her into that cave to whisper obscence secrets. Gone was the rational technician. She tried desperately to find her tongue.

"I – I don't know really. I don't think so."

"What about you?" smiled Lady Sarah catching the girl's black plait. "Do you have a lover?"

Patricia swallowed.

"It's time to go." She turned and freed herself.

"Or do you love her?" she thought she heard Lady Sarah's voice following her.

* * *

"So here we are! Away you go, you cool collected scientists." Lady Sarah's laughter made a hollow sound echoing along the underground temple. Patricia shivered in the shadows, the damp cold was getting to her. But even stronger than the pernicious atmosphere, was the fever of the experiment.

Dr. Swallow helped her set up the microcomputer, the N-field generator and the frame of generation – a sort of aerial. The torches and lamps were put out, and they waited in total darkness for the huge transient effect the hard light had caused to die down.

"I wish I'd done something useful with my life," Lady Sarah said in the sudden night. "Watching you two, I realize there is more to life than drinking, eating and screwing."

"You two", she had said, as if SHE were the outsider now. At the same time Patricia felt a woman's body sitting close to her, an arm holding her shoulders.

"Cross your fingers!" Carla Swallow said in her ear. It took her breath away. She didn't dare move a muscle as they sat together, warm waves twisting between her thighs. At last Dr. Swallow set the machine running, typing in the parameter she expected would start the computer in its search for a signal. Nothing occurred. Patricia didn't know how long had passed when Lady Sarah sniggered.

"Some helluva picture show, this!"

Neither of the other women laughed. Their dreams were hanging by a thread. Lady Sarah fell silent, but Patricia somehow sensed her moving around, intent on something. She had a crazy idea what she was doing to pass the time, but it was so outrageous that she dismissed it at once.

And then, with no warning the frame flickered; in a second or two a steady warm light flooded the area around the altar, as if it were a stage. They gasped with astonishment: a figure seemed to walk past them into the light. It was clad in a long dark robe with a nebulous headdress like a great shimmering spider that spread out from the head. With difficulty Patricia had to make a mental adjustment to the fact that it was not real, not a person who might see or speak to them. Then she suddenly realized that the imperious face under the headdress was very like Carla Swallow. Not perfectly but very similar. She watched in the stunned silence.

The woman lit an incense burner and a set of candles; from the glow appeared a wooden statue which had been hidden in the shadow behind the altar. The new light shone through the transparent shift of the priestess.

It became obvious she wore very little beneath her robe, the intriguing line of her hip and buttocks being silhouetted against the background.

She clapped her hands and from the shadows, another figure appeared. This one was a negress naked apart from a belt with hanging metal beads that just covered her modesty in her lower parts. She was beautifully proportioned – almost perfect – except for rather larger breasts than are usually seen in ideal figures. These two swung and bobbed with each movement, succulent-looking fruit which few, men or women, could view without some stirring of desire. But Patricia got the greatest start of all, staring at this image of herself. It wasn't quite right though. Her own nipples were much smaller than the large brown discs that topped those of the newcomer. And unlike her double, she had a mole near her belly-button. She was not the only one to have noticed the strange coincidences.

"It's you, Carla!" hissed Lady Sarah breathlessly. "Look! You and Patricia in another world!"

"Ssh, you'll disturb the vibrations." Dr. Swallow's voice was hardly a murmur, shaken by mysterious emotions. Patricia wished she could have seen her face, before she focused her eyes on the scene again.

The negress knelt before the priestess, bowing her head. The priestess got hold of her by her long dreadlocks and lifted her up. She seemed to be angry with her. Patricia's lookalike made a sulky face, as her mistress said something and pointed to her waist. She looked back sullenly, shaking her head, when she suddenly received a hard slap on her face. She cowered and removed her little skirt of

LAMAR VAN DYKE
'87

beads; and there she stood bare-assed before the priestess, who forced her head down onto the altar. The coffee-coloured buttocks were raised and, still without a sound, the other figure began to strike that vulnerable rear with a flexible rod. The behind writhed around until the girl was raised, then made to kneel again. The priestess removed her robe, and was revealed, pale and nude, and small-breasted. Her sex organ had been shaved, revealing a little puffed up mound of delicately divided flesh, and it was now on a level with the girl's face. The priestess pulled the girl's head towards her.

Patricia felt as if her own face were pulled towards the mass of flesh. It was her, naked and docile, at the knees of Carla Swallow. With a thrilling wave of guilt and pleasure she was suddenly conscious of the tight pull of her jeans riding into the lips of her sex. There she sat as powerless as her naked ghost, while a series of great throbs released pulses of warm juice that she could feel soaking her and trickling along her thighs.

Such a long poignant orgasm she could feel as the head of her twin was gently drawn forward; a pink tongue suddenly darted out, as if the deed expected of it were not new to it. And with a gesture of hedonistic abandon the priestess pulled the skin of her sex upward and stretched the flesh beneath so that her orange-brown folds were exposed and protruded. The tongue evidently worked eagerly, probing for something, then running along the slit to briefly vanish. The slave's mouth would occasionally gently bite and pull at the hanging flesh of the long outer lips in response to some urgent demand, and as her skill was seemingly very great, the priestess soon had her pleasure. Her face contracted in a grimace of sensation, her mouth stretched over her teeth, her eyes closed, her body became taut. There was a deadly silence in the room as the rounded flank of the priestess started to buck in pelvic thrusts, and she began to collapse into a squat, crudely rubbing herself on her neophyte's face, willing or unwilling. The scene suddenly faded.

* * *

A sigh escaped somebody, and the lights were lit by Dr. Swallow. Nothing was said. Embarrassment seemed to hold sway as far as the researchers were concerned. They walked out into a late afternoon sun, and only then did the atmosphere become more normal. Patricia was still troubled by a rhythmic twitching at greater and greater intervals. But the breeze soon cooled her leaving a pleasant fresh wetness.

Lady Sarah, however, seemed relaxed and her face had that indefinable air of satisfaction that comes after a climax. Perhaps Patricia hadn't imagined it after all. It fitted in with the woman's character, to uninhibitedly enjoy a voyeuristic experience with the help of an unseen hand. Dr. Swallow seemed to have difficulty meeting Patricia's eye, then deliberately overcame the problem by addressing her.

"Well, Patricia, we've got something to celebrate. We've just witnessed a video recording made in stone a couple of thousand years ago."

"The material doesn't seem to have changed much over the years . . . ." Lady Sarah smiled at her own joke, and all three women burst with laughter at last releasing the tension.

Despite the bottles of 'Aizoia Castle' and the festive spirit which ensued a scientific breakthrough, there was something constrained in the atmosphere over dinner that no one seemed to lift. Lady Sarah's conversation, skilled hostess though she was, fell flat; Carla Swallow remained pensive, more distant than ever; and Patricia was engrossed in the dishes for fear of facing either of them. It was a warm melancholy evening, full of the smokes of barbecue; the servant was apparently off duty.

"But how can you explain this by your X-rays, or whatever you call them? Are you sure you aren't kidding me?" This time, Lady Sarah caught her friend's attention.

"N-rays," said Dr. Swallow with a touch of impatience. "What do you think, Sarah? That we made it up for your benefit? And how, tell me?"

"You could have a film projector hidden in that machine." Lady Sarah shrugged. "How do I know? The figures were just like you, weren't they?" She brought up the forbidden topic defiantly. There was an icy silence.

"They were different enough," Carla Swallow finally answered with calculated sang-froid. Patricia could sense her effort, but that didn't stop Lady Sarah.

"How so?"

"I have an appendix scar that the figure didn't show." Dr. Swallow went on, her eyes straight onto Sarah's face. "And I don't shave myself."

For a moment she seemed to shake her opponent. Patricia repressed the vision of black wool curling between long white thighs that her words had conjured up.

"Besides, you must be mad if you think I could shoot that sort of movie."

"Of course, I am mad, my dear." Lady Sarah suddenly laughed. "That's why you always had me believe anything you wanted, and made me do as you wished. Oh, you haven't changed, Carla dear! Nor have I. That's why I still love you."

"You! You've always laughed at me!" Carla Swallow smiled at her with a long look of complicity. Forgotten in her corner, Patricia was in the throes of jealousy.

* * *

The bedroom was a stark place cheered only a little by the log fire that they lit since the spring air cooled rapidly at night. There was a large four-poster bed which had been renovated as a first step in refurnishing the ruin. A small couch was pushed against the wall, near the ghost machine. Dr. Swallow had insisted on keeping it within her sight. The place, with its crumbling doors, was hardly safe, and she wouldn't take a chance.

"You don't mind sharing, do you, Carla? Patricia can sleep in the cot," Lady Sarah said merrily, and direct as ever began to shed her clothes.

Like most English people, Patricia had a shyness about bodies that made her feel uneasy about undressing in front of strangers, yet curious about her hostess' revelations. The woman was naked to the hair in a few moments, and stood talking as if nothing were amiss. Lady Sarah's body was good for her age—she didn't look much over twenty, though like Dr. Swallow she was in her early thirties. Her blanched white skin was smooth as silk. Her bosoms were smallish with nipples of the palest pink. She was still the same exhibitionist obviously, walking about to show her thighs, slim but shapely, her belly rounded but not plump. Her pubic hair was sparse and wisp-like, and as she sat down, the bulging organ it covered momentarily opened like a flower of deeper pink. The outer lips, crinkled and slack, revealed smooth inner flesh, which was slender enough to quiver slightly as she moved.

Carla and Patricia undressed silently—watched by the naked aristocrat. Perhaps Carla Swallow was sensing the surreptitious glances of her assistant, because she turned away from her when she bared her top half—a muscular panther-like back rippling as she unfastened her bra. She put on a black silk pyjama top with golden motif. Then her trousers were loosened and lowered and Patricia caught sight of a pair of pale blue briefs with pink lacy effects, somehow unexpected in the soberly dressed Dr. Swallow. She pulled them down without fuss. The pyjama top half covered her bare rounded buttocks; so unlikely a view did it seem of the scientist, Patricia kept peering at them guiltily. They were slightly larger than she had thought. Dr. Swallow was deceptively large in the hips, though her overall impression was slimness. A tight and muscular bottom it was, yet as in most females, plump enough to tremble slightly as she turned and reached for her pyjama trousers. A brief shadowy suggestion of a hairy triangle was confirmed as she lifted her knee, raising the hem of her jacket with her thigh; her black bush bobbed into view for an instant.

Patricia was rooted on her chair opposite the bed, unable to move her eyes away. She must have made a funny picture, wearing only her long yellow socks which came above the knee. And she was still gaping when Dr. Swallow turned and looked at her—the atmosphere in the room had changed. Business, science, and friendly teasing had ended. The baring of the three women had added a strange tang to the air: a mixture of perfumes from under arms and other nooks and crannies, sweet-smelling soap and musky and sexual odour of secretions. The N-ray frame was sitting dead and dark in the corner of the room, but as they looked at each other, Patricia felt the ghost of the Azoic priestess and her slave amongst them. No one, not even Lady Sarah smiled any more.

And it was Patricia in the end, who lifted her knee to remove her fashionable woollen stocking and deliberately showed Carla Swallow her cunt. She felt a strange tiredness now, a careless feeling, as if she couldn't be held responsible for this exhibition of herself. And yet she knew exactly what she was doing. She let the raised thigh fall away and all the time there was this inner voice, *her* voice saying silently: "Look at this, Carla . . . all for you to rule as you want, with caresses or kisses. You can see it but no one else."

Carla's eyes looked openly, long enough to make Patricia throb before her. Then, like a mistress, she spoke, looking up the legs slowly into those opened thighs, her detached voice hardly real.

"Where did you get those?" Her gaze focussed on the two puffed-up orange-brown lips that parted slightly. Inside, soft vulnerable flesh convoluted and delicate, glinted with unmistakable white juices.

"Haven't you seen anything like that before?" Patricia heard herself say.

"Not quite like that." Carla Swallow added: "They are nice socks."

* * *

Once the lights were out only the firelight flickered. In the long silence, Patricia lay in agony. Why did SHE have Dr. Swallow in with HER? The she-devil! While she, Patricia, was left desperately aroused, a plaything ready for play, but with no playmate, no one to unwind the coiled spring. She didn't usually have to. She was too proud. But now she held her fat warm flesh and squeezed it almost angrily—rejected, after so crudely trying to seduce her Azoic priestess. As if Carla Swallow could care less about her assistant's hairy hot nest. She had never done that to anyone before.

"Goodnight, Patricia dear!" Carla Swallow's voice sounded warm in the night. Patricia didn't answer. She was too furious and guilty to speak, with her hand doing what it was.

"Goodnight!" The voice had a querying note. Patricia kept her mouth shut.

"She's asleep. She's only young and she's had a big day," said Lady Sarah.

"I'm not surprised, I'm very tired myself."

"I think she's got a crush on you, you know." A tinkle of laughter, then:

"You flatter me. She's a dear girl though. But she's quite straight. I visited her once when she was expecting a boyfriend . . . she was ready even down to being undressed."

"What if she was? Do you like her . . . enough?"

"I haven't got time for that sort of thing."

"No. But you like her, don't you?

"Why not? There's no way anyone could dislike her."

"As much as you used to like me?"

"Don't be a baby! We've all grown up now."

"So you don't care anymore?"

"I didn't say that . . . ." The voice was a little less harsh.

"But you still remember that day . . . ."

"Mmm, it's past now. I suffered then, but I got over it, eventually, Now I'm happy in my work."

Suddenly there was an intake of breath, and a muffled murmur of surprise. For a moment there was no sound but breathing . . . near panting . . . Then:

"Sarah, you had better stop that!"

"Don't you like it?"

"Take your hand away, please. Let's not start a silly struggle."

"Alright. But I'm not sorry I did it. It's bigger now than then, and just as nice . . . ."

"I'm going to sleep, I'm bushed."

* * *

Patricia felt even worse. Somehow Carla Swallow's rejection wasn't firm enough. Maybe if Sarah had . . . or if she herself were to . . . She squeezed. Her body stiffened. She had to concentrate not to come. She lay for half an hour, squeezing until she nearly got it over the top, then holding off, her bed becoming wetter and wetter.

"Patricia!" Lady Sarah's voice froze her. She wouldn't have answered but curiosity was stronger.

"Yes?"

"She's asleep now. Why don't you get in with us?" Deviless or not, it was too thrilling an offer to resist. Patricia got up, trembling and got in on the Lady's side. She had no trousers on, they were still in her bed, and as she crept in, long warm hands stroked her buttocks.

"I know what you've been doing." Lady Sarah whispered.

"So what?" she said on the defensive.

"So nothing. I've been doing the same. I know your trouble. You're all stirred up, aren't you?"

"What d'you mean?"

"You can't fool me. You're crazy about her, you've got the hots . . . and you know she's lying here near me with only those flimsy pyjamas on, and it's driving you nuts, isn't that true?"

"Ssh . . ."

Don't worry, she's well away. Admit it!" The hands were nice and knowing and delicately investigative on her ass. Patricia sighed.

"I guess it is. I can't understand it. I didn't think I was bisexual, but I am obviously."

Lady Sarah chuckled.

"She IS rather fascinating. Why don't you tell her? She might melt, you never know." She laughed again, mocking.

"She wouldn't. She's miles from that. Anyway I don't want to start anything, it would be unhealthy."

"Oh rot! Life's for living. I know it exactly. She's your boss, so aloof, cool yet beautiful in her way . . . It's there in all of us somewhere . . . ." Lady Sarah went on invitingly. "I tell you something. She isn't immune to your charms. No way!"

"How do you know?"

"She looks at you sometimes. She's too inhibited to give way, but she'd like to have you in her arms. She may kid you but not me. I know her too well. I have seen that look on her face ages ago, don't forget. That same green flame in her eyes."

"If only . . ." Patricia gasped as her buttocks were gently parted to accommodate a bold finger. "If only it were true . . . ."

"If you'd seen her eyes when you undressed . . . ." One hand moved onto Patricia's most intimate skin. "She would have kissed you there, if she could . . . or beaten your ass as she used to do mine . . . ."

A flow of creamy juice rewarded Lady Sarah for her attentions. She rubbed it along the crack, up to the anus. The girl was almost fainting in her arms with sobs that yearned for the caresses of a different hand. It was so simple really. Even as this body craved for Carla's hands, it was Lady Sarah who reaped it. She would enjoy it to the full, as long as she kept telling the stories the girl wanted to hear. To think of Carla's face if she woke up now! In her excitement Lady Sarah pushed a long red nail into the sensitive behind.

Patricia sat up, her heart beating.

"Why do you tell me all this?" she hissed passionately. "Aren't you jealous?"

Lady Sarah had retracted her claws. She was all softness again, fingers around Patricia's belly, circling her navel, appeasing the suspicion.

"Believe it or not, I only want happiness for her . . . my love is very unselfish. I think you can make her very happy."

"Don't lie about this. I can stand it if I think she's ice . . . but if I thought, just for a moment . . . she can't!"

Hands reached Patricia's breasts, and she sank back, her big brown nipples tingling with the surge of blood. Lady Sarah kept them pinched in her fingers.

"Of course she does! And she's not so inhibited now . . . . She's asleep, all warm and cosy, dreaming, maybe about what she saw today . . . ."

"I don't think she'd let herself think about that."

"She might dream about it . . . she can't stop her dreams."

"I bet she can. She couldn't let such a thing cross her mind."

"Why? What do you think she's got in her pants? Something just like yours."

As Lady Sarah's lips fluttered against the huge bosoms, her hand found Patricia's thighs involuntarily parting. Like a hunting animal, it grasped her hot wet vulva. There was an ecstatic protest, "Oh, no, not now . . . ." while liquor poured from the boiling flesh.

"You're nice . . . a nice generous handful . . ." Lady Sarah murmured, her breath burning on the tits.

"Don't make me come, please . . . ." The hand moved away, easily and tantalizingly. Lady Sarah knelt up and pulled back the covers.

"Look! There she is . . . sleeping peacefully."

Carla Swallow lay on her back, her mouth relaxed in a mysterious smile. Where her top and pants met, her belly was uncovered, rising and falling very gently and slowly. Her legs were slightly apart, one hand not a long way from her groin. Her breath occasionally produced a faint voiced sigh, a murmur of peace.

"She is beautiful . . . Look!"

Patricia knelt up, and the two women gazed wide-eyed at the sleeping figure.

"If we are careful, we can get her pyjamas off, and get her going in her sleep."

"Oh, no! If she wakes!"

"She won't. And if she does, she won't mind, you'll see."

"No, really . . . ."

The hand found Patricia's cunt again, a brief fondle which broke her last resistance. She was like wet putty at that women's touch.

"You . . . you begin . . . ."

"Just undo her jacket . . . one button . . . ."

Patricia slowly moved towards the hot body, and unfastened the buttons. A creamy olive skin appeared, shining in the firelight.

"There . . ."

The jacket fell open and Carla Swallow's apple-shaped breasts appeared with their little dark nipples like coins balanced on her flesh.

"Look!" Lady Sarah ran her hand very deliberately down from Carla's collarbone, down between her breasts and over her rising belly, to the top of her pyjamas pants. Then she reversed the movement, pressing the nipples at the top.

"Go on!"

With a trembling hand, Patricia imitated her movement, and as she did, she saw the sleeping nipples stiffen and rise like little cones of rubber. Instinctively she bent, and modelling her mouth on the woman's breasts, with soft jaw and tongue she sucked at her.

Lady Sarah looked with a smile at the large and warm brown rump raised before her. She liked it, the ideal rubbery toy to stroke, around the buttocks, between the thighs, back again, then around the front squeezing the soaking flesh until Patricia jerked. And then she had the girl moaning as she found her clitoris, a longish one, hard and distended, a female erection hidden in the dark fat folds of her hairy cunt. But Patricia didn't falter from her obsessional sucking, and Lady Sarah had to pull her away.

"Let's have her pants off. Then you can see what she's got and know what she needs."

Patricia felt on the edge of a cliff. It was an evil suggestion, yet the vulnerable form of Dr. Swallow seemed impervious to being awakened even by hands caressing her more delicate regions. Calmly Lady Sarah unfastened the pyjama cord and whilst Patricia lifted each thigh and foot, she pulled them down under the buttocks. A flash of coarse black hair appeared but even before Patricia had become accustomed to seeing the hidden hair of her boss, Lady Sarah crudely lifted the unconscious thighs and parted them as far as possible.

Patricia was faced with something she had never expected to see in her life: Dr. Swallow's cunt, wide open in front of her. It was a long slash of feminine essence surrounded by damp unruly hair which grew thickly on the bulge, all around the groin and again straggly on the inner thighs before disappearing under her in the division of her behind. The delicately crinkled brown outer lips parted slightly as her belly swelled. In between, her inner lips hung loosely. They were salmon pink and glistened with wetness, one a trifle longer than the other, guarding the dark entrance to the scientist's body. Like the opening of some sea shell in a rock pool it just perceptibly pulsated with some emotion, a tiny run of liquid gleaming in the light. Patricia's eyes feasted on the unladylike sight, roving up and down from one convoluted fold to another. But they always came back to the part that differed most from her own organs.

Carla Swallow had a great bulge at the top of her slit where the lips all puffed up as if covering some large fleshy protrusion.

"Tickle her there now. That'll give her a lift to her dreams!"

Patricia's trembling hands came to tickle the strange mound. There was a stirring. The flesh moved, parted, and the clitoris pushed upwards. It was enormous, a sort of deep orange thumb; and like a living thing it rose up.

"What is it?" the girl gasped.

"Her clitoris, what d' you think? I knew she had that . . . she had it at fourteen."

Patricia went hot and cold. So under her smart trouser suit, Dr. Swallow had this great finger of feminine aggression. And here she was with it tall and erect, yet essentially woman—an Azoian, if anyone was. Lady Sarah looked at it eagerly, no different from the rude little girl who had first stroked it.

"The priestesses of Aizoia used to eat buglewort to make them grow. And when we played, she ate it, because she was the queen. And maybe that's how this happened. Maybe not . . . . I wonder what she's dreaming about to make her so randy."

Patricia had slipped off the bed, shivering with shock.

"It's wrong. Leave her alone!"

"Come back, Patricia." Lady Sarah laughed. "I bet she's dreaming of you."

"I don't want to look at her like that. It's all your fault . . ." she cried out as she tripped on something in the dark, some horrible presence cold and metallic.

"Why, are you afraid? Damn it, what are you doing, Patricia?" Then Lady Sarah shut up.

The room had suddenly lightened. And as it did it altered. The walls retreated and they seemed to be in a great hall with almost infinitely distant walls, with long columns rising into a misty vault. In the room was a throne where a royal figure sat with flowing black hair and a midnight blue robe. Around her stood women in pale blue gossamer thin shifts—half a dozen of them. And before them carrying platters filled with fruit, exotic vegetables and nuts, stood slave women. They wore nothing except flaps of red material that covered their sexes. Behind they were bare with voluptuous buttocks, some large, some smaller. They poured wine for the pale-blue clad ladies of the court who fondled them or slapped them according to their behaviour. But the thing that struck the two watchers most was the face of the queen.

It was Carla, like the queen Aizoia herself, her face imperious yet alert and sensual. And, as they watched, a troop of newcomers was led into the space before her throne. Men and women of barbaric appearance, with costumes made of fur and leather. The men were chained and stood heads bowed before the queen. All but one of the women were merely bound by leather thongs around their wrists. The exception was a tall proud-looking woman with brown hair shot with yellow and black—a barbaric tigress who was carrying a golden chain, like Bodicea of old, the British queen paraded through the streets of Rome.

"That's my Aunt Zenobia," said Lady Sarah. "My God!" And this time there was almost terror in her voice. And then the royal image of Carla spoke.

"So this ends your proud rule, Queen of the Dark Marshes! How say you now, who insulted me at the court of Maximus? Like a beast, you are chained! Your servants are bound and helpless! And I may take from you what I will."

The tall creature sank her head to her chest.

"There is naught to be said. Only have mercy on our poor servants, for they did nothing but follow their queen."

"Your servants? Why, they shall all be slain, or given to the slavery of the queen of Egypt whom I wish to please, and who is cruel enough, so I hear. All shall go over to the cages below . . . ."

"I beg of Your Majesty! Not slavery for my handmaiden!"

"Slavery it shall be. Though I shall release one if you name her, to be your companion in captivity."

"Then shall it be Prunella, who attends me always."

"And who is she? Show her!"

"Come, Prunella!"

A brown girl—the image of Patricia—came forward. She wore a fine silk robe, unlike all but the queen's, of palest green.

"Ha ha! What a fool you are to think I had the intention to slay or enslave your servants. I but wished to know the one whom you loved. And so I do know it is she, who I see is a ripe fruit upon whom you dote. So shall I taste of this fruit before your very eyes, for she pleases me."

"No, I beg on knees that you do not! All the riches of my kingdom are yours if you wish it, but do not hurt this woman . . . ."

"Hurt her! I shall not hurt her, rather the contrary!"

"I implore you! Do not touch her! She is my dearest possession."

"Enough! Strip the queen of her garments! She shall show us how well the years and her gluttonous appetites have treated her body!"

The near naked slaves roughly approached the conquered queen, and though she was strong and struggled mightily, they soon tore off all that covered the voluptuous body, except for a tight band about her waist, and a small cloth that held her bosoms. The queen who was like Carla imperiously descended the steps. One leg emerged from her robe as she stood facing the humbled victim.

"Thus you are!" She suddenly snatched at the cloth and the royal prisoner's huge bosoms fell loose, great tender white orbs surmounted by large flat brown nipples.

"And thus! Like to a sow, it seems, whose udders are in some need of a crane to bear their weight! And how is the cunt of the Queen of the Marshes? All must see this unusual sight, for queens' cunts are seldom seen, no more their asses . . . ."

She snatched away the tight band, and the queen's hairy tuft of brown appeared, with easily visible and pendulous lips protruding from the join of the thighs.

"It reminds me of that of an ape, now that I see it, so gross and indelicate. Rotate now, that I know how fat is your ass, sow!"

Queen Zenobia hesitated, her cheeks flame-red.

"Turn! Else your favourite shall be taken forever."

She turned and her beautiful but large behind appeared, vulnerable, quivering in the light.

"Ha ha! It grows heavy to carry. It has spent too much time seated in a chair whilst its owner fattened herself on milk and honey." Aizoia/Carla approached and slapped the buttocks, then pinched them. "Show your cunt to those who look on, as slave-girls are obliged to at the market."

Zenobia knew what to do, and grasping her pubic hair, she pulled upwards, drawing all the folds of her most hidden flesh into the light, great pale brown wrinkled outer lips trimmed with coarse hair and soft damp lips hanging out from within, her clitoris large but limp and retracted.

"Shameless bitch! Your constant fornication has led to the enlargement of all that womanly flesh." She reached down and touched Queen Zenobia's sex, gently kneading it.

"Even now I feel its lewdness. Are you not a dirty slut, who wore a queen's raiment to disguise the body of a harlot?"

Queen Zenobia was not unmoved by the skilled caresses, and her face flushed.

"As I am defeated, so I am as Your Majesty says."

"So you are, and so shall you ever be. Hark now! Send away the male captives, for they may not witness what shall follow." The men were led out.

"Now all the captives may be unclothed—save Prunella." Soon all the captive women were naked. They stood sad and dejected.

"Turn from us and put your noses to the dirt of the floor whilst you kneel, asses raised. Thus are female captives seen by Queen Aizoia!"

The frightened women all knelt and raised their bottoms—a sea of soft buttocks, each with its cleft from which many different shaped cunts bulged helplessly.

"Let them be given wine to lap from bowls, like bitches."

Each woman was provided with a bowl from which she eagerly lapped wine, for all thirsted greatly. Their bellies quivered, their cunts dilated as they swallowed each mouthful. Queen Aizoia moved along the line, lewdly fingering and tickling the exposed organs, jabbing something into one orifice, sometimes another, the women squeaking as she did.

"Should you not kiss this one, since she is lost to you?"

Queen Zenobia was obliged to kiss each woman as they passed, on the unseemly nests that they presented.

"All must now be bare, for I am to disrobe and it is unseemly for the queen to be naked when others are dressed. Slaves! Turn from me, to the ladies. Disrobe them, and excite them with your hands and tongues, that they may enjoy what follows!"

She still stroked Queen Zenobia's sex, who was wriggled and sighed, for she was a sensitive creature. The women soon stood bare and with busy slaves before them, heads low. Aizoia called Prunella.

"Unclasp my robe!"

The girls did so, and the queen was nude, like all the others, but for a thin gold band at the waist that covered nothing. Her huge clitoris hung four inches of strange womanly sting. She smiled to the audience who all sighed in admiration.

"Undress your favourite, bitch!"

Zenobia stripped the robe from Prunella. She wore a modesty shift, but that, too, Zenobia removed. The brown succulent body of the girl appeared, nipples hard.

"Bid her turn and bend."

The girl did so. Her fat brown ass parted to show her glistening organ. The queen's clitoris stiffened and rose like the bud of a rare orchid as she looked at the offered pleasure.

"Thrust your tongue in her slot, that it may be well prepared, fat bitch!"

Queen Zenobia buried her head into her favourite's ass. There was the wet sucking sound of flesh against flesh. Then she got up from her work, her tears running as freely as the juice from her cunt.

"Open her to me!"

Her fingers parted the girl's last defense, a little contracting hole to accomodate the hard organ . . . .

* * *

And then all disappeared. Patricia heard Carla calling her name in the night almost hysterically. Suddenly she was afraid. If Lady

Sarah was . . . . She rushed to their bed. Someone grabbed her and she struggled furiously as Lady Sarah's hands searched for her thighs.

"Leave me, leave me, you bitch! Carla, help me!" Then words dried in her mouth.

The green eyes of Carla Swallow were flashing at her face, and her hands, the strong lustful hands of Dr. Swallow, were opening her. She seemed hardly to know what happened, but she convulsively jerked feeling the strange clitoris penetrate her. Oh, it was like being burned and stretched, a shower of sparks seemed to flood her belly. She saw Carla rear up. And rolling over, the woman mounted her, her hands feeling her passionately, one on her nipples, the other behind gripping the girl's fat writhing bottom. The fingernails bit into the succulent flesh foraging down till she held the coarse hairy crevasse between Patricia's stretched buttocks, as her own white ass pounded upon her like a steam hammer, faster and faster.

Patricia was briefly aware of the lone crouching figure of Lady Sarah watching them jealously, before she lost sense of everything but Carla's bottom that pumped her desperately. And the weaker she felt, embraced and probed by that strange flesh, the more strongly she seemed to pulsate in sympathetic rhythm to her lover, until she screamed. And the woman screamed above her, rigid and raised like an angry sea, before her body was seized by a convulsive spasm. As if a 20,000 volt shock was periodically applied to her, she shook, her taut wet belly slapping against the girl's. Patricia held her ass as they jerked up and down, riding the storm. And she smelled her and heard her groaning words of forbidden passion. Then her lust spent itself like lightning as her feet crossed around her lover's back, high in the air and her inside seemed to turn into a pulsating furnace; her toes and fingers reflexed in twisted curves, and she felt her whole body like a giant mouth opening and shutting rhythmically as if to eat the woman. Even in this last moment of naked lust Patricia had a vision of the earliest days of their meeting; her long thirst was being quenched. The Carla Swallow collapsed on her, and she knew nothing more.

* * *

It could just as easily be called the dream machine, Patricia thought. "The WET dream machine", Carla had said when she told her. Somehow she had lost none of her mystery nor her unattainable air. But she was too honest not to call a spade a spade. Months later, she had finally admitted to Patricia the whole truth. The N-rays were really generated by the ancient rocks; this, Dr. Swallow still believed. But they were generated in far stronger form by thoughts and dreams . . . particularly those that pertained to sexual matters. And thus as she had already begun to suspect in the temple, it was the highly charged Lady Sarah's lewd mind that had imagined the little scene between her companions . . . with slight errors concerning parts of their bodies that she could only guess at.

Her own dream, Carla Swallow analyzed clinically, had been stirred up by the sexual scenes she had witnessed, and picked up by the ghost machine Patricia had accidentally switched on. It was not the first time scientists were victims of their own invention, she had smiled. And that was the end of the matter.

They worked together as before. But sometimes at the end of a long day perhaps when Patricia was bending over a birdsnest of connections Carla would turn to her. "Would you like to drop round to mine tonight?" Whatever Patricia was doing was always cancelled.

FOLLOW THE WILD GOOSE FLIGHT

NORETTA KOERTGE

Introduction: This episode was originally planned as part of *Who Was That Masked Woman*? a novel about growing up lesbian in the Midwest. But because the book was getting too long, this adventure of Tretona at a Girl Scout Camp ended up on the cutting room floor where it's been smouldering ever since, just waiting for a chance to warm the needy reader. Enjoy!

Our paddles clean and bright
Flashing like silver
Follow the wild goose flight
Dip, dip—and swing.

—Canoeing song

New boots from Abercrombie and Fitch, a faked Red Cross life guard certificate (Tretona couldn't do the crawl), army surplus bug repellant (according to her brother Troy it was so strong that it dissolved ball point pens, the lacquer on gun barrels, and by implication the stingers off mosquitos), and other gear for the North Woods—all neatly packed in the trunk. Tretona was going to spend the summer at a Girl Scout Camp! She was feeling that mixture of power and anxiety that comes from talking your way into a job you aren't qualified for. For starters she had never been a Girl Scout, but she'd managed to parlay a long career in 4-H club, two church camps and a canoe trip to Minnesota with the volleyball regulars into a job as Unit Leader. The interview with Pepper, the camp director, had gone very well. Now all she had to do was impress the counselors under her and she would be all set.

It sure sounded like fun for the campers—swimming, boating, hiking, fire-building, crafts. Boy, she could have used some of that as a kid. 4-H had been one big drag—trying to keep your calf separate from the 25 other identical ones your dad was raising. (Generally, she would just give up on taming it and let it run with the others until time for the fair.) Sewing projects were worse—first the perennial apron which your mother pretended to like, next the little gathered skirt made out of a feed sack which no one would be seen dead in, and then finally a shirt. Tretona had managed to get some decent fabric, even matched the plaid and got the collar on, but then finked out on hand-making buttonholes (their old treadle machine didn't have none of them new-fangled gadgets) and put on snaps instead. It only got a yellow ribbon (which was the lowest there was, even worse than white and everybody got some kind of ribbon). Her mother was mortified. Or was she? Now Tretona remembered overhearing her words to the 4-H leader: "I suppose I can't expect my daughter to be any good in domestic science—I myself am such a failure as a housewife."

It was a familiar message—You're no good and small wonder because I'm no good either. But maybe her mother was in some sense pleased and signalling Tretona not to follow in her footsteps.

Pepper's map was exact (give that Big Girl Scout an orienteering badge)—if you go 259 miles North of Milwaukee, turn right at Copper Falls, left again at the red mailbox and follow the gravelled lane for 2.9 miles, you arrive at Pine Hills G.S. Camp—and there was Pepper at the gate, sitting on the fender of an old green pick-up. Cheery hello and then a look at the clipboard. Tretona's Unit was the farthest away—it was called Deerpath. Her assistants weren't here yet. She could drive up to the unit to unload her gear. But after that no cars were allowed past the gate—that was an absolute rule. Please not to ask for exceptions to be made. Bear left at the Lodge, carry on well past the Latrine (what better way to insure social cohesiveness than through your own group's Special

Speak, thought Tretona), and then follow the Indian markings blazed on posts—forbidden to desecrate trees—a cardinal camp rule. Pepper looked up, fingered her leather lanyard and smiled, "Glad to have you aboard, Getroek. We've got a great bunch of counsellors this year. It should be a good summer."

The sports car looked pretty incongruous sitting in the semi-circle of tents, so Tretona quickly dumped her stuff on the bunk bed, unpacked her Swiss Army knife and pocketed it, put on her new boots and deliberately scuffed them up against an oak tree. (At least she knew a few brands of trees—but if any of the kids had badges in that area she'd soon be left behind—god this was worse than trying to teach organic chemistry this past spring. At least that she had known once even if now she had forgotten it all.) Better start boning up. It was impossible to scuff up her brand spankin' new Girl Scout Leader's Manual so she tied it up in a red bandanna (carefully crumpling up the handkerchief first to work some of the starch out of it). Now let's get the car out of here—probably real G.S. types would find it decadent, so back past the childish hieroglyphics of a deer plus path, and a huge wigwam with a big circle of dozens of logs in front—it looked like a pow-wow site. For an instant Tretona wondered if recalcitrant campers were ever burned at the stake. Then the lodge with a big flag pole in front, complete with an obviously brand new flag, a forcedly cheery wave at Pepper who was talking to someone else, and then the temporary safety of the parking lot. A desultory look at the manual's sections on fire-building (alas no newspaper allowed and even pine needles were considered to be a bit sissified) and the platoon system (upon reaching the campsite, immediately assign duties to each platoon—the platoon groupings themselves, however, should have been long since established during the planning stage of the outing). Then some more cars drove by and the bugs were getting bad (damn, her mosquito dope was back at the tent) so there was nothing for it but to go back and meet some real scouts.

Pepper was tapping nervously with her pencil. "I must have your Christian name too, Miss Seagull." A stream of emphatic German came back from the woman standing on the other side of the clipboard. Tretona checked out her cute little bum and for some weird reason noticed now nibble-able her elbows were and then without thinking she jumped into the conversation.

"Maybe I can help," Tretona found herself saying. "For one thing her name is Siegl—it's probably pronounced with a Z and a long E, 'Zeegl', right?" Fraulein Seigl nodded emphatically. Tretona continued, dredging up some long buried scrap of dialogue from German 211, "Und Ihre Vornahme, bitte?"

"Ja, Vornahme, Christian name, I have already understood: Ehlee-suh-ko-see-ma." Finally Tretona took Pepper's board and wrote it down: Elise-Kosima.

"Too difficult for the campers," said Pepper, recovering quickly. "We will have to call you something else. I think a good name for you would be Sparky, yeah, why not?" And so Sparky or Schparky (for Elise Kosima's pronounciation came to predominate) it was.

Tretona sat by her at dinner. Elise was an Austrian exchange student over here to study opera singing. She had once hoped to become a great mezzo soprano but admitted without embarrassment that she just wasn't good enough. She came from a small village in the Zillertal. Yes, she had a dirdlkleid and knew how to yodel. Also would do a Schuh-platteln dance if there was a talent show. Her parents were Catholic. The motto of her village was "Liebe and Arbeit". Her father ran a hotel and had a Mercedes. Austria was a very poor country but the standard of living there was quite high, for example, opera, *good* opera, could be had for less than the price of a movie and the wine, well, there wasn't any real wine in America of course. Schparky had opinions about lots of things and her implied criticisms of America were totally without malice or guile. At first, Tretona found the comparisons amusing, but soon the old hackles began to rise and when Schparky blithely observed that Austrians worked harder than Americans, Tretona exploded.

"How can you generalize like that?" she said, trying hard not to sound hostile. Elise Kosima cheerily changed her claim—well she could only really speak of what she had observed—it was certainly the case that Austrian students and Austrian farmers worked harder. Tretona slammed down her fork. She didn't give a good goddamn if this woman was a guest in her goddamn country—this was too much. She started out quietly enough, her voice dripping with sarcasm. "I thought all that students in your country did was to sit around cafes, drinking Viennese coffee and plotting revolutions." Then she moved into a heart rendering account of her own long hours in the chemistry laboratory. Tretona was just starting to describe the hard life of the American farmer but stopped her tirade because of the signs of pain on Sparky's face. "Hey, I'm sorry. I didn't mean to disagree so violently." And then Sparky told her and the rest of the table, for by now everyone was listening, that Austrian students couldn't go to labs, because all the equipment had been stripped during the war. And there was still no money. Only post-graduate students at her university got to do practicals. And then they had to make their own weights out of cardboard and calibrate them each semester against the one good set locked up in the professor's office. Tretona pictured the 21 sets of shiny brass and platinum nuggets returned to the storeroom by her 21 sophomores last spring and she thought guiltily of the new single-pan balances ordered for the new freshmen to use next fall.

"Gosh, that's terrible," said Tretona. Sparky looked up expectantly. Her eyes were still pleading for comfort. Tretona cleared her throat searching desperately for just the right thing to say. "It must be particularly hard, too, because there were so many famous Austrian scientists before the war. To see a great tradition interrupted must be . . ." Pepper was rapping on her water glass with a fork.

Greetings to the old counselors. Welcome to the new. Lots to do before the campers come. Canoes and boats should already be in good shape, but need final check. Poison ivy patrol. Review sessions on how to teach basic skills, such as firebuilding and knots (Tretona was relieved to hear that). Will compile list of special talents among the counselors. ("You can be the resource person for jodeln," suggested Tretona in an aside, but Sparky didn't understand.) This year she had added to their training schedule on how to deal with campers' emotional problems, homesickness, bedwetting, crushes . . . everyone giggled knowingly. ("What is 'crushes'?" whispered Sparky—and totally without warning Tretona found herself blushing fiercely. "Tell you later," she mumbled.)

Pepper had picked Unit Leaders, but hadn't assigned assistant counselors yet. During training they would all sleep in Unit 1, Deerpath, because that was Pepper's favorite of all the units.

Tretona was still blushing. Two months ago she had applied for this job, then gone for the interview, told everyone about it, bought her gear, driven all the way up here—and never once had the implications of it crossed her mind. She was going to be spending two months out in the woods, sleeping, swimming, bathing twenty-four hours a day with people who were all female. Not a man around. If any situation was ripe for—all of a sudden she felt like some kind of wolf in sheep's clothing. And if that wasn't bad enough, now the first person she had to go and meet was Sparky. Talk about crushes—boy, she really had one and if she didn't watch out, she was going to be in trouble for sure.

Tretona deliberately focused her attention on the other counselors (better just forget about Sparky right now before it was too late). Most of them were in uniforms complete with badges, and hand-carved scarf holders securing their green handkerchiefs. They were a neat, handsome lot—ironed bermudas, good tans, good bodies—mainly thin although there were a couple of those chunky phys. ed. types. And when Pepper led them in singing "Learning to Live Together Under Watch of God" everyone knew it and joined in, everyone except Tretona that is, and (she could't resist turning to look at her) her neighbor. Sparky was already looking at her—big eyes, eyes full of questions and wants and desires and willing eyes, too. No, that was romantic stupid nonsense, then quick as can be Sparky was whispering in her ear, her voice full of sibilants and throaty consonants: "What is this song, please?" Tretona closed her eyes until the shiver that shot out of her ear lobe and straight down her spine had passed. Then she whispered back, carefully circling Sparky's ear with a soft murmur, "I'll teach it to you." Sparky turned her head before Tretona had moved back and their cheeks touched. Sparky immediately noticed the goose bumps which had popped out all over Tretona's arms and legs and took hold of her forearm with both hands. "What is this? You are cold?" No, no, no, very warm said Tretona's eyes. Touch us, too, said the mucous membranes—we are warm and wet and swollen with waiting. For God's sake cut it out—Pepper is looking said the scaredy cat brain. And then the formal part of the meeting was over and Tretona headed determinedly across the room—to nowhere but at least out of Sparky's sphere of attractions. Now for a destination—over there was a line for cider. Good, compose yourself, hands through the hair and a little tug down of the cut-offs. Then she almost cried out when someone took her elbow.

It was Pepper. "Tretona! How is it going? Are you meeting people all right? I'm so glad you've hit it off so well with Sparky. I was a bit worried she might feel—well, you know, foreign, out of it, but now that you've taken her under your wing . . ." Pepper was off to mix. Tretona got her cider and stood around looking for someone to talk to. Everyone seemed to be involved in hugging some long lost friend from previous years at camp. Finally she managed to sort of barge in on a conversation between Smokey and Arkie (obviously she had to make herself up a nickname right away). But when the discussion turned from Smokey's field hockey team at Ball State to Arkie's cheerleading at the University of Arkansas, Tretona gave up and moved on.

Sparky was back at their table, sitting erect, holding her cider in front of her like a chalice, staring at it intently. What the hell, thought Tretona. The director told me to look out for her. Sparky saw her coming and watched her every move, head held a little sideways, pert, bird-like. But now Tretona was resolved, and not embarrassed and they chatted easily about cider vs. apfelsaft and then hard cider vs. obstler (a kind of lethal schnaps made out of mixed fermented fruits). And Tretona said have you seen the lake yet so they went outside and Sparky taught her how to tell whether the moon was waxing or waning (having to do with the curving shapes of "A" vs. "Z" in the German words abnehmen und zunehmen). And Tretona said, why don't we sit here on the pier. And Sparky took hold of her hand and announced how happy she was to have an American friend. And Tretona kept the hand and leaned over to kiss her—but Sparky leaned forward and kissed her first—on both cheeks and then gracefully got to her feet and dragged Tretona off on a little hike around the waterfront and back to the lodge. Tretona was frustrated but had to admit that maybe it was all for the best. This way I can have fun flirting with her, she thought, without all the danger and hassle that doing the other would entail.

The next day Tretona picked up a camp name and she immediately felt much more at home. She had wakened early, sleepily reached for her hiking boots, and following the advice of some outsy-doorsy manual read long ago solemnly turned each of them upside down. Stitches was watching. "You're a good camper," she said. Tretona was pleased, but embarrassed. "Boots are a girl's best friend," she said inanely. (It was a paraphrase of an old dirty joke—

"Legs are a girl's best friend," said the girl who had been taken on a fuck-or-walk expedition, "but sometimes even the best of friends are parted.") Anyway Stitches liked the expression and from then on Tretona was known as "Boots – the girl's best friend," or "Boots" for short.

Learning-to-live-together with the grown-up Girl Scouts was easy. The big community values were being a good camper and loving nature. Tretona had no problems at all with the first one. She liked making little piles of kindling, neatly ordered according to size and combustibility. She liked making basic A-fires, or tepee fires, and log cabin fires – no anarchy allowed either at the woodpile or in the fire circle! She dug the knotting and splicing, the lashing of lean-tos, and the lacing of lanyards. She polished up her J-stroke an push-pulls and learned how to gunnel and do a bow-rudder. She quickly caught on that there were only two ways to do things in the woods – the wrong way and the Girl Scout way. But that was O.K. It was always made clear what was expected and she found to her amazement that arbitrary conventions no longer bugged her like they used to.

So – Good Camper, si, but Nature Lover? She wasn't quite sure why she found that whole bit so obnoxious. Partly it was because "Nature" seemed to include lots of excess baggage like the flag, Republican religion, and apple-pie morality. Somehow looking at a lake at sunset was supposed to make you feel proud to be an American, i.e., someone who was privileged to live in God's favorite free enterprise system. She and Sparky both started sleeping through the morning flag ceremony, until Smokey warned them that Pepper was taking attendance. "She'll probably take that damned clipboard with her up to meet Saint Peter," complained Tretona, but she started turning up and standing nicely at attention while the flag was unfolded and hoisted up the pole. It all seemed a little like a dress rehearsal because the campers weren't here yet – all this rigamarole was supposed to be for their benefit. And then Pepper was always interrupting with advice: "Keep the flag perfectly level – the star field must be unfolded last of all." And "Hoist the flag briskly. It should snap out in the breeze. Let's try it again, Chip."

In two days it was taken for granted that Boots and Sparky would canoe together, that if Boots was in charge of taking a patrol out to tie down the tent flaps before a storm that Sparky would volunteer, that if Sparky's group was doing K.P., Boots would hang around to help out. Boots convinced Sparky to put on bug dope and showed her how to apply it. (Austrians just used some sort of stick afterwards to stop the itching and Sparky nearly went wild the day she ran into black flies completely unprotected.) Sparky in turn doctored Boots' fever blister with some vile smelling foreign junk that cleared it up immediately.

All very jolly and seemingly very innocent but as the time for the big Overnight approached, Tretona started to get worried. Just two days before the campers were to arrive, all the counselors would canoe across the lake and camp out in two-person pup tents. The plans for pairing off began early—Smokey and Stitches, Arkie and Chip, and of course, so everyone assumed, it would be Boots and Sparky. On the other hand, she didn't trust herself alone with Sparky, under the stars . . . What if it rained and they had to put the flap down? What if their sleeping bag cocoons should touch in the night?

Tretona decided to let fate decide—and finally there were only three names missing from the sign-up sheet for tents, hers, Sparky's and Pepper's. Maybe Pepper would take the initiative. It would be an honor for "our visitor from abroad". And surely Sparky would be safe with her. But no use. "So that leaves Sparky and Boots in the ninth tent," announced Pepper.

It was a beautiful camping spot: plateau overlooking the lake, breeze to blow the bugs away. There were gourmet pocketburgers and perfectly cooked some-mores—after all we had to set a good example for the campers, didn't we? Pepper designed and executed a Ceremonial Campfire of exquisite symmetry. Never had the circle of voices blended so harmoniously: "From the hills I gather courage, visions of the days to be." For one crazy moment Tretona envisaged the hoards of little campers who would be piling off the bus in two days' time and almost giggled, but Sparky nudged her back into the proper state of solemnity. "Strength to lead and faith to follow—all are given unto me." Their eyes met. Would Sparky follow tonight? And would she have the courage to lead? "Peach I ask of thee, oh river. Peach, peace, peace. When I learn to live serenely." Yes, when or if I ever learn—

A gradual dispersal, discrete undressings behind trees and tents, quiet good-nights, beautiful-sky-isn't-its, big-day-tomorrows, watch-out-for-me-in-the-canoe-race.

Tretona jumped into her sleeping bag quickly, and watched Sparky tightening up the front rope. She had on finely woven cotton pajamas which pulled tightly over her round little bum as she fiddled with the hitch. The moon glinted off her short curls and made a little haze around the hairs on her shins. (She absolutely refused to shave her legs—that was probably the most foreign thing about her.) Tretona wondered what it would be like to run her tongue up along those fuzzy little legs—with a slight pause at the knee and then to plunge straight into the beautiful underbrush searching for a cave . . . Her saliva glands spurted and she quickly turned over to face the outside of the tent. No use getting all worked up. But to no avail. Sparky was lying beside her tapping her on the shoulder, whispering in her ear, excited, giggling . . . She wanted to go swimming. Can't, not without a lifeguard. Silly, silly Americans. Sparky was adamant. And so tippy-toe past the other eight pup tents, wide detour around Pepper's pine branch lean-to, noisier as they scrambled down the hill, now laughing in low voices as they peeled off the pajamas, one long look of mutual admiration and then a gasp as they hit the water.

Sparky took off for the middle of the lake with a strong crawl. Tretona, too smart to be obviously outdone and too prudential to enjoy the risk, paddled around in the road laid down by the moon. The water tickled as it moved between her legs. She turned over on her back and reached down with her left hand. The honey was still intact but her concave body started to sink. Determinedly Tretona began to experiment—all those ship-wrecked people must have discovered some way to while away the hours until they were finally rescued. Now into a languid float—head tipped back, hips up, back well-arched, arms dangling down, down, caress the buttocks, now in from behind, fingers straining to reach, but relax or you'll sink. The wonderful agony of leaving the body limp, all limp except for one little tight peak of tension, knotting, spreading, could she hold the float, no what a wonderful way to drown, sinking, sinking, sinking, still rubbing, still teasing until just as the breath was fading, the exploding warmth, running along muscles and then diffusing into all the little capillaries.

Tretona pushed off from the sandy bottom and broke through

the moon surface. Sparky swam up and pretended to throw a life-saving hold. "You were disappeared," she scolded. Their legs touched gently for a moment and then they were both pulling hard for the shore.

Shivers as they stood dripping in the chillier air. Tretona organized a caucus race—after promising to read *Alice in Wonderland* with Sparky later—and so they tore up and down the beach, making way too much noise. Then a sharp crack footsteps—they hit the dirt behind a bush. Now they could see Pepper up on the ridge fully-dressed. But she didn't see the pile of the pajamas lying on the rock in the moonlight—or perhaps she chose not to see. In any case, a very skillful withdrawal was called for and somehow they made it back into their tent without falling down or giggling or being detected . . . Whispering was out so Tretona waved a tiny bye-bye goodnight as they sneaked silently into their sleeping bags. But Sparky took hold of her cheeks and kissed her full on the mouth, a kiss sweet and gentle, innocent of tongue or passion or prolongment. A sisterly kiss? Maybe even a Girl Scout kiss. Tretona permitted herself a tiny, barely audible sigh and fell asleep.

The Last Day Before Campers dawned brightly. Breakfast was a tour de force—oatmeal with dried apricots cooked all night buried in coals, eggs fried in paper bags, biscuits baked in a stone reflector oven. It took hours though and it was ten o'clock when Pepper assembled them for a treasure hunt. "The idea is simple," she said. "Each of you will be given a set of clues and orienteering directions. The treasure you are looking for is each other! At the end you will meet the other people who will be in your unit. The three of you will be working together all summer. Good luck! And don't get lost!"

There was a buzz of excitement as everyone swarmed around reading their clues. One by one people peeled off in different directions. Tretona measured off 70 degrees as the sun moves from the axis of the Ceremonial Fire Circle and set off. Sparky was heading down from the lake. Pepper sure knew how to lay out a hunt; the clues were clear, but a little tricky. Tretona was reminded of the Sports Car Rally she'd gone on with Lu where the clue mentioned a Latin poet and everyone had shot off towards a nearby town called Homer, but Tretona, who was navigating, insisted they look a little further on the map and sure enough they found a village called

Virgil over in Greene County. Remembering that episode, when she read the clue "tree who holds its leaves tightly though winter winds blow" she resisted turning at the big pine tree (which had needles not leaves, strictly speaking) and sure enough there was a magnificent oak tree farther down the path. Now look for a stump—and there was Stitches! Now to combine the letters on the back of their clues: DE + ERP. "Deerpath! Deerpath, that's got to be it!" Stitches was excited. "I'm glad I'm with you, Boots. I told Pepper you were my favorite." Tretona mumbled and shuffled around in the dirt. "Yeah, I'm glad too. But where do you suppose ATH is?"

She really was glad. Stitches had every badge in the book, so she'd really be a big help, but she didn't make a religion out of scouting. At least she didn't seem to. Tretona looked at her sitting there on the stump. Neat (her shorts still had creases in them), thick glasses (she couldn't see the water from the high dive and always had to ask someone else if it was all clear), solemn as hell. She had a bunch of exquisite Indian designs embroidered all over her shirt—hence "stitches". Bet I could seduce her, Tretona thought, but clamped down on that idea right away. Jesus the kid might not even by 18 yet—she'd been a camper here just last year. Tretona idly wondered if that would count as statutory rape, or maybe child molesting.

Stitches had her ear to the breeze. "Someone's coming," she said. "It might be our missing ATH." Not bad, thought Tretona. The kid's got a sense of humor too. Crunching branches, little yips of pain—or excitement?—and here came Sparky! Both hands were full of berries. She offered them some while starting to munch out of her left hand. Stitches shot up and knocked her hand—the berries flew in all directions. A great kafuffle about whether the little black berries were poisonous. Stitches, sure they were and Sparky just as sure they were the same as good old Austrian Brombeere. Tretona finally took a counselor in each hand and marched them back to camp. That afternoon everyone dispersed to her own unit. Boots and Sparky and Stitches messed around Deerpath, putting the 24 little cots in straight rows, sweeping the floors, tying up the tent flaps in the approved fashion. Sparky brought in an assortment of colorful vines to decorate the tents, but Stitches objected, saying it was not right to destroy their natural surroundings. Sparky snorted and said no one was more careful than the Austrians about conserving wild flowers and rare plants, but surely common vines were not protected by the law. Again Tretona intervened. Sparky could decorate her part of the counselor's tent. No campers were allowed in there anyway and hence she wouldn't be setting a bad example.

After the Last Supper Before Campers down in the Lodge and Pepper's big pep talk, the three of them came back to the unit. The empty little cots looked sort of eery in the moonlight. There were three tents for campers—there'd be eight little noisy brats in each—three patrols which they'd take turns in supervising. "I'm scared," said Stitches. "What if some of them remember me from last year's Round-up when I was a camper too and won't mind me?"

Sparky chimed in, "What if they are not understanding my English?" Tretona had her own fears. What if someone breaks a leg on a hike, or one of them drowns on a canoe trip, or runs away and gets lost? But now it was time to be a good Unit Leader. (Strength to lead and faith to follow.) "Hey, you guys. Just remember those little girls are going to be pretty scared themselves when they get here. Lots of them won't have been to camp before. Some of them won't even have been out of the city all that much. They're gonna be afraid of owls and bats and those fish in Pine Lake which nibble on mosquito bites."

Stitches caught on immediately. "What's more they're going to be afraid of us. I can remember my first Unit Leader. She wore a whistle and used to whack her thigh when she was trying to get us to listen. Boy, she was mean—not at all like you, Boots. We'll be fine. Well, I'm going to turn in."

Ballet as each woman turned to her bunk, three bare bottoms smiled out blindly, shoulders hunched protectively over their private parts. Safely pajamed, Stitches and Sparky swung flashlights toward the latrine. Tretona, too lazy to follow, peed behind a tree and sat down on the step to watch the fire flies, diagnosed by Sparky as not quite as big as an Austrian Glühwürm. Down on the farm they used to trap lightening bugs in glass jars and use them for lanterns in the outhouse. If you killed one while it was glowing you could smear the phosphorescent stuff on your face and make temporary warpaint.

"Night, all!" Stitches went straight into her bed and collapsed. Sparky lingered at the edge of the tent platform. Tretona looked up at her longingly and desperately tried to think of some way to detain her. "Now I suppose you're going to tell me the moon is more beautiful in Austria." The night was picture postcard pretty—crescent moon in buttermilk sky framed by pine branches. Sparky just smiled, not rising to the bait. She seemed pensive. Then suddenly she sat down on the second step and leaned back between Tretona's legs. Without waiting for tension or embarrassment to build Tretona started massaging her temples and shoulders and arms. Sparky made little appreciative wiggles in response so Tretona kept going. Down the side now, careful not to explicitly touch the breasts. Next curve around in front, firm strokes around on the solar plexis, letting her elbows accidentally brush Sparky's nipples. On hooray for good German cotton, fine woven as silk, a perfect conductor for caresses, yet a perfect alibi for any innocent who wished to claim that nothing was happening, not really.

Sparky turned her head up and again there was that full sweet kiss. Tretona, prepared this time, did not attempt to escalate, but prolonged it, enriched it with a slight movement and if accidentally her tongue should flicker by, what harm is that?

Still kissing, keep up the concentration, shift Sparky around into her left arm and the right hand now set out on an exploration of the center pants seam. Oh what fine tiny Austrian stitches and a beautiful little Indian mound. Ski down the other slope, gently linked turns plunging down the fall line, slowly but inevitably. There, we're in the valley. Shall we gambol here? Sparky's arms were tightening. She abruptly broke off the kiss and gasped in Tretona's ear, "It is now time for bed, no?"

"No," breathed Tretona, deliberately misunderstanding and nodded her head towards Stitches who was now breathing steadily and noisily. "If we go to bed we'll wake her. Don't talk." And what better than a kiss to ensure silence and keep walking around on little pussy feet but don't creek the tent stairs. Encountering no resistance, Tretona moved down the side to play with the pajama pants fastening. Strange little German snaps. Clever really. Oops, they're open. (The first secret of seduction being to make every incremental advance so inconsequential in itself, that only the unreasonable person would object. Natura non fit salutum.)

Now the right hand could repeat the descent, inside this time making bolder sweeps, thus further loosening those useless restraining pajama britches. Too fast? Then pause to fondle the head, tiptoe with lips around the neck and carefully behind the ear—no grossness, no harshness. Now isn't this nice too? A tentative query into the Queen's soft domain. Vagina Regina. But Sparky was urgently whispering, "Please, Tretona. Please don't fuck me." Tretona temporarily puzzled—more by the word than the message. What to do? Discussions impossible, must keep monitoring the sleeping Stitches' regular breathing.

Time for another creative misunderstanding. (Seduction rule number 2: Always take people literally, especially if it's to your advantage, meaning of course the advantage of both of you.)

"All right. I won't if you say so. I'll just kiss you, O.K.?" which is exactly what Tretona proceeded to do. Quickly but without a hint of duplicity, the pajama pants dropped to shroud the ankles. Now strong legs spread—the basic A fire begins with an upside down V and now to lay the kindling carefully with tongue strokes and kisses. Tiny ones first, delicate little side branches and eminently inflammable, followed by bolder, thicker strokes piled on the middle, remember to blow on the fire occasionally to keep it going. "Then," as Pepper had said with considerable passion, "there comes a time in the life of the fire when you can throw in practically anything and it will burn." And so it was, with Sparky grabbing hold of her hair, lifting her hips to give the tongue Lebensraum.

Oops, an Austrian moan was wafting out into American woods. Nothing to do but to reach up one hand to cover that mouth—gently now, so as not to frighten her. And then Sparky's tongue was drumming on Tretona's fingers, clearly a vicarious attempt to pile more fuel on the flame. So Tretona stoked the fire and Sparky's body expanded with the heat while her thighs tensed and crackled with excitement. And the coals stayed hot and glowing until the moon started to set behind the trees.

* * *

"Here come the campers!" They were tinier than Tretona had imagined, hardly the Visigoths and Vandals she had been led to expect. By some miracle those assigned to Deerpath all found their bunks without too much fuss. And their Unit was the first to hike out of the Lodge area. Inspired, Tretona called a halt when they were well away from the others. "I have a secret to tell you. Did you see which unit got their gear together first?" The scouts looked blank. No one was going to volunteer so early in the game. "Come on. Who got out first?" Tretona was insistent. A little chubby scoutette finally broke the silence: "We did?"

"Right, *we* did. Deerpath was first. And Deerpath is going to be the best unit all around. Why? Because we're going to make it that way. All of us – you, me, Sparky, Stitches. But it's a secret because we don't want the other units to feel bad, O.K.? So just remember the Deerpath Secret – *Deerpath is best*. Let's get on up the hill now. Our unit is signed up for swimming this afternoon. But first, everything has to be put away. If Pepper inspects I want our unit to look the neatest of all. Got it?"

"Got it, Boots," a few of the campers were grinning now.

"That was a good pep talk," said Stitches later on. The three of them were resting on the dock while their campers took swimming tests. "You really got them cracking. You're a good leader." Tretona was pleased and looked over to Sparky for further confirmation. "Just like Il Duce," said Sparky. Their eyes locked for a second before Sparky turned away and jumped in the water. So she was pissed, thought Tretona. So much for seduction. Still and all, she'd sure seemed to like it last night. Better apologize, though. And so Tretona dived in and followed Sparky over to the raft. No use pussy-footing around (to coin a phrase).

"Hey, Sparky, I want to talk to you about last night." Sparky looked up startled and then averted her eyes.

"You were pushing on me," she said resentfully.

"Gee, I guess I was a little pushy, Elise. I'm sorry. It's just that I wanted you so much. And I must say, I thought you wanted me too, at least by the end you did, didn't you?" Sparky looked back at her now with full, sweet eyes, but she said nothing. "Look, we need to talk more. Meet me tonight out at Trapper's Point after the campers are asleep." Sparky didn't answer. But she came, and wouldn't talk. And so Tretona seduced her again – and again – all summer long. Furthermore she made sure the trains ran on time.

RESPONSE

ARTEMIS OAKGROVE

HOW DARE YOU.

How can you wish me thus: weakened and humbled before you
like a broken child, fearful of her own wishes?

Are you so wise that you can traverse the distance to hurl
yourself over my glacier, propel yourself into my inner most
passions with impunity?

Only by way of your soulful searching, gift-born sensitivity
and merciless psychic bonding.

Or did you slither under my barrier like a snake?

Dangerous. Worse than dangerous—peril utter and complete.
Ah, but what have *you* to lose? Shrouded in your isolation,
despoiled by time, experience, despair.

Longing, yes. You know. You thrive on it like bloodied fang
marks.

You did *not* go unnoticed—by anyone. Nor will you ever.
Carving your impressions with a sledge hammer when all
that is needed is a gentle nudge.

You do not lack for malice. Yours *is* the pursuit. My distance
is but a game for you. In so challenged you rise.
To reach only—for if you found your prey, limp in your grasp,
you would let fall the object of your quest upon the damp floor,
like so . . . much . . . dust.

No more difficult could your music be, far more expensive
than anything you had, for sale indeed. What price? Bidder.

Possess me! Why? Why do you wish this? Why
when you know me so well?

I have made way through my own keyhole. Alone.
I fear not loneliness, death, failure.

I fear my own thirst. As much as the desert in
which I perish.

You speculate if warm blood pumps through my veins,
one of many who do so with far greater exposure to my person,
voice, eyes, sighs.

It is a wonder that my skin does not fall away, brittle fragments,
victims of the opposing forces of my wintery veneer and boiling
passions.

And yet you pause to consider if I hesitate, breathe, blink in
recognition of your thievery.

If I did not see your famine or hear what you did not say
believe that my inattention is born of genuine innocence. I do
not look to see if eyes are upon me, only because I never
expect them to be.

I do not doubt your prowess, pursuer. All that you say is
so. My pretense crumpled, chastity uprooted, sex claimed with
one efficient blow. What then, she-cat? Lick your claws and
primp your tail pridefully?

Look at your whimpering conquest with scorn and disdain,
mindful of your next feast over some other . . . distant . . .wall?

JOURNEY TO ZELINDAR

DIANA RIVERS

The following is an excerpt from a chapter of JOURNEY TO ZELINDAR, a Lesbian fantasy adventure tale (Lace Publications).

Just prior to this portion of the story the Hadra (the women) of Samasi have been warned that the Zarn of Eezor is sending an army of his guards to invade the Yarmald Peninsula. Most of the women of the settlement are riding south to stop the army at the Red Line. Though her two lovers are among them, Sair, the teller of this tale, has been forbidden to go. As Sair was driven from Eezore, her birthplace, because of a gang rape by the Zarn's guards, the Hadra fear that her hatred of the guards would unbalance the psychic energy they need to hold the line against the guard. Instead Sair goes to a high spot above the road to watch the others leaving without her, then falls asleep and awakens at dark, cold and stiff.

The night birds were hooting already from the hills when I wandered back into the central circle. Save for Zarmell, all others had left the circle. She was tending the fire still, stirring the contents of a large pot. Seeing me she set down her spoon with a smile and reached out a hand. "Well, Sairizzia, are you calmer now? Will you have some tea?"

"Yes," I said gratefully, and sank down on a rock not caring this time if she mocked me. I drank my tea in silence while Zarmell stirred her pot. My mind was still on that distant road. At last I nodded my head toward her brew, asking my question without words.

"Potions, potions for healing," she replied to my nod. "Things that can cure the Spirit as well as the body. I have no kersh no Hadra powers. I am an outsider like you, Sairizzia, so this is my way—to be a healer. It is a thing I can do and a power none can deny." As she spoke she shook more leaves from her pouch into the pot and thrust some branches on the fire so that it blazed up again. "Often Neshtair become healers. Sharven made that same choice, but she went to live in Ishlair instead. It is she who will heal them at the line while I have potions made ready for their return."

As she went back to her stirring I sensed a long silence coming and wanted her to speak more. "Who is Sharven?" I asked, hopeful of some story.

Zarmell stared into the fire, making no answer for some time. Then she spoke suddenly as if just remembering my question, "Sharven . . . oh yes, Sharven. Who is she indeed? A very powerful Neshtair. She is healer not only to the Hadra at Ishlair but to the Kourmairi of the river settlements as well. No doubt you two will meet sooner or later." Zarmell set down her spoon and came to stand before me with her hands on her hips. "Sharven and I are as sisters though we are no blood kin. We even look alike; big women, women of bulk and substance—stature, not all muscle and bone the way you like them." With that she pinched me and laughed. I struck at her hand, but she took no notice and went on.

"Yes, we look like sisters, but we are not even from the same city. She is from Mecktash and her escape was very difficult. You must get her to tell you some night by the fire. She was upper caste, even danced for the Zarn once, but that was when she was a little skinny thing, a nibbit. However that is her story and she must tell you herself.

"Since coming to Yarmald she has chosen to become healer and herb woman and is very good at her work." She stopped and gave me a sharp look I could not read. Then, frowning, she continued, "We are strong women, Sharven and I, yet neither of us has any kersh. But you . . . ." Suddenly she picked up her spoon and shook it at me. "You will have it! I see the mark of it already!" She shouted this with a strange mixture of envy and triumph and then rushed on, "You could hear the speech of minds almost from the start. You came here young enough. They will train you."

With these words she waved her spoon so wildly I drew back, sure she would strike me with it. Her fierceness frightened me. I had nothing to say into that flood of words and so held up my cup for more tea.

"Yima leaves," she said with sudden gentleness as she poured from the pot. "The root is for dreaming, for visions, but the leaves are for soothing the soul." Her voice was as soft then as it had been harsh before. Smiling, she came and sat next to me putting her arm around my shoulder.

It was truly night now. The sky had darkened and the darker mountains rose against it as flat black shadows. Against them the lights of Semasi looked few and scattered. Zarmell's fire blazed like a bright heart at the center of it all and I felt strangely comforted by her size and the warmth of her body against mine. "You are sad, Little One," she said softly. "And I have talked too much and too wildly."

I sipped my tea for some moments in silence and then remembering my old promise to myself, I asked, "How did you come here, Zarmell? In what way did you leave Eezore?"

"Aha, so you finally have time to ask. I thought you so bound up with Hadra lovers you had no time for words with a Neshtair."

"Zarmell," I said impatiently, "Tell me your story or not, but do not tease me more."

She sighed and nodded. "Ah, yes, yes, I have a sharp tongue and sometimes it outspeaks me. Tarl is not the only one who should feel shame for her words." She glanced away with sudden shyness and asked, "Do you really wish to hear it, Nibbit?'

I put a hand on her arm. "Yes, Zarmell, I have wanted to ask since I first knew you came from Eezore and were not Hadra-born."

She got up to poke the fire again and stir her pot, moving about so restlessly that I almost lost hope of her speaking, but at last she settled on a rock beside me. "Like you I was born Shokarn in Eezore, but I am working caste. You have seen the brand on my forehead. This also is mine." She unlaced her wide leather wristlet and showed me the caste tattoo, purple against that light patch of skin.

"I was always Muirlla, always. Even from the time I was very young. I did not have to come among the Hadra to learn that." She gave a snort of angry laughter. "They did not invent the love of women, though sometimes they act as if they did. But in Eezore it is your death if discovered, so I learned to be very careful.

"Because I was young and strong then I worked at rough jobs, often men's jobs. Women who are working caste have more freedom in some ways. There is no need to keep them unspoiled goods for some find husband." She spit into the fire. "There were always other women like me on those jobs and sometimes we met in secret with each other. But I found no happiness in that. They seemed too much like men. They may have thought the same of me, for I was a tough sort then. So I was always looking and hoping, but carefully, for there was much danger.

"There was a shopkeeper on a street close to where I lived and I passed her every day. She was young and pretty and always smiled at me. After a time we began to greet each other and trade a few words. One evening, taking all my courage in hand, I stopped at her stall and with a little bow said quite formally the words I had practiced so many times, 'It would please me much to know you better.'

"She did not take offense but smiled sweetly and answered, 'That would please me, too.' It was almost as if she had been waiting for my words.

"Trembling I held out my palm to her in the sign of friendship and she drew in it the sign of the Muirlla, all the while looking into my eyes." As she spoke Zarmell took my hand and opened it. With her finger she traced that sign in my palm and I remembered having wondered at it red painted on the walls of Eezore. For what seemed a long time she stared at my hand as if searching there for the past before she went on.

"I looked down expecting to see that mark burned into my flesh like a brand. My hands shook. I could not believe my great good fortune and yet was much afraid, more so than I had ever been, even at dangerous work. It was not just the risk to my life that made me tremble. It was this new adventure opening before me. I blushed and grinned and looked down at my feet while she told me the way to her rooms.

"Quickly I went home to bathe and deck myself in the only good clothes I owned, a white shirt with red embroidery, a long skirt of a red and orange patterning. Dressed so I thought myself quite fine enough for anything I even brushed out my hair, a thing I had not done in weeks, and put a flower in it. Back in the streets I went with my heart high and full of joy thinking I had found my love at last. But when I knocked, the door opened on a dim room and two guardsmen sprang at me. They began slapping me about and making accusations.

"Death was clear in front of me. I knew I must move quickly. They both were drunk enough to be unsteady on their feet and thought me a great fool, not much to deal with. After all, one does not send the Zarn's army to bring back one Muirlla. But I had learned much keeping life in my body on the streets of Eezore and I always carried a knife. They asked me foul questions and poked at me with their swords. Then one, for sport, thought to see what I had under my skirts. He came close enough so I could give him a hard knee in the groin. As he bent in pain I had my quick knife twice in his back. With a groan he dropped to the floor. I grabbed up his sword. The other guard had time for one shout only before I had him through the gut with it. He was not expecting any trouble, only thinking to have some fun before delivering me to death."

She spat again and said fiercely through her teeth, "All this kersh is fine and honorable, but there are times I would rather see their guts spilled out before me on the floor." With that she gave a harsh laugh. I nodded in agreement, knowing well enough what she meant.

"I did not wait to see what that one shout would bring, but ran to hide in the sewers. These I knew well from my work. Soon I could hear many feet running above me and the sound of shouting so I knew I was being hunted. That is how I escaped Eezore, crawling through the sewers of the city in my only good clothes. I was many years safe in Yarmald before I could bring myself to wear a skirt again. The rest you know, Sairizziz, for you yourself have come the long road to cross the Red Line."

She sighed and leaned back, shutting her eyes. "I have often wondered about the little shopkeeper, if she betrayed me or if we both were watched and reported to the guard. Perhaps she died of torture in the square thinking me the traitor. Oh well, if that is so she is long since at peace and I am glad enough to be here."

"Did you ever find your true love, Zarmell?"

"I never looked again, Nibbit. Here I am free to love women without fear. Many women, as many as I want. That is enough for me, more than enough, Sair. That is heaven." She laughed. Then she pinched my arm again. "Well, Little Sister, will you share my cloak tonight? I have had my eyes on you for a long time and now you are well again."

I drew back shocked and offended. "I am with Tarl," I told her sharply.

Zarmell shrugged. "Well, only for warmth and comfort then. I know well enough where your heart is. But Tarl and Halli will share cloak this ride, of that you may be sure."

I looked about me. It seemed dark and cold beyond the light of the fire. Also the charm of the night was upon me. I had no wish to sleep alone in my small stone hut with only my fears of the coming battle to keep me company.

"Only for warmth and comfort then," I answered. She made no reply, but raised her eyebrows at me and went to bank the fire.

When we lay naked together in her cloak, Zarmell seemed all mountains and valleys to me, large round forms so different from Tarl's tight-muscled body. I was shivering by then as I had been too much exposed to the sun that day, so Zarmell wrapped her arms about me, pressing me close against her breasts and belly. I could feel the warmth from her body burning into mine and giving comfort. She put her face against my hair, telling me to sleep, and for a long while I lay rocking in that cradle of bodily ease. Then a heat came between my legs and with it a restlessness.

"Zarmell," I whispered. She made no answer. I whispered her name again, then spoke aloud. Still no reply. I took her hand and slipped it between my legs. That hand lay there, large, warm and motionless, making me more desirous, but giving no relief. It seemed I had what I had asked for – warmth and comfort only and now it was not enough.

"Zarmell," I said louder, pressing my legs insistently against that sleeping hand. For awhile there was no response. The very slowly her fingers began to move like some small creature exploring on its own, a creature unconnected to that large still form. Sensations ran up my body so that I shivered again, but not with cold. With her other hand she drew the hair back from my neck and I could feel her teeth there in small sharp bites. Her hand at my private self moved faster now, her fingers inside and delving. When I tried to turn, she threw her leg over mine and pressed me down with her arms so that I found myself held firmly under her sensuous weight.

"Lie still," she whispered fiercely in my ear. Her bites grew sharper and her hand moved faster, taking me to the edge of pleasure. Just as I was at the point of struggling, she flipped me over with her easy strength.

I felt her body on me, soft and heavy. She spread my legs and her large breasts brushed down my body to settle hot and full between my thighs. When her head pressed up against me I gripped her fingers, pushing them into me. I would have taken her whole hand inside had it not been much too broad.

With a sudden and amazing shift I was riding a wild horse, leaning far forward, galloping across an endless field. The speed was terrifying. It would surely kill me. I would fall and die but I shouted to the horse, wanting to go faster still. The hoof beats on the ground rushed up through my body, wave after wave. I could not contain it all. I was breaking apart, coming loose in the wind. With another sudden shift I was riding the great breakers of the ocean, a fierce joy in me as they crashed against the shore. One, higher than the rest, bore me up screaming and then drew back suddenly, beaching me on the sand.

I lay still that way for what seemed a long time with only the murmur of the waves and the sound of my own voice receding. At last Zarmell turned me around so that I was lying on top of her, bound in her arms. I clung to her as to an island and pressed my face into her breasts.

"A wild ride, Little Sister," she said softly, caressing my back with damp gentle fingers.

"How did you do that?" I asked when I could speak again.

She laughed. "I only took you where you asked to go. Is that not true?"

It was, indeed, true. I felt a deep easing in my body and in my spirit too. Then suddenly I thought of Tarl riding to that strange battle. I sat up with a cry, guilty and in pain. "She may be killed and I lie here thoughtless, taking my pleasure."

Zarmell hit me lightly with the back of her hand. "And would it lend her strength if you beat yourself instead?"

As I still sat there shaking my head, she pulled me down impatiently. "No, Sair, she would be glad for you. Believe me, in some ways I know her far better than you do."

I turned then to caress her in turn, but she shook her head. "Not tonight, Nibbet. We are both too tired. And besides, I came with you on that ride. It was surely one of the best." There was much pleasure in her voice and some pride also. I curled up against her. This time we slept.

We were roused in the early morning by Yima poking at the fire.

"I am sorry, daughters. I had no wish to wake you. I only meant to warm myself a little."

Zarmell laughed and winked at her. "Come, Yima, you also meant to see who I was sleeping with." Yima grinned at us both.

"Well, Zarmell, I see you have finally caught Sair in your cloak." Saying that, she poked some flames out of the coals. The flare of the fire lit the gray morning.

"Yes, Mother, and I live to tell you she was well worth waiting for." Zarmell seemed quite pleased with herself.

At those words I pulled away, not liking to be spoken of as a prize catch.

"Tell me, Zarmell, who else are you casting you net for?" I asked her sharply.

"Many far and wide, Little Sister, but as truth be told, I have had my eye on Kedris for awhile."

I sat up shocked. "Zarmell, you must not. She is but fifteen and still a child."

"And do you think yourself an old lady at eighteen? I, for one, do not see much difference. But you need not fear for her, Sairizzia. She is quite safe from me. Right now she is enamoured of her mother and will be of no use to anyone until that passes."

As Yima was shivering, Zarmell drew her under the cloak and we hugged her into our warmth. She dozed comfortably between us, but I soon grew restless, wanting to be on my way and when the sun rose I slipped out from the cloak and poured myself some tea. Yima opened her eyes. "You are up early, Daughter."

"I am on a journey of my own today if Sharu will take me."

Zarmell sat up. "Let us help you pack."

"Let me do for myself this day." I bent to kiss Yima gently and with rough loving knocked Zarmell back down with my shoulder.

"Thank you, Sweet Sister, for the night," I whispered to her and slipped my hand under the cloak to give her nipple a quick pinch. She laughed and swung her hand, catching me with a sharp slap on my bare leg.

"Ride well and find what you need, Nibbet," she called after me.

palm leaf of Mary Magdalene

CHERYL CLARKE

Obsessed by betrayal
compelled by passion
I pull this mutant palm leaf, orange
from my childhood of palm sundays.
Weave it into a cross, pray to it,
wear it as headband and wristband,
strap it round my ankle.
Magical as the pentecostal holy ghost.
Turning to fuchsia in afternoon light.

More than once an olive skinned nun pulled her
skirts up for me; later bribed me with a wild
orange palm leaf; thought its color a miracle
awesome as the resurrection; whispered it was
the palm leaf of Mary Magdalene, laughed;
side to side, stroked her unfrocked breasts
and shoulders with it; tied my wrist to hers
with it and took my forgiveness.

Mary Magdalene's palm leaf to you, dearest whore.
Flash it cross your sex back and forth like a
shoe shine rag more gently with as much dedication
while I (and the one you sleep with tonight instead
of me) watch and wait for the miracle
weave it into a cross pray to it
wear it as headband and wristband
tie your ankle to the bedpost with it
tongue of the holy ghost
palm leaf of Mary Magdalene.

*SWEET CECILY**

DENNISE BROWN

*Cec' uh lee: 1) a *very* proper English girl's name. "Sweet Cecily" 2) a beautiful feathery green herb whose anise-like seed pods are so sweet you cannot resist eating them.

"Clare, dear, take note of this for me, will you?"

"Yes, Miss Todd."

"Are you ready, then?"

"Yes'm."

The tall young woman paced the sun room as she spoke, and when she finished, commanded, "Read it back to me, Clare, now, if you please." She stopped her pacing long enough to listen, then nodded, tapping her riding crop against a highly polished boot. "That will do. Yes, I believe that will do. Now, can you hop down to the village and see that it gets to the *Chronicle* office by noon? It should make the Saturday edition. That will be best, I'm sure."

* * *

Cecily's corduroyed legs sprawled on the floor of her flat. Saturday morning, no rush today, and she luxuriated in it. A thick mug of tea squatted at her elbow. The wan morning sunlight filtered through the curtains and warmed her right hand. She turned the page, "perusing the classifieds", as she put it. Her eyes were caught by an entry in the "Help Wanted" page on her way to the "Flats for Sublet":

> Very personal secretary wanted by busy writer. Must be willing to type adult material. Some filing required, complete phone screening. Assorted other duties. Live-in position with generous time off and paid vacation. Salary commensurate with willing attitude toward all duties. Must work under strict discipline. Call KL5-5214 after 10 p.m.; ask for Miss Todd.

Live-in position, eh? Now that's an intriguing idea . . . solve two problems at once. Cecily let her gaze wander around the room, pausing to pat and stroke the pieces of furniture with her thoughts. She was sad to be losing such a good flat but the letter had been clear: The building had been sold and everyone was to make immediate plans to move. And her job was at a dead-end; who knew how long she'd even need to stay in this part of town?

Well, it wouldn't hurt to just call, get a little more information . . . .

* * *

I feel silly being here. I feel silly being here at this hour. I feel silly being here at this hour, dressed like this. I was never very steady in high heels. And I wonder *why* she specified all black?

Cecily wiped her hands on the front of her skirt; it was one of those silky dance skirts, the only skirt she owned. Lucky it was black Miss Todd wanted. Cecily felt her palms dampen again. Every time she moved she was aware of the skirt clinging to her hips. Why is this Miss Todd person so concerned about how I dress, she wondered grumpily.

Just then a long silver car purred to a halt in front of her, and someone – a man? a woman? – in a grey uniform opened the driver's door. Was *this* Miss Todd? Cecily was still trying to take it all in when the woman in grey stopped in front of her and touched the brim of her cap.

"You'll pardon me, Miss, but are you Cecily?"

"Yeees. That's me. I mean, I am . . . ." Cecily stammered.

"Then please . . . ." the chauffeuse said, opening the extra-wide door to the back seat.

Cecily stepped in and before she finished wondering if this was quite wise, the door closed behind her, the chauffeuse climbed behind the wheel and the silver coach pulled away from the curb.

The clear piercing blue of Miss Todd's eyes gripped Cecily, caused her heart to catch in her chest, to pause before resuming its steady beat.

Then a strong hand was proffered and a baritone voice: "Cecily. I am Miss Todd." Cecily, aware of her damp palm, tried to pull her hand out of the firm grasp. Miss Todd held it just a moment too long, then released it. "Cecily."

"Yes."

"I am glad to see that you followed my instructions about clothing precisely. Proper dress is so important."

Cecily felt pleased by Miss Todd's approval, and started to settle back into the cushions of the back seat.

"Just a moment, please, Cecily, lift your skirt behind you so that the fabric does not touch the seat. I want you to do that. I trust you followed my instructions concerning knickers . . . ."

A slow flush rose over Cecily's face. Yes, she had followed the instructions in all their intimate detail—including the omission of knickers. She knew that no one could tell, looking at her, that she wore nothing under the black skirt, but it made her feel peculiarly vulnerable and aware of that part of her anatomy. She felt the soft leather against her buttocks as she settled herself into the sumptuous luxury of the car's interior. She'd never seen or felt anything like it before.

"And would you keep your knees just a bit apart? I'm sure you'll find the ventilation soothing. And now, if you have any questions concerning the position advertised . . . ."

* * *

"That's it! The old bugger! He can just sod off. I'm packing it in!" Cecily shoved her books, her notepads and pencils and the wrinkled brown lunch bag into her satchel, snatched up her tea mug and sailed toward the door.

She was sitting on the bus toward home before the full ramification of what she had just done began to sink in. She stared out the window, seeing nothing.

Cecily jumped when the driver turned to her, "Miss?" Oh, yes, it was her stop, She jingled the coins into the fare box, smiled a distracted thanks at the driver and turned toward home.

You did it! You really did it! A jubilant voice inside her rejoiced and her feet danced a little tap step of joy on the sidewalk. Yes, you did do it. You certainly did it this time—abandoned your post, Cecily, responded a mother-voice, and her slowed footsteps carried her to her flat.

She let herself in, wondering if there were any sherry left. Better yet, brandy. And where had she stowed that bit of paper she'd used to scribble the address of that tall woman, that Miss . . . Miss Tweed, was it? No . . . Miss . . . Miss Todd. That was it, Miss Todd.

She fished around in the chaos of the top desk drawer and pulled it right out. It's time, Cecily told herself firmly, to pay Miss Todd a call.

* * *

She stood on the front steps of the imposing house, and took a deep breath. Press the buzzer, you ninny, she told herself firmly. She did so, hearing a reassuring chime from inside the house. Then the heavy door opened, revealing a woman wearing a black dress and white apron. "Yes, Miss?" the maid inquired, her gaze taking in Cecily's flushed face, the satchel in her hands.

Her eyes showed recognition even as Cecily spoke. "Hello. I'm Cecily Paige-Jones. I'm here to see Miss Todd . . . she told me to come . . . I mean, I told her I might come . . . I'm interested in the secretarial post . . . if it's still open." Her words tumbled over one another like puppies at play.

A smile spread across Clare's honest face as she began, "Miss Todd is out just now . . . ."

"I could come back, I suppose," Cecily interrupted.

"No, wait. Miss Todd is out of town just now, she won't be back for a bit, but she left word . . . now what was it? Oh yes, I remember . . . she said, if you appeared—and she seemed to be quite certain you would—you were to have the Green Room. Do come in and follow me, please."

* * *

Cecily deposited her small satchel on the chair by the bed, then looked around her. The wallpaper's pattern of roses was repeated in the down coverlet which rested on the dark wood bedstead. She reached out a hand to touch the carved bedposts; as she did so, she caught sight of her face in the oval mirror filling the headboard. Her skin was flushed, her eyes sparkling grey. Something about the house caused little ripples of heat to run up and down her legs.

Suddenly she felt impatient to explore this house of many rooms. The door to her own quarters let her outside, where she followed the winding path through low shrubs of sweet smelling herbs, tall stalks of lupine and blue delphinium. From beyond, the salt scent of the sea was a sharpness on her tongue. She took the curved steps up to another door and pushed it open.

No one seemed to be around, so she studied the breakfast room where she stood. A silver samovar stood ready on the table by the wall, and cactus plants filled the window overlooking the sea. She stepped into the living room—one end filled with a huge fireplace whose mantel bore the motto: I was musing while the fire burned. Lamps with beaded shades glowed dimly; the walls were covered with red blaze. She walked under an archway of greenery and found herself in a small solarium where she spied a huge white wicker chair, hunkered down, that faced the window. One could take her cup of tea and curl up in that chair and be cozy for hours, Cecily thought happily. But here, what's this? Before her was a door, half-covered with twining stems of greenery, that opened into a tiny room whose walls were lined with shelves of books.

Inside the corner room there was a plump sofa and two chintz-covered chairs. Two of the walls were windows that gave a view out over the roar and crash of the sea. Why, it's a secret library, Cecily observed, wondering what sort of books a person like Miss Todd might read. She stepped over to the shelves and pulled out a book.

Easing herself down in a chair, she started to read. It was a story of a woman . . . kept by a man . . . she went to work during the day . . . spent the nights in chains . . . the man whipped her, or had her whipped, at night.

The story was unfamiliar to Cecily and she knew she could have thought it awful, but what she noticed was a growing heat between her legs. She crossed them and, without thinking, began to rock just a bit.

* * *

Cecily hastily shoved the book into the drawer of the lamp table next to her and tried to smooth her expression as she called, "Come in."

The door to the drawing room opened slowly. She had not remembered quite how handsome Miss Todd really was in her navy turtleneck and tan jodhpurs. Nor did she remember the riding crop tucked into Miss Todd's boot.

"I hope you have enjoyed your visit. I am not surprised to see you, but glad that you made your decision so soon. If you need any help with storing items from your flat just ask my maid, Clare.

"I assume you have considered my offer carefully. If you promise to agree to my terms, I assure you that you will find your stay here . . . beneficial.

"I am going to leave you here for awhile to reflect upon those terms, and when I return, I shall ask for your promises. Think carefully and deeply, sweet Cecily, because we are quite isolated here, and there is really nowhere to go should you change your mind later. And—remember—this will be the last time I will ask your permission."

* * *

Thin yellow morning light filled the air; a robin's call awakened Cecily. She opened one eye, looked around at the wallpaper roses, and, closing that eye, let her mind catch at images of last night, of solemn promises by candlelight. Then, with her eyes squinted shut, she poked her feet toward the floor, encountered her slippers, and padded off to the bathroom. She finished her shower and was toweling her hair dry as she walked back into the bedroom, thinking about last night and Miss Todd, recalling the black boots, the riding crop.

"Cecily." She stood still, startled, caught unaware by Miss Todd's presence, real, not just her memories. "Cecily, come here." Cecily's slippers took her three steps straight ahead, stopping face-to-face with Miss Todd. "Cecily . . . ." Miss Todd repeated, running her hands up the girl's neck, pushing her hair up, making chills shiver down her spine. Grabbing her hair, pulling her head back, that touch of control that turned Cecily's knees to water as Miss Todd leaned over her, kissing her warm lips. Miss Todd slipped her other hand under Cecily's robe, spreading the robe open, pushing it aside, her arm encircling the girl's waist. Miss Todd drew her closer, felt the shiver that passed through her body, heard her breathing quicken. The tall woman still held Cecily's hair, pulling her head back, bending to kiss her again.

Their lips touched, soft, warm. Their breath caressed each other's cheeks. Miss Todd's lips, firm and searching, moved over Cecily's mouth, the tongue touching lightly, then more insistently, parting the teeth, probing, finding the back of the teeth, the jaw, the tongue filling her mouth, pushing, finding that point that Cecily felt in her center, that point of surrender.

Cecily shivered, felt her passion rise, her whole body reach toward Miss Todd—just as Miss Todd stopped, breaking the kiss, pulling harder on Cecily's hair, pulling her head back, feeling the heat in Cecily, the lust still in her mouth, their lips just a fraction of an inch apart. She wanted Cecily to know the depth of her own desire, to know and own in her heart how much she, Cecily, wanted this kiss, how much her lips desired it, how she could taste it in her own mouth . . . and she wanted Cecily to know, just as strongly, who would decide whether that desire would be met.

Slowly, firmly, controlling Cecily's head by the hand in her curls, Miss Todd pulled the girl back onto the bed. Her legs hung down over the side. Quickly, Miss Todd rolled her over, pulling the robe up from her fully awakened body, using it to tie her wrists together. With both arms around Cecily's hips, Miss Todd stood up, stroking Cecily's back from shoulders to bum, running her nails down the girl's back. Each new sensation washed over Cecily and as Miss Todd leaned over, their mouths found each other, a kiss or two, firm or lightly brushed.

"Cecily, sweet Cecily," Miss Todd began, stroking her long fingers down over the rounded curve of Cecily's nether regions. "How beautiful you are like that, how lovely your cheeks are . . . only one thing is missing . . . they are pale and need colour in them. But that can be remedied . . . ." And a quick smack landed on Cecily's backside. It stung a bit, and Cecily jumped from the surprise but found she liked the unexpectedness of it.

Miss Todd alternated strokes with blows, saying, "Cecily, your bottom is much more becoming now. How rosy it is, how sweet!" She slipped a knee between Cecily's, nudging her legs open wider. When Miss Todd leaned forward, her clothed crotch rubbed against Cecily's nakedness. She hesitated a moment for effect, then delivered a particularly stinging slap. Cecily pushed back toward her, her sex dripping, the scent of her in the air, vibrant, and Miss Todd added insertion to the sting, slipping two fingers of her other hand into Cecily, feeling the inner walls grip her fingers.

Cecily could no longer distinguish between being slapped and being fucked. She gave up trying to understand what was happening and gave over to riding the waves of pleasure that started deep within and spread to fill her. Her knees could not hold her, and she slid down until she felt the soft comforter beneath her belly. Miss Todd had pulled back and rolled her over, leaning down to taste her sweetness, and Cecily moved into unexplored realms. Her body tensed and loosened, tensed again, loosened until at last it could loosen nor more, and she let Miss Todd turn her gently onto her side, then Cecily slipped over the border to sleep.

Miss Todd covered her then with the clean white sheets and the creamy wool blanket. She kissed the girl's forehead, wished her a sweet sleep and good dreams, and slowly turned toward the stairs that led to the rest of the house.

* * *

That evening, Clare surveyed the dining room with satisfaction. Tiny crosses of light from the chandelier caught in the crystal goblets and shone there as if under water. A small silver vase, at each place held a single rose: Miss Todd's was deep indigo, nearly black; Cecily's, white; and, for the other guests, red, flame-orange and violet, exactly as Miss Todd had ordered. She would be pleased. All was in perfect readiness for the dinner party—birthday party, Clare corrected herself, remembering the special cake with sparklers that sat in the kitchen, waiting patiently.

Cecily waited in the den for Miss Todd and her guests. She made a last minute check in the mirror over the fireplace, lighted by the candle sconces on either side. Her reflection showed a young woman of medium height, whose chestnut curls and grey eyes were emphasized by the whiteness of her gown and her pale complexion.

She was a bit nervous, though she wasn't quite sure why. After all, this was a birthday party . . . surely nothing too demanding would be asked of her at a birthday party. Miss Todd had sent her a new dress with very specific instructions concerning her attire for the evening. A faint blush stained Cecily's cheeks as she remembered the new white garters with blue rosettes, the white silk stockings, the dainty white bra with narrow ribbons for straps, resting neatly atop the tissue paper in the box that held the dress, all folded in layers and layers of pink tissue paper.

She had dressed slowly, careful to remember all the preferences concerning her person that Miss Todd expressed on earlier occasions. This was a special night and she wanted Miss Todd to be proud of her. Now, what had she heard Clare say about tonight's guests?

It's Amelia's birthday. Amelia, tall, red-haired and imperious. "Like a queen, she is, Miss," Clare had said. Then there was the one she'd only heard called "The Master"—a dark, stocky woman with blazing eyes. "If The Master wants anything, *I'd* get it right away, Miss, if *I* was you," had been Clare's veiled comment. And the third, who was that? Oh, yes, the sporty one. "Played soccer, she did, when she was a girl. Varsity team at St. Anne's from her very first year. Captain she was, the last two," was Clare's information. "Tall and blonde she is—hair's quite short and her eyes, they'll look right through you, they will. They remind me of, what is it?—they remind me of blue pools you could drown in, you not bein' keerful. And the strangest thing about those eyes of hers—the dark part in the center, you know, they don't look quite to be the same size in both eyes. It's eerie-like, I say, can make ye a bit uncomfortable, that can—sometimes when she looks at me like that, I get t' feelin' that she's from Somewhere Else. Somewhere other than this earth, y' know, that perhaps she was not quite naturally born, if you know what I mean."

With that teasing comment, Clare's volubility had run down. "Her name? Well, all I ever heerd 'em call 'er is Hall. A rather funny name, should you be askin' me, as weren't." And with that, Cecily had to be satisfied, for Clare would say no more.

A quiet "click" startled Cecily from her reverie.

"Do come in, my dears, and meet Cecily. She really is a smashing secretary. I couldn't manage without her." Miss Todd's boisterous tones sounded straight off the hockey fields. "Amelia, this is Cecily. Cecily, Amelia. Today is Amelia's birthday, how know."

Cecily hardly noticed the long green velvet gown with satin cuffs and collar, the pretty face with red-gold waves of hair, for she was drawn by the eyes of this woman—warm eyes, eyes which could caress or punish.

"Come, come Cecily, don't drool. Although it's true, Amelia grows more attractive day by day. Master, this is Cecily. Cecily, my friend, here, prefers to be known as "The Master", and so you will address her." A long swirl of black cape, the collar standing up around a broad country face, dark eyes with a Gaelic hint of mischief, a chipped tooth giving a hint of vulnerability.

"And Hall—this is Cecily. I think you will like her. Cecily, this is Hall." Cecily felt herself lost in those blue eyes, barely registering the clear forehead, the handsome face. When she returned she found both her hands clasped in Hall's large firm grip. She focused on the thumb, trying to see something specific to help her feel less lost, and noticed that the bones of Hall's hands were large so her thumb came out wide to the side and her handspan was quite broad. Good hands for the soccer field.

"Hello, Cecily," came a low, pleasing voice. "You look lovely in white."

Cecily blushed in response to the close scrutiny of the three newcomers.

"I believe dinner is almost ready. In honour of the special nature of the present we have for Amelia, shall we dispense with the cocktails and simply start with the champagne?

"Time for your birthday champers, love," Miss Todd told Amelia while pulling a large bottle of Mumms from the silver container on the sideboard. "Would you bring me that towel, Cecily, there's a love? Ta.

"Sheila's mum gave it me," she reminisced, pointing to the silver ice bucket. "She's quite the one. The first night of our hols, Sheila and I did it at her place, and in comes her mum, sits on the foot of the bed and serves us tea! I was starkers and quite mortified. Had to pull the bedclothes over my bare bod."

Miss Todd shook her head, dismissing the memory. "Now, where was I? Oh, right—Amelia. A toast to Amelia on the thirtieth anniversary of her birth. She's a bit of all right, isn't she?" All the women raised their glasses, gazing admiringly at Amelia, their elegant friend. "Tits up!" Miss Todd proclaimed.

"Here," said Amelia to Hall, offering a plate of hors d'oeuvres. "Care for a bikkie and an olive? Have a nibble. Do you recall, dear, ages ago when we were best girls, the first time we went dancing, how you always stepped on my toes?"

Hall's clear blue gaze regarded her with affection. She reached out her large hand, stroked Amelia's arm. "Yes, love. I always get clumsy when I'm nervous."

Miss Todd's voice interrupted their revival of bygone times to move them along toward the meal. "Time for a bit of din-din, ducks. Come, follow me."

The dinner which followed took place in a haze and a fog for Cecily. Her last clear thought was that the roses' colours were precisely chosen: hers white, Miss Todd's blue nearly black—Hall's violet, The Master's orange-flame and Amelia's bold red.

In the pause that marked the end of the meal, Miss Todd said, "Amelia, would you escort Cecily to the trophy room? Here is the key. The rest of us will be along in a moment."

Cecily felt shy beside the elegant woman. Amelia wrapped her warm hand around Cecily's cold one. "Come along, my dear. I believe 'the fellows' have something special in mind for tonight, a surprise of some sort."

Cecily was surprised when they stopped at a door she did not remember seeing in any of her tours of the house. Amelia inserted the long silver key, turned a quiet latch, and they walked in.

"You've not been to the trophy room before," Amelia stated, seeing the wide-eyed look on Cecily's face.

There was a fire burning on the hearth; over the mantel were two crossed riding crops. A large green felt-covered billiard table filled the center of the room. Ominous eyes peered down at Cecily from every wall from the stuffed heads of animals she didn't recognise.

"Sit here." Amelia moved a foot stool over in front of the fire and pointed to it with her toe. "No, no! Not *on* your skirt. Lift the skirt first, then sit. Spread your skirts around you. That's better. Hasn't Miss Todd had time to give proper attention to your training?"

Cecily wasn't sure of the correct answer to this question so she was glad when the soft click of the door latch signalled the other's entrance.

The one they called "The Master" strode over to where Cecily sat, the long cape swirling out behind her like a bishop's cope. "Stand up." Her smile did not signal amusement. "Turn and face Amelia. Now kneel." She stepped back.

Miss Todd came up and put her hand on Cecily's shoulder, ignoring the question in her eyes. "Amelia, our little surprise for you tonight includes the services of sweet Cecily, here, my *very* private secretary. She will do whatever you may command or desire. And we are here to assure that she does."

A certain light came into Amelia's eyes, and her breath slowed. Cecily could see her green velvet bodice rise and fall. Her own pulse beat loudly in her ears because she knew she couldn't guess what might be required of her on this night.

"Do you prefer her undressed?" Hall lazily stepped from her perch on the billiard table, and was standing behind Cecily in two quick steps.

"I do," said Amelia. "But slowly. *Very* slowly. Turn her and show me . . . ."

Master was at Cecily's other side. "You heard her. Show her what she wants."

Cecily took a faltering step backward, unsure what to do next.

"Turn, love." Amelia motioned patiently to the inexperienced girl.

Cecily turned, feeling her full skirts swirl about her, making her aware of the slight breeze fanning up along her legs.

"Hold her," The Master instructed Hall.

Cecily moved her shoulders to test Hall's firm grip. Some vague idea of leaving passed through her mind, but the grip tightened. "Oh, no, love, you're not going anywhere," Hall advised her.

Cecily shot a glance at Miss Todd – was this true? The ice she met in those eyes told her more clearly that her presence was commanded, not requested, then the "Be still, Cecily" which followed.

The Master stood behind Cecily, so close that Cecily felt the woman's warm breath on the back of her neck. Large fingers skillfully undid the tiny buttons, moving from her neck to just below her waist.

Those same skillful fingers slid across Cecily's breasts, pausing to feel the nipples harden as she peeled back the bodice, exposing pink skin and white lace. Hall stepped toward her then, reaching for the tiny catch of the bra, where it nestled between her full breasts. Hall slipped the catch open, letting Cecily's breasts drop and sway.

Cecily shivered under their gaze.

"The knife," demanded The Master.

Hall's hand snaked to her pocket. Cecily heard the distinctive click of a blade locking open and closed her eyes. What were they going to do? She saw The Master walking toward her carrying the open knife, she felt the steel against her shoulder, drew in a breath to scream, then felt a little "clip, clip" as her bra straps were cut neatly.

"Thank you," The Master said as she returned the knife to Hall with another chilling click.

"This is too beautiful to resist," Amelia murmured, rising from her seat by the fire, striding over to Cecily. Amelia bent over her, moved the lacy fabric of the bra aside, gathered the girl's breast into her hand, drew it to her mouth, sucking and licking till the nipple pulled tight with arousal. "Such voluptuous tits," she murmured, stroking them, her fingers lingering over the nipples, before she returned to her seat by the fireplace.

Cecily stood before them with her breasts exposed, her nipples alert. She closed her eyes and felt a deep blush spread up her neck and over her face.

"Very nice," hissed Amelia, breathing heavily. "Very nice. I like the stockings. You have excellent taste, Susannah."

Briefly, through her blush, Cecily registered that this was the first time she'd heard Miss Todd addressed by her given name.

Standing behind Cecily, Hall continued the undressing, reaching around undoing buttons one at a time, slowly, until she reached the white stockings, the garters, finally cupping her hands around Cecily's nether cheeks. Amelia stood in front of Cecily; she could wait no longer. She reached her hand in beneath the fabric of the gown, stroking Cecily's skin. The girl shuddered, feeling the cool hands on her hot skin. Amelia pulled Cecily toward her.

"Cecily, look at me," she said, tilting the girl's chin up, waiting until the girl's eyes met hers. "I want you to do this of your free will, Cecily. We go no further unless you agree." Their gaze met, and Amelia waited, searching the grey eyes before her for that place where trust was born. This Cecily had a spirit she admired, and she would not have it broken. Softened, perhaps, but not broken. She let that caring slip into her own eyes, and waited.

Cecily whispered, "I agree."

"Kneel," ordered The Master. "Start there." She pointed to Amelia's green satin high heels.

Cecily bent her head to Amelia's foot, kissed it and licked it. Slowly she nibbled up to the ankle, up the leg. Since Amelia's skirt was slit quite high she worked her way up to the knee and above, to the top of the stockings, to the first fringes of dark sexual hair. Amelia sighed, took a step to spread her legs wider, and settled on Cecily's tongue.

Cecily licked and stroked the outer lips with her tongue, tasted Amelia's juices, felt them start to flow. With that flow, her heart opened; she longed to hear Amelia's cries, to taste her pleasure.

"Enough for awhile?" Hall broke in. "Amelia, dear, I think you need to calm down a bit, if you expect to last the evening. It's Cecily who needs warming up, and we'll be glad to do the honours. If you'll sit over here," Hall pointed to a leather chair in the corner, "you'll be able to see us all."

"Cecily, please come here." Hall waited for her beneath the strong beam that formed the top of the double doorway. "Give me your hands," she said, drawing a leather strap from her pocket. She quickly bound Cecily's wrists and fastened the strap to a large hook in the beam.

Amelia's quiet, amused voice warned, "Be careful now, there's two of you and only one of her."

"Take another step wider," The Master said.

Cecily complied, though her toes just touched the ground. Hall's rough hands stroked her shoulders, back, buttocks, thighs, again and again. "This will do, she should mark nicely," said a voice that matched Hall's unique eyes.

Amelia walked slowly toward the girl, standing in front of her. "Cecily, " she said, "I want you to pay attention."

The whipping began. All Cecily could hear was the crackle of the fire, the hissing of the whips through the air, and the quiet sound when the lash struck. The women were skillful, laying in strokes from either side, overlapping each other's blows slightly for greater sting.

Each lash of the whip moved Cecily toward Amelia, who spoke

to her, "Cecily, I want you, I want to see you like this." She reminded the girl of her beauty—and of her strength. With each blow, Cecily felt her torso move toward Amelia, and desired her with her blood's new heat, but could not touch her—and felt the lash again. As the whips raised their welts on her back Amelia questioned her, "Cecily, do you like it?"

And Cecily, her mind lost in the sensations, murmured, "Yes, I like it. Oh, yes, I like it."

"Yes, *Mistress*," Amelia corrected.

"Yes, Mistress, I like it." As the lashes were laid onto the backs of the girl's thighs, Amelia asked again, "Cecily, do you want it?"

"Yes, Mistress, I want it."

And again, as they marked Cecily's backside, Amelia queried, "Cecily, do you need it?"

And, after a long pause, Cecily sighed and reached deep inside her for her answer, "Yes, Mistress, I need it."

When Amelia could tell that Cecily was at her limit, she signalled to Hall, "Just one more." She saw Cecily throw her head back, trying to take the blow, to push her limits, and she honoured that in her heart, and bent her head to Cecily's neck, felt the flush and the flash of knowing that this woman was hers in some deep way, that there was a river-deep connection between them.

"That's enough. Let her down. Take her to her room."

* * *

When Cecily opened her eyes in the dark of her room she saw Amelia's fiery hair in the moonlight, felt her hand stroking her face.

Amelia put one finger over her lips, signalling silence. "It wasn't a dream, sweet Cecily. Come with me now, as quickly as you can." Cecily arose and pulled her clothes on. As she closed the door of her room behind her the last thing she saw was her single white rose, a pale reminder of an unforgettable evening.

* * *

When Miss Todd went down to breakfast the next morning, she found a white envelope sitting at her usual place, just above her knife and spoon. Slowly she reached for it, as if she could read through the envelope, and knew what it contained. She pulled out a square of white pasteboard, and read:

Dear Miss Todd,

I wish we might have spoken in person, but I had to leave late last night. Mistress Amelia has offered me a position with her, and I have accepted.

Thank you for all you have taught me. I shall never forget my days here, or you. Please say my goodbye's all around. Thank you, Miss Todd.

Sincerely,

Cecily

Miss Todd turned the card over in her hands several times, as if trying to make the few words yield more information. She would miss Cecily; she had grown quite fond of her. And she *was* an excellent secretary. However . . . . Miss Todd rang the bell beside her plate. Clare appeared in the doorway.

"Yes, ma'am.

"Clare," Miss Todd said, weariness in her voice, "take a note for me, will you?"

Clare nodded, pulling a pencil and pad from her apron pocket. Miss Todd took a deep breath, then exhaled. "Very personal secretary wanted . . . ."

(UNTITLED)

JEANE PARRIS

I have trouble having lunch with you.
A waft of Shalimar interferes surprisingly with the taste of
  won-ton soup,
And highly-pressed table cloths carry memories of slick, white
  sheets.
I can't keep a straight face about spare ribs either,
As I've brushed crumbs out of the strangest places.
The touch of a hand as salt cellars are exchanged,
Sends shivers of memories to places where hands have been;
Gentle, tentative, searching, sensitive hands,
Eager, but shy, at learning.
And my pragmatic, visual imagination plays havoc with dessert.
When it is mounds of vanilla ice cream,
Waiting to be devoured.
No, I have trouble at lunch.
But I shan't give it up.
Lunching is a luscious prelude—
Appetizer, shall we say—
To dinner;
Long, long dinners,
With the appetites of sight and smell and taste
Satiated rapturously.

*COME WHEN YOU NEED ME**

JEWELLE GOMEZ

The revolving door swept around easily, drawing the warm fall air of 12th Street into the Arcady Residence for Women where it quickly took on the sweet smell of face powder and expectation. The acrid scent of unemployment and newsprint remained on the curb. Inside, the lobby struggled to maintain an air of gentility. Chintz chair covers were washed and pressed to pass inspection by visiting parents; magazine stands held *The New Yorker*, *Red Book*, *Woman's Day* and other magazines that boasted soft focus drawings or vibrant colors evoking success. Residents brought in their own copies of *Backstage* and *Variety*. Only the superintendent carried the *Daily News* with its angry photographs of Attica inmates in rebellion. Few of the women asked to borrow it to see how Rock-

*from a song by Joan Armatrading

efeller met the challenge. Instead they leafed through *Vogue* or watched the television at the back of the lounge.

Roslyn was propelled by the door into the bright room which was heavy with worn oriental carpeting and draperies. She patted her short Afro as the woman at the desk looked up briefly. The few residents in the lobby did not stir, as if afraid to appear anxious. Roslyn glanced around the room not expecting to recognize anyone, not being surprised. Still the scent was welcoming. She could imagine one of these white women dusting herself in a fragrant-cloud of powder, one foot perched on the tub in the communal bathroom at the end of the hall.

Roslyn's thoughts swirled around the smells of the women while she moved automatically to the stairs and the fourth floor. She thought about stopping to pay her room bill but was too tired to go back down the half flight. Her back hurt and it felt good to hold onto her pay one more day even if the rent was overdue again. She just wanted to go to her room and collapse.

She hesitated at the public phone on the second floor landing but decided against calling home. Her mother didn't need to hear another sob story about cattle call auditions, racist casting directors or bizarre New York City street life. And Gale was so obsessed with boyfriends and babies talking about a career with her was like speaking another language. Roslyn remembered the high school nights they'd spent together sharing dreams of their future: Gale would headline at the Apollo; Roslyn would be her business manager. They had planned to be inseparable. In bed with their brown limbs entwined everything was possible.

"Say it loud, I'm black and I'm proud." They'd shouted the James Brown refrain at each other at school, in bed, everywhere until the power of the chant was irrefutable in their minds. Then Gale had her first marriage. The word 'asunder' was burned into Roslyn's mind.

Roslyn pushed down the tears which threatened to spill over. She could feel the frenetic energy of pursuit in a woman who rushed back to her room, her bath towel dropping behind her as she searched for the right key, the right perfume, smile, or reference to face her night. Two others passed her on their way down. The scent of "White Shoulders" hung over the stairs. They didn't notice Roslyn, still she bent her head to hide her face and hurried to her door. She was fumbling with the key, unable to get it to turn properly when the door was yanked open. Roslyn stared blankly, then thought, "My God, they've given away my room!" The tears overflowed and she leaned against the doorway choking them back.

"Hey girl, what's the matter . . . come on . . . ." the woman, Leean, said reaching out to take Roslyn's arm. Roslyn recognized her; she was the only one in the residence hall who ever spoke directly to her. Roslyn then looked at the door and realized she had the wrong floor. She started to giggle and said, "I'm sorry, today is not my day. I'm ok, really."

"You're just the person I wanted to see."

Roslyn was perplexed. She'd spoken to this woman on the stairs and in the lounge. They'd even watched television together once or twice. She liked the way the woman's blue eyes twinkled behind her round, goldrimmed glasses and the way that her curly brown hair fell unpretentiously to her shoulders. A "no-nonsense" kind of look that stood out in the miasma of up and coming "stars" she'd seen in the residence hall over the past six months.

"Leean, right?"

"Right. I'm about to move out of this way station and was sort of looking for someone to celebrate with. Come in and have a drink of champagne with me . . . please. If you don't I'll just have to share it with the matron."

They both laughed at the thought of sharing anything with the solitary stern, middle-aged woman who guarded the lobby during the night as if she were in charge of a pasha's harem.

Leean's room was strewn with suitcases and a few boxes stacked to eye level. "I've finally gotten the theatre to hire me on as a regular assistant stage manager and I found an apartment," Leean said as she poured champagne into a paper cup. "Drink up, we've got to kill this bottle before it gets warm."

Roslyn sat on the only free space, the bed, and gave Leean her congratulations.

"Everyone calls me Lee, OK? So you want to tell me why stopping at the wrong room sent you into hysteria?" Roslyn didn't answer. She'd said little to anyone for six months. She gulped down the champagne and stood, about to leave. "Come on, in theatre we call this a melodrama. We got a beautiful girl; we've got tears; we got the Tower of London!" Leean said looking around her room, laughing.

"In a nutshell," Roslyn said, "I'm tired of white advertising men telling me I'm too light for this commerical or too dark for that one!" The mocha brown skin was perfect foil for her challenging, dark eyes and short-cut natural hair. It was Lee's turn to be confused.

"I was lucky when I got here," Roslyn said. "I just happened to walk into the Pink Teacup and they just happened to need a waitress. I didn't know they were about the only restaurant in Greenwich Village to hire black waitresses. So I'm lucky, right?" Her voice took on a shrill edge. "If one more white-belted tourist puts his hand on my waist when I'm taking an order or calls me 'gal' I think I'll pour pork chop grease in his lap. He'll see just how black I am!"

Leean laughed, the lamplight sparkled off the golden eyeglasses. "Yeah, I know."

"What the fuck do you know? What white man ever told you you weren't black enough, huh?" The rage of the day crackled in the air.

"We all have to know some small part of that. You ever try to stage manage a crew of ten men who you're positive go home and beat their wives for contact sports? I've got to bust a two by four with my bare hands in front of them every other week just to get their attention. The point is sharing it with someone so you don't go crazy." Lee poured more champagne into Roslyn's glass without asking.

Tears seeped out from under Roslyn's lowered lashes, rolled down her cheeks and fell neatly onto the white cotton blouse that strained around her large breasts. One tear settled in the center of the lacy handkerchief which lay pinned open like a flower in her breast pocket. She sipped from her glass then said, "I just can't figure out what to do next. My back is killing me. I'm about to get cramps and I don't even know anyone here to borrow a tampon from . . . ."

"Tampons, um . . ." Lee approached the stack of cardboard boxes. ". . . let's see . . . two by fours . . . toothpicks . . . tampons!" She lifted the top two boxes neatly and deposited them on the floor. The muscles in her upper arms hardened under her freckled skin. When she bent down, the line from her hips flowed full from her waist. Her body looked firm and round under the dark tee shirt and jeans. The auburn aura of her skin glowed in the deepening twilight; the lamplight fluttered under the pink scarf draped over the lampshade.

Lee tossed Roslyn first one tampon, the another and another, turning it into a barrage until Roslyn fell back onto the bed engulfed in laughter. "How about a back rub? That might make it feel a little better." Roslyn turned over, grateful to be touched even if only for a moment. Gale had known just where to massage, making the pain easier when they were kids.

Lee knelt beside Roslyn on the bed and began a slow, rhythmic motion along her spine and sides. She kneaded Roslyn's neck until she felt the muscles relax and as she did she described the tiny apartment she'd discovered. Soon she straddled Roslyn, the denim of her jeans taut against her crotch.

Roslyn laughed out loud and said, "My best friend, Gale, from back home, says that if a woman offers to rub your back she's a lesbian trying to get you into bed."

Lee maintained her rhythm on Roslyn's back and said nothing for a moment, then softly, "They also say that orgasms get rid of cramps."

"Really?"

"Both are true," Lee said continuing to massage upward on the bony center of Rosyln's back. Roslyn said nothing but Lee felt the tension gather again in Roslyn's neck when she touched her shoulders. As she continued the motion the energy melted away and Roslyn's neck and shoulders released their tension.

"Do you want to?" Lee asked. She rested her hands at her sides. The answer came so softly that Lee had to bend forward and ask again. "Do you want to make love?" When she heard the quiet "yes" she stretched her body out on top of Roslyn's back. The full curve of Roslyn's ass fit comfortably into the hollow below Lee's belly. Their legs became tight lines like tracks: bonded together yet separate, as Lee pushed against Roslyn's back. Her small round breasts pressed close to Roslyn's starched blouse. She rubbed her arms tenderly while kissing the bare skin between Roslyn's hair line and the stiff uniform.

"Please turn over." Lee raised herself on her hands and the tips of her toes while Roslyn wriggled over onto her back Roslyn could not stop looking at the ripple of strength in the arms of this woman who held herself above her so easily Lee lowered her body onto Roslyn's. A soft moan escaped as she felt the heat of Lee's cunt on hers. Even through the denim the dampness wet her pink, rayon skirt. "You didn't answer me, Roslyn," Lee whispered teasingly in her ear as she gently brushed her breasts through the white blouse. She rubbed the outside of Roslyn's thigh with one hand as she again demanded an answer.

"I want to hear you tell me what you want." Roslyn struggled to find her breath. Her body moved in rhythm with Lee's. She could not open her legs wide enough, nor find the words to say what she wanted.

"Yess . . . please, please, please." On the last word Lee put her hand under the thin, shiny material of the uniform and brushed the inside of Roslyn's thigh. Her legs spread easily then and Lee gently probed the outer edges of her cunt. She touched the hard curly hairs which rimmed the mouth, then found the clit, feeling the warm secretions fill the opening. One finger slipped in easily, then another and another until she filled Roslyn and the rubbing motion pressed her thumb against the hardened clit.

She whispered in Roslyn's ear hoarsely as her body took up the motion of her hand, "Is that what you want? Anything you want, this is just for you."

Roslyn gasped for breath in counter rhythm to her hips which rode along under Lee's hand. She could manage only one word, "yes," over and over until she came and the sound filled the room.

They lay still for a moment but Roslyn wanted something more. She needed to feel the same openness in Lee that she had offered so she said, "You said it's about sharing . . . ."

"Yes."

"Then share with me." She turned Lee over onto the edge of the bed making her legs hang over to the floor. Lee leaned backward, her body supported by the tight muscles in her forearms. Roslyn slipped down to the floor beside the bed, unzipped the jeans and tugged them down around Lee's ass. For a moment she was fascinated by the expanse of pale skin. She had never seen anyone white so naked, so exposed. She marvelled at the contrasting colors and textures of their skin as she nibbled at the edges of Lee's cunt. The hair was soft, almost straight and a bit lighter than the chestnut brown of her head.

Roslyn pulled the jeans lower until they hung loosely around Lee's ankles. She pushed between the full thighs that had looked deceptively thin under the pants. She licked the inside and then the top of Lee's cunt and then quickly began her search for the clitoris. She held the mouth open feeling the hardness of it against her tongue. She submerged herself in the wetness and the movement of Lee's hips around her head. She pressed her finger against the opening, then entered when she felt Lee's body straining toward her. She pinned Lee there with the strength of her mouth and the syncopated rhythm of her finger. The muscles of Lee's arms tightened like rope; they trembled, yet were solid support as she thrust her cunt closer to Roslyn's mouth. She came, half sitting and almost silent.

Lee pulled Roslyn up onto the bed, turned off the lamp beside them and held her close in the darkness. "You always need three things," Lee said, "your art, someone to love and something to eat. I'd say we're doing Ok tonight?" They laughed loudly, then drifted off to sleep.

Roslyn woke with a start at 6 a.m. Lee lay with her back to her on the single bed. Roslyn was sure she was late for the soda commercial audition she had at nine. She slipped out of the bed as quietly as she could. Lee barely opened her eyes but said, "You'll come back this afternoon, right?"

Roslyn whispered "yes" and ran out the door, upstairs to shower and change. She took a quick glance at herself in the mirror as she left her room hoping she looked enough like a major member of the Pepsi generation. After the audition Roslyn felt like she hadn't done badly. The men were patronizing, as usual, but she'd done alright. She took her time walking back downtown to the restaurant to relieve the woman who'd taken her shift for her. She did not get off work until 8 p.m. When she got home there was no answer to her knock on the third floor. She continued upstairs to her room where she found a bunch of almost limp daisies tied with a ribbon to her doorknob. She took them inside, going over the audition in her mind while she undressed. She climbed between the covers and lay naked beneath the sheet looking at the flowers in the mayonaise jar on the dresser. She waited to hear Lee's knock on the door and fell asleep.

Roslyn was up early the next morning for the breakfast shift. The day sped by and she walked the Village after work, splurging on a pair of earrings with the money left over from paying the rent. She bought the *Times* and stood reading the rather terse coverage of the Attica riot. When she got back to the Arcady there was something in her mailbox. The afternoon receptionist handed her a postcard picture with two tabby kittens curled up around each other. On the back was scrawled "sharing" and nothing more.

Roslyn took the card up to her room hesitating a moment on the third floor before walking on. She lay restless on her bed trying to read the rest of the paper. The kittens reclined silently beneath the daisies. She'd finished her period with fewer cramps than she'd expected but was still exhausted. Leean's face stayed in her mind. She didn't understand why she didn't come to see her or let her know where she was. She tried to remember which theatre Leean said had hired her. Their talk seemed so long ago now. Lying in bed thinking about their night together, she hungered to feel her touch. She also felt freed. All of the feelings had come together in that day. Somehow they had come to the surface and she was not weighed down by the aloneness any more. When she'd called her mother in the afternoon she described her audition with laughter. Her mother sympathized and laughed with her. Roslyn smiled remembering her mother's deep laugh, then fell asleep with one hand cradling her breast, the other resting between her legs.

She awoke before the alarm sounded and was up and out an hour early. She walked quickly through the Village to Balducci's where she bought a pastry and sat on a stoop watching the traffic. She decided to save the newspaper until she had her coffeebreak at the restaurant. She was looking forward to seeing Bernice who'd left her in the middle of an improbable and hilarious story about her weekend. Roslyn saw now how much she liked the other women who worked at the Pink Teacup. She'd not talked with them much but she loved listening to their stories. They sounded so like the black women who were her mother's friends back home.

Each carried a history of independence and wildness that could not be mistaken. They folded their handkerchieves with the same care for style as did her mother and gave the same attention to the artwork that was their lives. They would never appear in any of the magazines in the Arcady lobby, but their beauty seduced Roslyn today.

Bernice was big like life not bigger than life. Rachel was too volatile, Hettie too bossy, yet each was perfect. The broad expanse of their bodies gave a hint of the love, lust and friendship they could sustain. They were so much like the women back home Roslyn almost laughed out loud at herself for missing it until now. Their voices, movements, smells were ancient elements of affirmation.

When she entered the restaurant the smell of coffee, frying bacon, porkchops and garlic made her feel faint with joy. She sipped a cup of coffee as she spread the pink crocheted edges of her handkerchief in her shirt pocket. It sat saucily on her breast. She enjoyed watching Bernice as she moved swiftly down the narrow aisles between the tables. Her hips rolled rhythmically under the pink and white uniform. The hard edges that had frightened her now seemed familiar. These were the women her mother went shopping with. They came over to play cards or sat under hairdryers with her at the beauty parlour. The morning moved quickly.

On her break Roslyn scanned the trade papers, circled a couple of leads, then tossed the paper back into her bag. By 3 p.m. her shoulder ached and the spongy shoes she wore were both too hard and too soft. At the back of the restaurant she leaned over to touch her toes, trying to get the blood flowing for the final half hour. The bell over the front door rang, she straightened up and grabbed two menus. White people always came to soul food restaurants in couples.

Lee entered, sat at the counter and ordered coffee. Roslyn put the menus down uncertain what to do next. Should she rush over and throw herself into this woman's arms or knock her from the stool?

"I'll get it Bernice," she said.

"Umph," Bernice muttered as she turned back to the heat of the broiler.

"Milk, sugar?"

"Milk, no sugar."

Roslyn set the cup down and met Lee's gaze. "Will there be anything else?"

"No, I'm just waiting for you to get off."

"Really?" Roslyn's throat was tight. She hid the questions beneath her easy actor's facade.

"Yeah, that's all the last three days have been. Beside moving my stuff into the new place and loading in a show at the theatre. That and waiting to see you."

Roslyn started to speak but saw there was no room or time here. She finished the last twenty minutes, then changed into her sandals and replaced her starched uniform blouse with a tee shirt. "See you tomorrow, Bernice," she called back over her shoulder into the kitchen. "I'll be in a little late though, is that ok?"

"Yeah, baby, ain't nothing happening here I can't handle."

Lee swung down off the stool, her face split with a grin. Out on the street they walked stiffly until Lee said, "The new apartment is small but it's got lots of sun and I know exactly where the tampons are."

"Yeah, well I'm really interested in seeing your two by fours."

"Lady, you can see anything I got."

On the new double bed their bodies were washed with the golden light of the setting sun. Lee lay across Roslyn's body thrusting, touching, pulling until the room was dark. After she came Roslyn rose onto her knees above Lee. She sucked at Lee's breasts, then played gently with the small opening. She stopped suddenly and said, "I don't want you to leave me like that again, unless you mean it to be goodbye."

"I wanted everything to be perfect when you came." Roslyn said nothing. "I guess I was afraid of everything going too right. My job, the new place, you . . . ."

Roslyn began to touch Lee again. The gentle pressure of her fingers escalated to a fiery motion that enveloped Lee's body. Roslyn's fingers drew the moisture from inside her cunt. She thrust deep inside and watched the spreading night around them.

"Yes," Lee moaned as Roslyn played across her clit with her thumb. Roslyn pressed her lips to the bridge of Lee's nose, her mouth, her neck, hungry for the taste of her. The movement of their hips and hands was independent of their thoughts.

"Yes," Lee shouted as her body released all the desire she'd been carrying for so long.

They lay silently for a while until Lee whispered Roslyn's name in her ear. This new place, this new thing felt good. That was all there was to say.

PUSHING IT

JULIE A. KREINER

Innocent as a puppy you said. Safe. Just wanna sleep.

Well I fell for it didn't I? Or pretended to, Lady of the Next-Day Phone Numbers.

We were both lonely I guess. Both wanting to have a body beside us. Wanted to feel we weren't the only ones alone in the endless night.

We turned to each other at the same time. In the dark we found mouths. Kisses impassioned by need. Hard flung, hard received. We wanted too much to be gentle. Our minds racing ahead of our actions. Touchings tinged with memories of past loves, work unfinished. Kisses covering up words we never said to those who should have heard them. All we want is the escape by physical touch. A free pin-wheeling fuck.

Hands touching. Rushing to feel the other's moistness first, fingers pushing for a climax. Trying so hard we miss the point. Trying so hard we come back to reality to find we forgot the reason we started all this.

But we huff and puff some more. Never say die the motto. Well we must have run down the batteries the drugs gave us. Must have steamed off the alcohol. Must have . . .

Cause it's morning and we wake apart. Feeling shy. Feeling silly. Still feeling lonesome but we pretend to ignore that in the daylight.

You saunter off to your day. I smooth the bed and hop in the shower. Check for tell-tale bed sharing signs. Finding red scratches on my thighs it occurs to me that they will remain long after I've stopped thinking of you. Stop thinking of last night.

A soul seems so expendable when one wants to give up. Doesn't want to be reminded of the harder way of time and patience. But lord knows how I fear the day when I'm strong enough to reclaim it, and it will walk right past me—not knowing who I am.

LA FEMME CHÊNIÈRE

LINDA PARKS

A story of ruthless women, who have nothing to lose—except their lives . . .

Cal Maynard swung her cutlass, bringing the heavy blade down across the stunned sailor's neck, separating head from body with one clean blow. The three remaining Spanish sailors looked on in total horror, then abandoning their short-lived defense of their ship, they turned and fled across the hyacinth-covered marsh.

Cal screamed a victory call and together she and her crew of women began to push their captured victims into a tight group on the beach. Belle Howard had one man on his knees, with her pistol against his skull.

"Don't!" ordered Cal. "We need him!"

So far the women's plan to overcome the Spanish ship, *Rain Song* had worked. The skeleton crew offered little resistance as the ship rested between cargos on the almost deserted strip of beach near New Orleans. The women now had control and had only to rig the ship and catch the tide to seek refuge along the coast of Texas, within the thousands of little lagoons and coves that nestled there.

Belle turned and swaggered toward Cal, her ruddy face in a rage, her pistol in hand. She also carried a bandoleer into which were thrust three more pistols and several knives. Her satanic features were now distorted even more with long pent-up hatred for her leader.

Cal stood motionless, letting her arm hang loosely at her side, seemingly unconcerned about Belle's threatening approach. The cutlass seemed lifeless in her hand.

"Don't ever tell me what to do!" shouted Belle. She paused, turned and aimed with deadly accuracy at the bending figure of the Spanish sailor. The gun exploded and the heavy ball smashed into the victim's head, leaving behind it a gushing mass of flesh and bone, as the man's body crashed into the sand.

Cal struck quickly, her cutlass springing to action, striking Belle a glancing blow across her right cheek, ripping a gaping slash that spurted blood in great red streams. Belle fell backwards, grabbing at her face, screaming in pain. She struggled in the sand, while Cal stood over her watching with remorseless satisfaction.

Then she put her booted foot on Belle's stomach, pressing down. "Now this is what anyone who will not obey orders will get."

Belle's screaming continued as she moved and bled into the earth.

Cal pointed to two women. "You, Alta and Centa, take her onto the ship."

Immediately, two tall women jumped to the task, one on each side pulling and dragging Belle's now limp form up the walkway. She had mercifully lost consciousness.

"The rest of you. Tie the men's hands behind them—tightly. Put them into the cargo hold. Lock them all up except the ones we need to set sail and get us headed out of here."

The year was 1816 and the place was the Louisiana coast, as the crew of women pirates, aided by reluctant sailors sailed the *Rain Song* toward the safety of the open sea.

Once in safe waters, Cal ordered that Belle be brought to her on deck. She stood leaning against the masthead, looking upward at the clear blue skies, her face almost pretty as she smiled into the sun. Her clear blue eyes were a reflection of the sky itself, and her small, perfect teeth gave her face a definite attraction. Her black

CHRIS GRASSANO

hair framed a copper complexion, as the wind blew it wildly. She stood in her coarse cloth shirt, hanging down over knee length trousers, which were tucked into leather boots. She wore a wide belt into which she had thrust her butcher knives, powder flask and other possessions. Her main piece of armament was her long heavy-bore gun, which she carried at all times, along with the wide-bladed, curved sword with the basketlike hilt that was made of leather.

Belle was dragged and thrown down in front of her. The deep wound was now swollen and her face was distorted. Edges of the cut had turned a deep purple and dried blood and flesh caked the young woman's hair and clothing. She looked up and, through dry parched lips, spoke to Cal. "Why? God, why did you do this to me?" Her voice trembled and faltered.

"You did not obey orders!" came the gruff answer.

"But that man. He was the one who raped me and killed my husband. I knew him. I had to kill him," whimpered the injured woman.

"The reason makes no difference. You did not obey my orders. You endangered our entire mission. You agreed when you signed on to obey me without hesitation."

Belle stammered. "I couldn't help it. I couldn't."

Cal turned to her crew. "This is the time for any of you who can't obey my orders to get out. If you stay, you must obey."

None in the group stirred.

Cal looked down at Belle. "I could never turn my back to you now." Then she gestured to the two women who stood as guards, their arms folded over ample breasts. "Take her. Bind her tightly and blindfold her."

So Belle was manacled and blindfolded as she tried in vain to fight. "No. Don't kill me, Cal," she begged seemingly disregarded by Cal, as she stood without a sign of emotion on her lovely face.

Then, Belle's lover stepped up. She was a strong, ravishingly beautiful black woman. "Cal, I'm asking you not to kill her. I'll look out after her."

Cal looked directly into Nan Decatur's black eyes, which did not blink or turn away from her stare. "Begging for her life?"

Nan nodded, and then dropped her eyes.

Cal smiled. "What's it really worth to you?" Then she added quickly. "I'll meet you later and we can talk more of this."

Nan knew what her greedy leader meant. It would not be the first time that Cal had used another woman for her sexual lusts in order to grant a favor. She used her control over the woman in a ruthless manner.

"Sure. Why not?" answered Nan. She turned to help Belle to her feet and gently took the ropes from her wrists. Cal watched as Nan walked away from her, half-dragging Belle. She watched Nan's well-formed buttocks moving under the tight trousers and she felt a twinge within her thighs as she imagined the lovely woman naked and at her whim.

Cal's own lover was watching. She was a dark-skinned Cajun, with black, beady, snake-like eyes that darted quickly from Nan's moving body to Cal's lustful eyes. She strutted boldly to Cal's side, moving against her.

"Another one?" she asked openly and arrogantly.

"Jealous, my pet?" Cal smiled, bending to kiss the lips of the shorter woman. "My silly Alta."

Alta Bertrand was no fool and she knew not to anger her lover with further comment, so she let Cal lead her below into their cabin.

As the great oak door slammed shut, Cal struck Alta with her open hand, knocking the smaller woman to the floor of the cabin.

"How dare you question me in front of the others?" she hissed. "Take off your clothes. Quickly."

Alta's eyes flashed both anger and anticipation now, as she knew what was coming. She began to rip off her binding clothing to prepare herself for her lover's sexual attack.

Cal removed her own clothes slowly, deliberately, as Alta watched the woman she adored. She loved Cal's smooth skin and small, perfectly formed breasts. She saw the pink nipples jutting outward as Cal pulled off her boots and removed her trousers. Her black triangle of soft fur hid the wet oasis that Alta thirsted for now, as she felt the old desire and weakness of lust overcoming her, and she bent down on her knees in front of Cal.

With a despairing groan she began to ravish the damp pouting lips, as Cal stood with her legs spread out, watching as her slave eagerly worked on her. She watched intently, until her own rising tide of passion could no longer be suppressed and she moved to lay back upon the great bed that filled the corner of the small room. She cried out in sensuous delight as Alta moved with her, never breaking contact with her lover.

Alta loved it when she reduced Cal to this clinging, moaning, aching woman gasping out in sheer passion, as she busied herself with kissing the nestled bud of womanhood that she sought to arouse to its fullest desire. She buried her face within Cal's thighs eagerly, as she felt Cal's body trembling and she knew the moment had come for complete release.

The orgasm crashed down upon Cal, filling her with uncontrolled throbbing sensations that almost made her cry. Tears filled her eyes as she gasped out in total abandon, and Alta let her own hungry mouth savor the reward, as she heard Cal murmur, "Take me. Take me now!"

Cal recovered quickly and became herself again, demanding and eager to satisfy her greed for Alta's body. Alta knew the fervid look in her eye and she knew how deep Cal's appetite was for her. She prepared to give herself to Cal completely.

Cal brought out a huge leather-bound wooden penis and held it as she watched Alta strike the familiar pose, leaning down over the bed, with her buttocks facing Cal and ready for the rear attack of the instrument that Cal now quivered in anticipation of delivering into her willing mate.

It was now the cruel mistresses' turn to become the ravaging benefactor of sexual delight as she brought the leather weapon into contact with Alta's seething passion. Slowly she pushed, using one hand to hold the instrument and spreading Alta's flesh with the other. The instrument slid in a bit, and Alta gave a whimper of desire through open lips.

Cal pulled it out and then pushed, inflicting pain and passion with the strokes that she now began, thrusting in and out deeply of the submitting Alta. With deliberate deep strokes she relentlessly pursued her lust, until Alta was screaming in orgasm and begging her to use her even more. She continued to thrust time and time again, while Alta squirmed and pushed back onto the pole that impaled her, wanting to come again and again in her selfish sexual lust. And she did.

Again and again Cal struck with the adored instrument of love and torture, until finally she fell to her knees in spent passion, gasping for air. She pressed her lips to Alta's buttocks and kissed her gently and whispered words of soothing considerations in a moment of rare closeness between the two women.

The two lovers lay together, locked in a tight embrace and slept for awhile.

Weeks went by, as the women prepared and trained, while nested safely in a hidden cove close to Galveston Ile. They knew that it was the territory of Jean Lafitte and his band of pirates and that not many other ships would venture into this area of danger. But their refuge remained undisturbed as they forced their male prisoners to teach them all they knew about sailing the great craft, and how to fire the big cannon should the need to.

One day as they practiced sailing, Cal went to the galley and found one of her crew struggling with a young sailor. "Mademoiselle Pirate, help me escape and I will spare your life."

The man had ripped the blouse from the shoulders of her young crew member and he was forcing her to the floor in a tight embrace choking her as they went down.

Cal struck the man across the head, stunning him for the moment. "Tie him to the masthead," she ordered.

As the man stood tied to the great beam in the center of the ship, Cal ripped his shirt from his back, exposing his browned flesh to the eyes of the women who watched with glee.

"Bring me the whip!"

The sailor turned, "You are a brazen wench. You will die for your deeds."

"The only one to die will be you!" promised Cal. She sent the whip flying and digging down on his back, digging out flesh with each swing and cracking loudly. She kept on whipping the boy, until Alta cried out, "You will kill him, Cal; let us have some fun with him first."

"Yes," cried the others. "This is too easy." The man had already passed out and was not feeling the beating.

They untied him and he fell to the deck in a heap.

"Throw some water on him. Wake him up!" shouted Cal.

Nan worked over the young victim until he was fully awake.

"Now take off his boots and trousers," screamed their captain.

Soon the man stood naked, held up by his arms by two strong women.

The other male prisoners began to grumble and yell.

"Take them all below!" ordered Cal.

Then she returned her attention to the helpless man. She reached between the his legs and grabbed and pulled savagely. He screamed in pain and tried to pull away from the tight grip of his two captors. They held him and jerked him roughly. Cal continued to hit and pull at his privates until the man could barely stand at all.

"How does that feel?" she asked laughingly. "Isn't that what you like?" She got right up in his face. He spit out at her.

For an instant it seemed that Cal would surely cut him in two with her cutlass as she pulled it from her belt. Then she stopped. She wiped her face and smiled. "Tie his hands behind his back."

"Shall we blindfold him?"

"No, I want him to see what is happening," hissed Cal, her face still red with rage.

Then the boy was dragged to the side of the ship, where Cal was placing a big plank over the side, reaching out over the water.

"I've been wanting to watch someone walk the plank," she laughed. She pointed out into the sea. "Look at what we have for company." Fins were darting over the dark waters, as sharks searched for food.

The sailor was crying and begging for his life. "Please do not kill me; I will obey you. I will serve you always." The more he begged the more Cal and her crew laughed. His begging reminded them of their own pleas when the men had attacked their settlement and had raped them and killed the men who tried to protect them.

They forced the man up onto the plank and Cal began to prod him with the point of her sword. The fellow tottered on barefeet along the rough board to the very end of the plank. He stopped, looking down at the water so far below and the fins that were coming closer and closer to the ship.

"Look!" They must already smell his blood."

He turned and looked at Cal. "Please!" he cried.

"I've had enough of this," said Cal. "Walk on!" she commanded.

The man stood, silent, unable to move another step to his doom.

Cal pushed the sword deeper into his already bleeding back and the man tumbled downward, hitting the water and going under.

The women leaned over the side to watch. His body bobbed back up and he was screaming as the sharks began to tear at his flesh and then suddenly he was gone.

Very calmly, Cal spoke, "Bring the rest of the men up on deck."

Facing the prisoners, she threatened, "Any man who touches one of my crew will die just like that fool. I promise you that if you obey me and help us willingly, I will set you free – adrift in a boat – when we are finished with you," she lied.

The men only stared at her as they stood in the chains that bound their legs and kept them helpless to struggle or fight back.

"Get them out of my sight," screamed Cal. "They sicken me."

The ship headed back into the secret cove where they made their camp while they waited to attack their first Spanish ship, as they had planned for so long.

Every day that went by, Cal wanted Nan more. She would watch her as she helped the poor Belle, who had lost her mind and walked around in a helpless, hopeless daze most of the time. Sometimes when Nan walked by so closely to her, Cal's thighs would ache, but Alta was always there by her side, watching.

Then one morning, Cal devised a plan and sent Alta inland to the river to get fresh water. Alta knew what was going on, but there was no way she could refuse her captain's orders, so reluctantly, she and several others of the crew set out to get the much-needed water. Her heart was breaking as she left the camp and turned to look at her love. Cal was already stalking the aware prey, and Nan was leading her down close to the water's edge.

Cal found her there, in the sunlight, with her copper-colored skin glistened in the water as she washed herself in the briny liquid. Her great swinging breasts were free of covering and Cal's eyes devoured them.

Nan came up on the beach and sat down on a covering, leaning back and showing Cal all of her beauty. Cal strode down and knelt beside her as Nan leaned over into her arms. Cal's mouth kissed a scalding trail over her face, neck, breasts. The fires were raging in both women as their bodies mingled and their hands sought each other. Cal guided her fingers over every inch of Nan's soft submitting skin, and Nan gave herself to her eagerly, without struggle. Cal sought the dark sweet cavern of love and found it to be as hot and savory as she had imagined a thousand times. She fell upon Nan until she was filled with her aroma and wet with her passion.

Not a word passed between them.

The day finally arrived for the long awaited journey to the sea to seek their treasure. They had trained well; they were ready. The crew lined up in front of Cal. The men prisoners were made to kneel on the sandy beach in front of them. Each woman put a pistol to the back of each sailor's head, and upon Cal's signal, they pulled the triggers and blew each man's brains out. Stepping over their bodies, the women boarded their ship and set sail to test their skills and to seek their fortunes.

A merchant galley was sighted. It was an American ship. The crew was disappointed, because they knew that even Jean Lafitte did not attack an American vessel.

But Cal was determined not to give up this ship. "It will make it all the better," she promised. "They will not suspect an attack at all."

The women quickly donned their skirts and threw shawls around their shoulders to hide their weapons. They put on hats with lace, as they knew the captain of the ship they now closed in on would use his glass to survey them. What he would see was a ship filed with helpless women. No danger would be suspected by the ship's crew.

Nan stood at the bow, showing off the very best of her alluring qualities, as her breasts peeked up out of thin blouse. Alta and the other women as well, would have the captain's eyes bulging out as he spied through his glass.

And the ship that would soon fall victim to the women's trick took the bait and was heading straight for the *Rain Song*. The men on board here were cheering an yelling and waving and acting like the idiots and fools that they were, as they thought they would soon be seducing the poor females aboard the ship they would soon board.

Cal laughed as she watched the ship pulling up alongside and the captain's leering face was smiling back at her in all his innocent stupidity of the moment at hand. The ship was soon tied alongside the *Rain Song* and the captain of the now-doomed ship was swinging on board, with a scant handful of his own crew, to welcome the women he beheld.

"Greetings. What mischief has befallen you to have no men aboard?" he called, coming to face the beautiful Cal.

With that, Cal smiled and said, "My dear captain, you are now my prisoner. Tell your men to throw down their arms, or you will die right here and now."

The captain kept smiling until Cal pulled the big pistol from beneath her shawl and stuck it against his nose. It was all too easy. Soon the captain and his crew were on lifeboats floating away from their ship, as they cursed and yelled threats against the women who merely waved to them. Not a single shot had been fired.

Cal ordered the *Rain Song* to be scuttled while she and her women crew moved aboard the fully-loaded cargo ship. The women sailed their new prize *Ocean Queen* back to their safe nest.

As they began to unload their cargo, Cal went to search the captain's cabin more completely. Hiding in the big closet, she discovered a stow-away: a ragged girl peering at her through tear-stained eyes.

"Come out of there!" ordered Cal. "What are you doing hiding in there?"

"I stowed away at Big Chênière," replied the young woman.

Cal surveyed her find with lusting eyes, finding that the girl was not unattractive. "How old are you, Lass?"

"I'm nineteen," came the answer.

"Are you a virgin?" inquired Cal with renewed interest.

"Yes."

Alta came into the cabin. "Well, what have you found?"

Suddenly Cal turned on Alta. "Leave this place. Don't ever come near me again, unless I call you. I must have peace or I shall die."

Alta stared, then turned and slammed the door very hard.

Cal took off her belt and put her guns and knives on the desk. Then she opened the cabinet and took out two glasses and a bottle and slowly poured out two brandies. She held one glass out to the girl who took it and sipped at the liquid.

"What is your name?" asked Cal.

"I am called Lydia."

"Lydia. What a delightful name," countered Cal. "I am Cal. I am the captain of this crew of women pirates."

The girl smiled faintly.

"I want you," admitted Cal. "I want you now. Here and now."

Cal was never one for playing games or having patience, as she pursued the trembling woman in front of her. "I want you to give yourself freely. Will you do that?"

"I do not understand," queried the girl.

"I am going to make love to you. I do not want to force you. It will be so much better for you and for me if you do not fight me."

The girl's eyes widened. "But I will fight you. Indeed, I must," she cried out in despair.

Cal looked intently at the girl. "I am going to have you. Fight if you must."

Cal moved to her with fire in her eyes. She stood behind the girl, running her hands over Lydia's hair, down her neck to the small breasts. She began to unlace her dress while the girl stood motionless and quiet.

As Cal loosed the binding lace, Lydia sprang up and ran to the door trying to open it. Cal was on her at once. "Don't fight me. Stop it," she ordered.

"Never. Not until I die."

Cal laughed, "You'd be no good to me dead," she put her arms around the girl pulling her close to her and, forcing her mouth open with her own, she began to kiss her over and over, until Lydia was breathless and weak. Cal could feel the struggle lessening; she could see in Lydia's eyes the tide of desire pressing in as she laid the girl back on the bed.

"Don't. Please don't," protested Lydia weakly. But Cal's mouth met the girl's and she kissed her deeply, moving her hands over her breasts, feeling the girl's small body responding slowly, her breath quickening with every kiss and every probe of her hot tongue.

Lydia's arms tightened around Cal. Then Cal pulled away and began to undress. The girl watched silently as she sat on the edge of the bunk. Then Cal was naked. Lydia saw before her a beautiful young woman, whose skin was smooth as satin. She closed her eyes as Cal began to remove her clothing as well. Then Cal began to kiss the naked girl again, and she lightly stroked the insides of her silky thighs. The girl's body shook and her legs opened for Cal's touch.

Greedily Cal kneaded the girl's body with her skillful fingers while her tongue darted here and there over her, teasing her and inflaming her with passion. Cal brought the girl to the brink of madness with her mouth and fingers and then bent to the girl's wet sweetness and partook of her freely.

Cal took Lydia several times within a few hours thinking to make the girl her slave, but unintentionally all the while, Cal was falling in love for the first time. From that day on Cal was as much her slave as Lydia was to Cal.

The women pirates began to build their community in earnest. For many years, there were rumors of a pirate ship of women that ran the coastal waters off Louisiana and Texas, but no one could ever prove that such a crew existed. The victims didn't talk much about their attackers. No one seemed much interested in searching for the women pirates. So, the women lived and loved at LaFemme Chênière undisturbed. No man ever discovered their secret cove. No man ever will!

FEMININE

CHOCOLATE WATERS

The word has become hateful.
It reminds you of little-girl voices,
clutch purses, ankle bracelets,
clean underwear in case you get hit
by a truck.

Feminine.
The word has lost its woman,
its essence, its puissance,
its delicious smell.
It reminds you of deodorant sprays,
of "female troubles,"
of not-enough-iron in the diet.

Feminine.
The word has become declassé.
They scorn it in class rooms,
in locker rooms, in faggots.
They scorn it in political matters,
in women's bars.

Feminine.
The word has lost its noblesse,
its butch-butch-butchiness.
Feminine.
The word had lost
its balls.

CHALLENGE

ARTEMIS OAKGROVE

It was with happiness that Kaheya and I walked along the wide sidewalk in the bracing spring air toward my Thunderbird. I had given into, quite easily, Kaheya's schoolgirl plea to attend a social at Le Tour, a private club situated in an improving neighborhood where, once a month, the young set were allowed in for a night.

Just eighteen, Kaheya was now and, to her young mind, at last old enough to attend these special gatherings; tonight had been her first. I had more reasons for accompanying her than my desire to share in her gaiety. I had been as much her chaperone as her date, for these events were usually attended by a handful of characters who can best be likened to vultures who prey on the unaware. It was just this sort I had come to protect my young lover from as well as to silence those who would reveal to her the unkind tag she had acquired without her knowledge: "Avalon's pet."

Twenty years Kaheya's senior, I was told often by my friends that

I should know better, that I was taking advantage of her innocence. These friends could not accept that after my first year with her, I was still very much in love with this delightful presence who walked contentedly by my side, leaving the dance safely behind us.

Our eyes met in a loving embrace that held for three paces, then she encircled my arm and drew closer. Her doeskin gloved hand smoothed the black ranch mink of my sleeve, inviting me to caress her. I knew that, above the objections and gloomy predictions of her peers and mine alike, our love would endure. She tantalized me, this lamb.

Before I could respond to her touch, my internal alarm was set off, raising the hair on the back of my neck upright. Suddenly our path was cut off from all sides by three women bent on malice.

How could I have been so stupid? Why tonight, of all nights, had I parked so far away? I clutched Kaheya's hand hard and underneath the black kidskin of my glove my knuckles were white. Poor dear, she had no idea why I'd hurt her with my rough grasp or what these three intruders wanted.

The tallest of the three, Jo, spoke and set my nerves on edge. "Fair maiden of stone, at last we have apprehended you, and out in the open unprotected by your fancy buildings, friends and cars."

Her voice was so full of contempt and hostility it frightened me, but I didn't show it. Kaheya was afraid, I could feel it. She took my lead and contained her response to this very dangerous situation.

My Thunderbird was less than a block away; I could see it. Still, it might as well have been across town for all the good it was doing me. Jo was right, we had no protection, and our vulnerability was the ace up her sleeve. There would be no talking my way out of this confrontation as I had done in the past.

Jo's recklessness was well known. Rugby, motorcycle racing and mountain climbing had made her strong, taught her that she had nothing to lose by forcing my hand. Her friends weren't necessary to guarantee her success tonight, but she didn't know that.

They were a packaged deal—Jo as the leader—and her pack. I avoided any hint of visual challenge in Jo's hot, brown eyes and sought out Brady's gentler, less honorable, blue ones. Brady's coloring was like mine: jet-black hair set against startlingly pale white skin. On me it was wintery, detached. Brady wore it like a dare. I didn't trust her and was glad Jo had a firm grasp on Brady's borderline evil.

Along for the ride, as always, the thrill-seeking Cally. Harmless by herself, she was sly and unpredictable in the company of her fellow musketeers. She wore Brut and, despite my refinement, that common scent awakened a deeply buried, caged animal in me. I shook loose of the snare of the fragrance and cleared my head to determine the best scenario to be hoped for. It was not good.

They had been stalking and threatening me for weeks, meeting with my disdain at every turn. I had hoped that when I had discovered Brady and Cally drinking on the job and fired them that I had seen the end of their growing antagonism toward me. I had believed, erroneously, that once they had gone, they would forget about their quest to make me notice them as something more than laborers in my office design firm. Now it was worse, now they had a score to settle. Jo, by her very presence, showed me she no longer wished to remain in my employ. I was sorry for this; she was a good worker.

It could be said by some that I probably deserved what was very likely going to happen to me, but Kaheya was guiltless of any wrongdoing. She must be spared any harm at all costs.

Through the hat netting draped before my eyes, I extracted Jo's intentions and methods. It didn't take much to see, from her cruel smile, that she knew me better than I had thought. The others were circling like wolves and my spine stiffened when Cally reached out to stroke my coat. Her hand came to rest on my backside, but I ignored it.

Yes, they had divined my weakness and were prepared to use it against me. Brady stopped to eye Kaheya and, for a moment, she looked like she could swallow my delicate charge in one swift motion. Kaheya recoiled fearfully, unable to match my calm any longer. Her young heart was unworldly, trusting and more than vulnerable. Sacrificial doves had better survival skills. I pulled her tightly to me to reassure her and prepared to speak. It was too late for verbal games; they had me and I knew it.

"Let her go. She can't bring you any sport, Jo." The spring air had turned to ice water in my throat, and I was surprised to see my words had a calming effect on the threesome. Their stance relaxed the tiniest bit, and then I knew for certain that it was me that they wanted, not the honey and light clinging to my side. It was sport they wanted, but, still more, they wanted common denominators, parity. I suspected they would have it before the night was over.

"You're clever, Avalon. And you think fast on your feet. I like that in a woman. Come with us and we'll let the girl go, unharmed. Otherwise . . . ." Her smooth speech trailed off into allusions that could awaken terror in the stoutest of hearts. I was grateful for my double-edged gift for registering emotions in the pit of my stomach instead of on my face. If my fear betrayed me now, Kaheya and my dignity would suffer the same fate.

"Do I have your word?" I asked coolly. Jo was many unsavory things, but she *was* trustworthy.

"Will you come with us, quietly?" she sparred.

"I will," I promised. My word was as good as Jo's.

Jo stepped aside and motioned for Kaheya to leave. I reached into my pocket for the car keys, handed them to Kaheya and spoke rather meanly to her. "Go home, right now." My attitude shocked her into action and she obeyed me without question, breaking free of the circle of doom, blinded by her fear.

The four of us watched her cross the street and head up the block to where I had so foolishly parked. She drove away in the sleek, black car, leaving me to my fate.

There was no longer any need for them to block my retreat by surrounding me and, for the brief moment before I was compelled to follow them to Jo's Landrover, we appraised one another. They were savoring the delicacy of chilled victory; I struggled to detach myself and secret away my pride to a place inviolate.

Clearly, I had underestimated these three. Looking at them in toto, the only unattractive feature about them was the firmly-rooted chip on their collective shoulder. To them, the reason for my consistent shunning was our difference in class and background. Oh, if only I could survive this ordeal without revealing to them the real reason why I had gone to such great lengths to put them down, discourage them, put distance between their very potent selves and my heavily governed self! Please, dear god, don't let them unearth my fatal attraction to angry women, to Jo's overwhelming strength and appeal, Brady's dangerous charm, Cally's flippant hedonism.

The trap was set and I felt myself drawn to the bait like a starved deer. The sound of the spikes of my heels echoed in my ears as my

external self was escorted in a somewhat less than delicate manner to the vehicle. The cool, icy, maiden of stone was ever prideful and not far from defiance on the exterior. Inside, she was slipping into an unstable volcano. It was as if I were standing outside myself, watching this ridiculous scene play itself out.

The ride to Jo's house was rough and reckless, although Jo wasn't driving. She didn't trust her associates alone in the back seat with me. They were in front.

I was stiff and straining against the feel of Jo's large, confident hand exploring my thigh. I found myself wondering what satin felt like to someone as coarse as Jo; my absurd obsession with tactile responses meant nothing to her. She wanted me to respond to *her*, in some way—fear, disgust, passion—anything but my hated aloofness.

I knew better than to put a wall in front of a mountain climber; she'd scale it just because it was there. When she rappelled herself down the other side, a burning pool of desire would await her. *Oh, Jo. Don't.*

My reverie was broken by Brady, who had been watching me, studying me, almost scientifically. She reached back and lifted the netting of my hat to get a better look. *Brady, do you have any idea why a woman like me wears a hat, much less one with netting? For power. There is so much power in hats and protection behind the finespun veil of black. For decency . . . .*

She saw something of my nakedness in my pale eyes and smiled.

The jeep lurched to a halt in front of a small house in a neighborhood full of small houses. It didn't look like where I would expect to find any of my abductors living, least of all, Jo.

My sense of judgment was restored when I was escorted to the back of the house to descend some broken cement steps to a basement entrance. I was the only one comfortable with the silence. Silence was my ally, a well-worn weapon that defended me with unswerving dependability.

It wasn't until the door was closed firmly behind us that they overcame any remaining vestiges of awe and respect they might have had hidden away deep inside themselves. This subterranean den of theirs—I could see now that they all lived here—was the backdrop for reducing me to their level. Among the gym shoes, trophies, empty beer cans and general uncleanliness, I was to trade my dignity for the safety of the love of my life; my pride to protect her innocence.

Jo shed her bulky army coat and threw it over the back of a questionable looking chair. I wanted a cigarette, and my need was made worse when Brady reached into her letter jacket for a pack and lit one for herself. Cally turned a table lamp on behind me and joined the others on the couch. The effect put them in darkness where I couldn't clearly judge their responses. It put my eyes in the shadow also, thank god.

As if by instinct, when the first command was uttered, I knew how they wanted it done: slowly and with more grace than a porno movie. It was Jo. "The hat."

From those two words I detected regret in her mellow voice. She wasn't eager to dissipate the vision I had created: lightbeams scattered through my outline. She had wanted me for so long and now she ran the risk of being disappointed by the real thing. The others weren't sensitive enough to know of this poignancy, and their impatience filled the air.

So, I obeyed her order and removed the long pearl pin that fastened my symbol of power to my hair. One hand lowered with the pin, the other with the hat. It would have been unwise to act on my own by moving from my assigned spot to lay my hat in a place of my own choosing. I awaited directions.

The strange chair, I was told, was to be the receptacle for the likes of Perry Ellis and Cardin. I swallowed my mounting disgust and impaled my hat on the arm of the chair.

Cally's voice startled me, to her delight. It was wicked and hollow. When she told me to remove my coat, I realized that I had not heard from her yet because she was too aroused to speak. This was the side of her that I had not thought possible in the many encounters I had had with these women. My heart sank as I let the coat slide seductively over my shoulders and into my hands. She was my only hope: the difference between sport and rape. The playful quality I had observed in her before had fled. I dropped the coat and my hope coyly, but artfully, on top of Jo's coat.

There were no more thick pelts to hide the increasing panic in my breathing. A moan sliced the inquietude, and I knew that Jo wasn't disappointed any more. My damnable cool was thawing and she was responding to it overly much, showing me the strain she had been under. Her relaxation was directly proportional to my increasing tension.

"Let your hair down," Brady ordered confidently. The scales had finally tipped in their favor and no one in the room was ignorant of that fact. There was a slight tremor in my hands when I reached up to undo the pins in my hair. But Brady got what she had demanded. Raven silk slowly caressed my neck and face.

A hiss of challenge was elicited from Brady—the one I was most worried about—when I made an unconscious, defiant flick of my head to toss the stray tresses from my face.

To my dismay, they were learning how to handle me. Even in the best of circumstances I must be approached slowly, with thought and firm resolve. Any sign of weakness on their part and the scales would tip back to my side and remain there. As each one of them demanded something more of me, my chances of gaining control of the situation diminished. They were getting an appetizer, whetting their palates on my mounting nervousness, and I prayed their carnivorous stirrings wouldn't develop into cannibalism.

"Damn." Cally's voice was electric when I stepped out of my satin evening dress and exposed my pendulous, well-shaped breasts. I fixed my eyes on the horrid velvet picture of a naked woman above this uncivilized trinity and tried to blank my mind of responses. My slip went the way of my dress, but I sensed that my panties were another matter. I removed them carefully, taking them over my garters and reverently down my legs. My attempt to place the grey lace garment on the chair met with a forceful snap of Jo's fingers. She motioned silently for them and I tossed them to her without feeling. She caught them deftly and crushed them in her fist like rose petals.

I hadn't realized it before, but Jo had moved up to the arm of the sofa. She was excited, almost beyond her capacity to contain it. I couldn't help myself and I smiled at her. Any other time and this would have been comedic. Here I was standing in a dingy apartment wearing alligator shoes, grey silk stockings, a garter belt and black leather gloves, waiting for orders from three women who had only heaven knew what in mind in the name of revenge; and I was smiling at the ringleader.

Jo clasped her fist with her other hand and brought the mass to her mouth. Her eyes were searching over her hands, contemplating me.

"Jesus Christ, Jo! Are you just going to sit there and look at her all night?" Cally had grown more impatient.

Please don't say I'm beautiful.

"She's beautiful!" Jo extoled.

My smile left. Hearing Kaheya say I was beautiful was like a limeade in summer—refreshing. *From you, Jo, it's a travesty.*

"Turn around, lover. Let's see the merchandise." Brady was the only one with some semblance of control and for some reason I found it demoralizing. I did as I was told, which Cally enjoyed. My firm buttocks appealed to her greatly.

Jo, woman of action that she was, stood and unzipped her slacks purposefully. She peeled them over her muscular legs and beckoned me to kneel before her. She took up her perch on the broad arm of the sofa and presented me with her needful sex.

Jo's voice was deep and guttural when she spoke. "Lick me off, baby."

I had to bend at the hips to reach her, which left my backside vulnerable to the very eager Cally. I was proud enough to do my best to please Jo. I wouldn't have it said, after all this, that Avalon was a lousy lay. Jo didn't object when I used my hands to spread her moist vaginal lips apart to receive my able, albeit reluctant, mouth. Hisses of delight greeted me when I kissed and flicked my tongue about her flesh, and I was thankful for her clean, good aroma and taste.

Cally wasted no time resuming her fascination with my rear. There was no way to prepare me for the intense, searing pleasure I experienced when she spread my buttocks apart and had begun to thrill me orally in a place where I had never been approached before.

In distress, I acknowledged the signals my body was giving me: hot skin, deep breathing, burning fluid bathing my crotch and filling the room with my distinctive, feminine scent. Against my will, my body responded to this theatre and, to make matters worse, Brady took up residence at my breasts. She milked them, pinching and tugging at them alternately and with increasing severity.

Concentration was not possible; I rushed from one sensation to another. Jo moaned loudly and writhed forcefully. My god! So did I. Wet, maniacal sounds from Cally urged me on. Brady was silent, but her breathing had become harder and faster. Her attention to my breasts hurt and felt wonderful at the same time.

Jo was only partially aware of who was servicing her. Now only a portion of her arousal and enjoyment came from her sense of finally conquering the mountain she had longed for. Despite myself, I *wanted* her to find fulfillment.

The symphony of sensations overwhelmed me. The chorus of moans and wordless pleas drove me wild.

Jo grabbed fistfuls of my hair and forced my mouth harder into her need, no longer aware at all of me or her surroundings.

Of utmost importance to her was to peak, to reach the summit. Like a score in rugby, a win at the track, she must, at all costs, have the thrill and satisfaction of victory. Her body had taken over, and it took what it needed from me.

I cursed my congenitally weak jaws and the distraction of their pain. Normally, when cunnilingus was mutual, I could use my own need to cancel out the pain. My pleasure wasn't a consideration in this plan. By design, I could only know unforgiving desire, not contented satisfaction.

"Oh, god!" Jo screamed.

I expected her to respond vigorously, but she had built up far more sexual tension than I had imagined. I could feel the impact of her release in the marrow of my bones. When she finally unhanded me, she collapsed against the wall behind her. Her head rolled from side to side and she swore senselessly, but quietly, through her staggered breathing.

The shock waves of Jo's response sent Cally over the edge with her. When I looked back, I spied her in a heap, victim of an orgasmic faint.

Suddenly, a chill overtook me from nowhere. I raised up and turned to look at Brady. When she had left the scene, I couldn't say, but in the deepest pit of my heart, my worst fears had begun to take form.

She wore three things: a wicked smile, a shirt (presumedly to hide her femaleness) and protruding obscenely from her shirttails, a dildo that she had strapped on.

My large, fearful eyes amused her and made coming closer all the sweeter to her. Cally was still out of it and Jo searched the ceiling for relief, which left me essentially alone with my nemesis.

"Kiss it, baby. Make it wet and ready for me," Brady demanded. Her excitement had lowered her voice and a sharp edge patterned her words.

I dared not disobey her, but how was I supposed to make it wet when my mouth was dryer than dry? I kissed it tentatively. My shyness encouraged her savagery and she forced it into my mouth. I could not find an association in my mind for the taste of that thing: foreign, unreal, was all I could respond with. It was real enough to her, however. She seemed satisfied with my feeble effort and removed her symbol of power from my tortured mouth.

I was straightway knocked off balance by her and forced to the floor. She mounted me with deadly aim; mercy was a thing of the past. The blinding fury of her humping forced my breath out of me. I couldn't speak and any attempt I made to get her off me only resulted in her redoubling the attack. The speed and accuracy of it kept me from dwelling upon how badly it hurt and frightened me. I didn't, then, know how else to respond to her but with passive silence. It was of no real concern to her, I could see; I needed only to be there and be afraid.

Then without warning, she lifted her upper body off me and paid token homage to her climax. It was as though it had happened unexpectedly and was a nuisance to her. When it passed, she looked me squarely in the eyes and I knew in that instant I was in real danger.

I had seen demons in nightmares, they were tame by comparison to what I witnessed in Brady's eyes. This was where she wanted to go all along, her passage was complete.

If I had known fear before, this was my introduction to terror. Her work began with a sound backhand to my face that sent me into a tailspin. If I screamed I never knew it.

When something resembling lucidity returned, my full complement of senses conspired against me to magnify the effects of her attack. The cold floor was at once colder and less forgiving. I heard nothing apart from her foul grunting and vile insults, her breath was stench itself. My mouth tasted like what I had always imagined poison would taste like, and I shall *never* be able to clear from my memory the murderous look on her face.

I had never begged for anything in my life. Fortunately for me, my inner self had more sense than I. What was one more betrayal on the part of my body at this point? I could only suppose that the expression on my face was that of one who sought mercy—for when I cast my look upon Jo, who was watching me, it shocked her.

Suddenly, I was no longer a mountain to be conquered, an opponent to be bested, I was a human being. This wasn't sport any more, it was rape.

Jo reached down and grasped Brady's shoulder. "Brady. Eh!" she shouted and slapped Brady hard on the side of the head. "Cool it, man."

Clemency. If relief was rain, this was a flash flood.

Jo seized control of the situation. "Take off, Brady. I want her to myself for awhile."

Brady let go with her vicious laugh and replied, "Sure, Jo."

What a perfect talent for contempt Brady had. She unfastened her dildo from her hips and stood, leaving her machismo buried deep inside me.

Jo reached her foot over me and prodded Cally to consciousness with her boot. "Blow, buddy," she instructed and pointed to the door.

Brady dressed and helped Cally to her feet. "Come on. Let's go shoot some pool and get high."

They both left as though nothing unusual had happened. Jo bolted the door behind them and returned to kneel beside my ravaged body. "Avalon, what have I done to you?" she whispered remorsefully.

I was touched by her tenderness and sincerity. It had never occured to me that she had a conscience. I was more profoundly moved when she removed the dildo and gathered me up in her incredible, powerful arms, then carried me to her bedroom. She placed me gently on her bed and smoothed the hair away from my face. I would rather she hadn't turned the light on; my emotions were as near the surface as they had ever been and I couldn't corral or trust them.

"May I have a cigarette?" I asked respectfully, like a child asking for dessert.

"Yes! Yes, of course. Where are they?"

"In my purse." My reply was framed with a defeated sigh and I wondered if this was what a broken will felt like.

She lit my cigarette for me and let me smoke it in silence while I stared blankly into space. It wasn't until I went to put it out that I noticed her holding the ashtray for me as though she were the servant and I the queen. Her eyes were filled with wonder.

"Kaheya must be very special for you to go through all this to save her."

I shut out her painful words and looked away, but I answered quite frankly, "Everything that is good in this world is in . . ." my breath caught and a lump formed in my throat, "Kaheya's . . . heart. Damn you, Jo." I couldn't keep my tears at bay any longer. They spilled out in rivers. I sobbed and wept uncontrollably. Me, the maiden of stone, who hadn't cried in years.

Jo lay close to me and pulled me to her with her authoritative arms. "Cry it out, angel. I deserve every one of your tears and all your scorn. I wanted to bring you down to my level, but I was fooling myself. It can't be done. Alongside your bravery, my mountain climbing looks foolhardy and self-destructive.

"You were right to shun me. I've behaved barbarically and cruelly to you because I hated you. You represent everything I'm afraid to be and I wanted to destroy you because of my own fear. When you fired Brady and Cally, I got so angry I couldn't stop myself from wanting to hurt you."

The contrast of virility and compassion I found in Jo's steady, reasuring grasp and her soothing voice opened all the right doors for me. I cleaned my face with the handkerchief she had given me, but I couldn't look at her.

"Can you ever forgive me, Avalon?"

I couldn't speak. Not because I was angry with her—I wasn't. I was losing my ability to resist her. Lying there next to her made me feel safe. She was *so* strong and appealing. My skin was getting hot again and I couldn't stop it. Why wouldn't she give up like I wanted her to? Weeks ago.

Before, when I had met women of Jo's ilk, they slipped and fell on my outer layer of ice. But not Jo. How could I stop my breathing from growing harder? The movement rubbed my breast against Jo's shirt sleeve and made my nipple stiff. *Damn you*. She knew I'd responded to her charms and she let me.

A high voltage current flowed through me and awakened my desire. *No—don't look into my eyes—you'll see. See I'd weakened.* But, my defenses were gone and she pried open my inner doors like a jewel thief.

Her eyes weren't full of contempt anymore, but desire. Was it hers or a reflection of mine? I couldn't tell any longer. Her mouth had softened and looked inviting now that the cruelty had left her lips.

No—Jo! Don't kiss me. I wouldn't be able to . . . . But she kissed me and I didn't pull away. My moans were small and far away, not like hers. Hers seared through me like hot pokers.

"God, Avalon. I want you so badly."

"Jo . . . ." I panted. "Oooon." The feel of her mouth on my nipple was unbearably sweet. I'd lost all hope of resisting her. It was easy to urge her lower. My scent filled the air and we were both intoxicated by it.

I was completely out of control and reduced to monosyllabic raving. "Eat me. Oh, eat me!" I wailed.

And she did! It was as if she knew me intimately. I didn't have to teach her anything. She handled my clitoris so adroitly with her tongue driving me insane. I screamed and writhed fitfully, but I couldn't dislodge her. Like everything else in her life, she pushed me to my limits and beyond.

I couldn't contain my screams. "Jo!" My orgasm crashed down on my body like waves from a stormy surf. Jo joined me in heaven and held me in her magnificent arms. Her gentle kisses were like beacons showing me the way safely to shore. I was beached on a new horizon.

"Avalon—baby, lover—I had no idea it could be this good. You're terrific." Jo's voice was low and breathless.

Suddenly, I realized I hadn't been brought ashore by some benign wayfarer. I had been lured there by a siren. I was awash with shame. "Jo, stop it!" I pushed her away and found my landlegs to stand. "Please, just stop. It can't be like this between us. It won't work."

Something in my voice brought Jo to her senses and she blinked away the spell. Reality settled into the downturned corners of her mouth and she nodded her head sadly. "You're right. This has been madness, all of it. I'm sorry." She stood and followed me into the front room and helped me get dressed again.

I saw the beginnings of a black eye in the mirror of my compact and clucked out loud. I put my lipstick on angrily and lit a cigarette. I was recovering my sense of who and what I was. The wall was firmly in place again, but I couldn't allow myself to think about whether or not Jo would perceive it as a challenge again. All I wanted was to get away . . . from her . . . from this awful apartment . . . from the memory of what had just happened. I brushed my hair quickly and replaced my hat.

Jo offered to give me a ride home but I couldn't bear the thought of being near her or her intense appeal for a moment longer than I had to. The hotel district that flanked the freeway was close by so I knew a cab could arrive in a manner of minutes. Jo called one for me.

She helped me with my coat and turned me around to face her. "This won't happen again, Avalon. You have my word. Brady and Cally will forget about you if I find something else to occupy them."

She walked with me up the steps then around to the front of the house; the cab had just pulled to a stop and she helped me inside.

She held the door open as she spoke, "You've shown me a new mountain to climb, Avalon. It may take the rest of my life to do it, but if I can become half the person you are, it will be worth it."

I looked at her, my mouth set firmly and my stony veneer in place. Her sincerity was unquestionable but I was beyond showing that it mattered to me. I wanted to tell her that it was my wish that she succeed but instead, I replied with a stiff voice, "I'll expect your resignation on my desk Monday morning."

Jo closed the door of the cab carefully, saying nothing. I doubt she had expected anything different from me, I never looked to see. I gave the driver my destination and slumped wearily back into the seat as he pulled the cab away.

My thoughts turned to Kaheya and all her sweetness, and I wondered if I'd let myself ask for her love and tenderness to help heal my wounds.

Biographies of Contributors—
THE LEADING EDGE

Pat Califia—is a Radical Pervert who has written widely on sexual politics. Her work includes SAPPHISTRY, a sex-education book for Lesbians (Naiad Press 1980), and a regular column in *The Advocate*, "The Advisor". She is currently working on a book of pornographic short stories, MACHO SLUTS, to be published by Alyson Publications, Inc.

Regine Sands—lives and works in New York City.

Dorothy Allison—is the author of THE WOMEN WHO HATE ME (Longhaul Press, available from Firebrand, 141 The Commons, Ithaca NY 14850) and RIVER OF NAMES, a book of short stories to be published by Firebrand Books, and is working on a novel based on the characters in "Predators".

Ann Allen Shockly—Author of LOVING HER, THE BLACK AND WHITE OF IT, and SAY JESUS AND COME TO ME (All from Naiad Press).

Anahn Nemuth—is in hiding from the lynch mob demanding the other 417 fantasies.

Sandi Strack—was born in 1960 in Dublin, Ireland and has been drawing and painting fanatically since the age of 6. Now a professional artist working mostly with ad design, her fantasy is to someday have a huge studio where she could spend her life doing paintings and sculptures of mythical and mystical women/ creatures (mermaids, faeries, silkies, dragon ladies, witches and magical beings . . .)

Merril Mushroom—she is not Alice but has known her well.

C. Bailey—comes from the West. Leather Country. Boots, the fine creak of her leather pants as she moves; vest, black leather jacket, gloves: she mounts her black Nighthawk Motorcycle. And Rides.

D.L. Harris—is a writer of prose and poetry, who has a deep love for erotica; she describes herself as a storyteller/ thought-provoker, who thru her writing hopes to make you smile, laugh, cry, and most of all, think. She is currently putting the finishing touches on her first book of prose and poetry. And collaborating with two other women writers on a book. She also has been published in a Northwest women of color anthology called GATHERING GROUND (Seal Press, 312 S. Washington, Seattle, WA 98104).

Charlotte Stone—is half French and half English. She was born in Bayonne, France in 1948. She lives in the large port of Felixstowe in the county of Suffolk on England's east coast. She has published several fantasy novels in English and French, as well as short stories. Woman to woman sex is a strong theme in many of her works though not all. She contributes regularly to British woman's magazines on subjects as diverse as discus throwing, astrology and sexual relationships between women. She has worked in the past as a teacher, astrologer, shop-assistant and scullion. She is currently a writer and journalist and has a strong involvement with Telecommunications and Computing.

Lamar Van Dyke—was born in leather diapers and although it took her a long time to grow into her black leather jacket, she has managed to fill it out sufficiently and add numerous accessories. Her business and her pleasures are tattooing and piercing. In her spare time she manages to be a drag king and performing artist. She has shown her artwork in Seattle, Washington.

Noretta Koertge—teaches Philosophy of Science and women's Studies at Indiana University. Previous publications include two novels, WHO WAS THAT MASKED WOMAN? (1981) and VALLEY OF THE AMAZONS (1984), both with St. Martin's Press and an edited series of articles *Philosophy and Homosexuality* (1985) with Harrington Park Press. She is currently completing a futuristic story about a utopian community entitled PYRAMID.

Artemis OakGrove—author of the THRONE TRILOGY (1984–86 Lace Publications).

Diana Rivers—is a fifty-five year old ex-New York artist/writer living in the hills of Arkansas on women's land in a house all built by women's hands, including her own. She has been writing short stories of our own lives for the past 10–12 years and getting them published in such magazines as *Feminary*, *Conditions* and *Sinister Wisdom*. She has also had a story published in LESBIAN FICTION and another about to be published in an anthology by Silverleaf Press (Westport CT 06880) called CROSSING THE MOONSTREAM.

Cheryl Clarke—first published in *Conditions*: Five, The Black Women's Issue in 1979. Since 1979 her poems, stories, essays, and book reviews have appeared in *Sinister Wisdom*, *Ikon*, *Thirteenth Moon*, *Heresies*, *Black Scholar*, *Sojourner*, *The Advocate*, *The New York Native*, *Hanging Loose*, HOME GIRLS: A BLACK FEMINIST ANTHOLOGY, *Lesbian Poetry*, and THIS BRIDGE CALLED MY BACK: WRITINGS BY RADICAL WOMEN

WOMEN OF COLOR. She is the author of NARRATIVES: POEMS IN THE TRADITION OF BLACK WOMEN (Kitchen Table Press, 1983, Box 2753, New York NY 10185) and LIVING AS A LESBIAN (Firebrand Books, 141 The Commons, Ithaca NY 14850). She is a member of the editorial collective of *Conditions Magazine*, which is in its ninth year of publication. Currently she is listening to write a new book of narrative poems.

Dennise Brown—spent several happy past lives as a medieval nun and an Egyptian priestess. But times are hard for such as she, and bowing to the twentieth century, she earns her living as a computer programmer. She nourishes her imagination and her herb garden in Bellevue, Washington.

Jewelle Gomez—is from Boston and lives in NYC. She is a reviewer for *The Village Voice* and *Hurricane Alice* and the author of *The Gilda Stories*. "All we are saying: give peace a chance."

Julie A. Kreiner—was born in 1958 outside Chicago, schooled in Iowa, received a more complete education in Boston and contemplated these lessons in New Hampshire. As a writer, she turned these "teachings" loose on paper and "Pushing It" became one in a collection of prose poems/ reconstructed realities. She now lives in Sedona, Arizona and works at one of the town's newspapers.

Linda Parks—is a highly acclaimed writer, poet, critic and civil rights worker. Her writing focuses on justice for women and human and civil rights for women in prisons. She has written a novel, JUST HOLD ME (1986 Lace Publications).

Chocolate Waters—has published three collections of poetry, short stories and rubberstamp cartoons: TO THE

MAN REPORTER FROM THE DENVER POST, TAKE ME LIKE A PHOTOGRAPH and CHARTING NEW WATERS (Egg Plant Press, 415 W. 44th St., #7, New York NY 10036). Her fourth collection, THE COMING OUT OF CHOCOLATE WATERS: I WAS A CLOSET WOMAN, is looking for a publisher. She writes and works in New York City where she has lived since 1981.

THE RAGING PEACE

Vol. 1 Throne Trilogy

by *Artemis OakGrove*

$7.95

"Dykes on the prowl for nighttime reading, THE RAGING PEACE captivates."

—GCN

DREAMS OF VENGEANCE

Vol. 2. Throne Trilogy

by *Artemis OakGrove*

$7.95

"An overwhelming, breathtaking plot filled with revenge, violence and spiritual turmoil . . . far more than just another SM book."

—KSK

THRONE OF COUNCIL

Vol. 3 Throne Trilogy

by *Artemis OakGrove*

$7.95

". . . concludes the compelling fantasy of a love between two women that withstands the passing of centuries, the barriers of time and memory, reincarnation, earthly trials and spirit war."

—Bookpaper

TRAVELS WITH DIANA HUNTER

by *Regine Sands*

$8.95

"From the first innocent nuzzle at the 'neck of nirvana' to the final orgasmic fulfillment, Regine Sands stirs us with her verbal foreplay, tongue in cheek humor and tongue in many other places eroticism."

—Jewelle Gomez

A THIRD STORY

by *Carole Taylor*

$7.95

Ms. Taylor's wonderfully funny novel takes a candid look at university life and explores what can happen when the wrong people discover the heroine is a lesbian.

JOURNEY TO ZELINDAR

by *Diana Rivers*

$9.95

Sair lived a sheltered life in her city, Eezore. Her father kept her innocent of the world and its wicked ways. When this bright innocent young woman had to marry the captain of the Guard, she had no idea what her fate would be when she refused his marital caresses. Given over to the Guard to preserve her husband's injured pride, Sair was raped and tossed aside to die. JOURNEY TO ZELINDAR is Sair's exciting tale of survival, learning and growth from her rescue by the Hadra women to her eventual telling of her tale to the archivist of Zelindar. Travel with Sair across the Red Line to the powerful mysterious world of the Hadra; learn their secrets and dreams that such a world really exists.

JUST HOLD ME

by *Linda Parks*

$7.95

This romantic novel about women loving women, faith and determination will hold you fast in your favorite reading chair from the intriguing beginning to the hope-filled conclusion.